T H E
BIRTHDAY

ALSO BY CAROL WYER

THE BIRTHDAY

CAROL WYER

Bookouture

Published by Bookouture in 2018

An imprint of StoryFire Ltd.

Carmelite House
50 Victoria Embankment
London EC4Y 0DZ

www.bookouture.com

ISBN: 978-1-78681-537-8
eBook ISBN: 978-1-78681-536-1

This book is a work of fiction. Names, characters, businesses,
organizations, places and events other than those clearly in the
public domain, are either the product of the author's imagination
or are used fictitiously. Any resemblance to actual persons, living or
dead, events or locales is entirely coincidental.

PROLOGUE

The children's screams lifted high in the air and pierced Elsa's eardrums like knives slicing through her brain. The desire to strangle them – all of them – became overpowering. Bloody headache. It had turned her into a demented witch. She batted away the urge. She couldn't think straight when she had one of these bad headaches. They blocked out reason and all she wanted to do was shut herself away and hide under her bedcovers until the pain became manageable. They'd been occurring more frequently the last six months and the medication was no longer having the effect she desired. She'd have to ask for a higher dosage.

The doctor had diagnosed them as tension headaches, brought on by stress. Hardly surprising given what she'd been through the last year.

In the barn, two boys were fighting over a toy dinosaur, each tugging with all their might, determined to possess the plastic object. *Such ferocity over something that only cost three pounds from the craft shop.* Elsa drew on all her reserves and, clapping her hands, called for attention. The last thing she'd needed was to find herself in charge of today's birthday party: twenty overexcited five- and six-year-olds, racing about feverishly and oblivious to any of her commands.

The birthday girl, wearing a baby-pink dress on which was pinned a large fuchsia badge bearing the number six, and with sparkling pink hairgrips holding back her thick, black hair, was the culprit behind all the squealing and shouting. It was Harriet Downing's special day and she was milking that for all it was worth. Elsa plastered on a false smile and announced it was time to visit the petting zoo. She was greeted with more shrill cries from Harriet's friends, all hyper after sugar and soft-play, and eager to launch themselves on the animals housed in pens near the specially adapted barn that was Uptown Craft Centre and Farm's main function room.

Elsa Townsend was part-owner/part-manager, a role she'd inherited through her marriage to and subsequent divorce from Barney Townsend, who'd set it up as a garden centre five years ago in May 2010. Barney loved plants and gardening, but it was Elsa who'd spotted the potential for development and bringing in new clientele – ones with lots of pester power: children. Garden centres attracted only one type of person, those who enjoyed gardening. By converting some of the outbuildings into animal pens and providing birthday parties, along with arts and craft days, Elsa had turned the place into a goldmine. The bigger and busier it had become, the more pressure it had placed on the Townsends' relationship, and as Barney withdrew more frequently to his greenhouses and planting areas, so their marriage had suffered.

Earlier this year, the Townsends had finally given up on their failed marriage and had divorced. Elsa owned half of the business, but Barney had sold his share to Alistair Fulcher, a self-opinionated, swaggering know-it-all, and Elsa was left working with a man she could barely tolerate. It was Alistair's fault she had been stuck with the birthday party on her day off. He'd messed up the work rota and 25-year-old Donna, who should have been in charge today, had managed to get time off to visit her sick gran. Elsa snorted. *Sick gran.* She wasn't born yesterday. Single Donna and the very much married Alistair Fulcher were obviously having an affair. She'd spotted the secretive looks between them in the office. Why else had Alistair suddenly announced he had to go to Nottingham, leaving Elsa in charge of everything that day? She only had two helpers and one of them, Janet, was busy elsewhere for the moment. Elsa looked around for 24-year-old Guy Noble who'd disappeared to prepare the animals for viewing and had not yet returned to assist her. Controlling a large group of children and baby animals required at least four adults, yet three was all she had today, and at the moment she had no idea of the whereabouts of the other two.

The children were scattering; some had fastened onto the tug-of-war going on at the far end of the barn and were watching it, adding encouraging shouts; two girls had begun performing handstands against the wall and another group were… well, Elsa couldn't work out quite what they were up to but it involved huddling together and periodically leaping about shrieking. Harriet Downing had separated herself from the main group and was giving Elsa a look that said, *If you don't sort this out, I'm going to tell my mother what a rubbish time I've had.* Elsa couldn't face reimbursing Mrs Downing, or explaining why Harriet hadn't had the birthday party she'd expected. The woman had been quite specific about her requirements and had hinted, if all went well, she'd recommend the centre to her vast network of mothers and friends. Elsa didn't usually accept a booking of twenty children without having at least one or two of the parents stay behind to lend a hand – it was tricky to keep an eye on all the squabbling or overexcited children, especially once they'd eaten, but Mrs Downing had wanted all Harriet's classmates to attend and insisted it be a drop-off only party, so Elsa had reluctantly agreed. She did a quick headcount. Twenty. As if by magic, Guy appeared and she let out a sigh of relief.

'Look, here's Guy. He's going to take you to meet our new baby lamb, Billy. He's only three days old. Who wants to pet him first?' She grimaced at her own artificially pleasant voice. Her head pounded. She'd grab a couple of pills and catch up with Guy.

'Me!' came the collective scream, making her wince.

'Okay, okay!' laughed Guy. He was a natural with children. They seemed to like his big, honest face, shaggy hair and clunky boots. Elsa supposed he looked like a friendly giant to them. He ambled forwards and the children flocked towards him, instantly quiet. She exhaled again and signalled she was going to the office. The crowd of children trailed out of the barn after Guy. *Like the Pied Piper leading the village children away,* she thought before the last child disappeared from view.

Elsa scurried past the stables, where three ponies, wearing bows and fake unicorn horns, were tethered, waiting to offer rides to the children once they'd finished the petting tour. Each birthday party began with food and games in the outside barn: Pin the Tail on the Donkey, Grandmother's Footsteps and other favourites; it continued with a trip around the animal enclosures, where children were encouraged to hold or stroke or even feed the animals; and culminated in a short pony ride around the grounds. It was nice when they had a summer lamb, and the birth of Billy had been a bonus.

She sidled into the office she shared with Alistair and rummaged in her handbag for some medication, popping two pills into her mouth. Her head was now thudding so much she could barely concentrate on what she was doing. She took a generous swig from a bottle of water she kept on her desk, swallowed hard, then sat with her face in her hands for a few moments. She needed the throbbing to ease before she could face the children and pony rides. Guy would be fine for a few minutes without her. Janet would be helping him, making sure the animals didn't bite or bolt. The two of them could cope. She needed a holiday. Maybe she'd book a trip and leave Alistair to run the place. That'd teach him. He ought to pull his weight more, not constantly leave it to her. *Bloody Alistair.*

The pain began to dull but she had little energy to stand and return to the party. Guy would alert her to any problems. Birthday parties! It had been a stroke of genius to come up with that idea. Each event brought in considerable profit, especially when the children asked their parents to buy the farmyard models, soft toys or any of the numerous craft gifts available from the shop they had to pass through on their way to the exit. She shut her eyes, tried to relax her shoulders and wished Barney had stuck out both their marriage and the job. They'd worked well together.

Her thoughts continued to flow and it was a shock when she looked down at her watch and realised she'd been in the office for almost twenty-five minutes. It was time for the pony rides, and then the parents would arrive to collect their offspring. After that, she'd take off and head home too. The thought cheered her and she ambled back out to the yard in time to see the children trooping out, the first group with Guy and the second with Janet. Voices rose again in excitement at the sight of the horses.

'Unicorns!' screamed Harriet. The chattering, like flocks of noisy starlings, intensified as the children spilled towards the stables at speed. Twenty children. No. Nineteen. Elsa counted again. Janet only had nine in her group. She hastened across to join them, pulling Janet aside.

'Janet, there's a child missing.'

Janet shook her head. 'No. Guy and I split them up when they came into the enclosure to calm them down. They were pretty excitable. He took ten and I took nine.'

'There were twenty children.' Elsa's heart fluttered. The look on Janet's face chilled her blood.

Janet called out, 'Can you all line up, please? No touching the ponies. Remember what I told you earlier about frightening the animals. We don't want anyone bitten, do we?'

Her voice was calm but as the children got into two lines, Elsa's pulse quickened.

'Can't I just stroke it?' asked Harriet, breaking from the others to approach the first pony. 'It's *my* birthday.'

'In a minute, Harriet,' said Elsa, a little too firmly. Harriet's bottom lip jutted out and tears welled. Mrs Downing would be most unhappy that her precious child had been admonished, but Elsa didn't care about that for the moment.

Janet spoke calmly. 'Can you tell me who's not here?'

The children looked about in puzzlement. One of them – a girl with braided hair and a gap-toothed smile – eventually raised her hand. Elsa remembered she was called Audrey – her own mother's name. 'Ava Sawyer's not here,' she said. 'She went to the toilet, but that was ages ago.' There was a buzzing among some of the children.

Harriet, who looked sulky at having the attention removed from her, spoke out. 'She's always going off on her own.'

Elsa ignored the remark and spoke to Audrey. 'Why didn't she tell me? I told you all to ask if you wanted to go to the toilet.'

'She said she knew where it was. You were busy with Freddie and Thomas. She couldn't wait.'

Elsa's heart bashed against her ribcage as her breathing quickened. She'd been defusing an argument between the two boys who'd been fighting over the dinosaur during the party. One had accused the other of cheating at Pin the Tail on the Donkey. She hadn't seen the girl slip out of the barn. She was in charge and she hadn't seen Ava Sawyer leave. She must have miscounted earlier. Elsa swallowed hard. This was her fault. A child had gone into the centre unaccompanied and not returned. She might still be lost somewhere in the vast centre. She fervently hoped so. The alternative was unthinkable.

Janet went to search the toilets in case the child was trapped inside a cubicle, or ill. The remaining children lost interest in Ava's absence and gradually became restless, kicking at stones and grumbling at being kept from the ponies. Elsa felt the tension mounting again. She had no option other than to let Guy lead the first couple of children – Harriet and her best friend, Rainey Kilburn – off on a pony ride while she kept an eye on the others. Janet raced back, concern on her face, and shook her head. She was accompanied by two of the craft centre's staff.

'Nobody there. Ted and Kristin haven't seen her either.'

'What does Ava look like?' Elsa asked Audrey.

'She was wearing a yellow dress. She has glasses.'

She remembered the child: doll-like with a porcelain complexion, long, blonde hair and in a lemon dress that hung on her skinny frame. She'd not seemed at ease with the others and held back when they were playing games, as if she didn't feel she belonged.

She spoke quietly to Janet. 'Alert all the staff. Shut the centre and put out a call on the public address system.' Even as she uttered the words, she had a sinking feeling it was going to be fruitless. Ava had been gone for a full forty minutes, and if somebody had come across her, they'd have accompanied her to the tills, or taken her to a member of staff. Elsa looked around at the faces in front of her and willed the girl to be found with every fibre of her being.

'Has she gone home?' asked Audrey.

'I don't think so,' said Elsa. 'I think she's still here.' As she spoke, parents approached the yard with smiles on their faces and her heart lurched again. She recognised the woman with the same delicate features as her daughter. Ava's mother had arrived.

CHAPTER ONE

TUESDAY, 25 APRIL 2017

Tony Mellows edged around the enormous quagmire that masqueraded as a building site. The bloody weather had been against them ever since they'd begun the sodding job. The weather forecasters were a bunch of tossers. They'd said it would be dry today and yet here he was, up to his ankles in mud, and the rain was pissing down, yet again. It'd rained all day. He shook his head to dislodge the drops in his thick hair.

There was no end to the wet weather, but deadlines were deadlines, and they had to excavate the site. The new owners wanted huge greenhouses and modern buildings erected in time for the big launch in July, and even if nature was trying to thwart them, they had to carry on regardless and clear the scrubland.

He signalled to the driver of the large JCB bouncing across the rutted field, its bucket rocking and clanking as it laboured to the far side. Bob, the driver, grinned back and mouthed, 'Wanker.'

The recipient of the derogatory remark was standing next to Tony, dressed inappropriately in a steely grey suit, white shirt complete with cufflinks, and red tie. He spoke to Tony. 'So, when do you think you'll begin erecting the new buildings?'

Neil Linton held an umbrella bearing the Poppyfields Garden Centre logo over his coiffured head. Head honcho on this project, he looked like a man who'd keel over with a stroke or heart attack pretty soon if they didn't deliver on time. He was a weaselly-looking character with a pinched complexion, who managed to look permanently angst-ridden. He drew deeply on his cigarette – the third since his arrival that afternoon – and flicked it onto the sodden ground. A thin wisp of pale, silver smoke rose from the stub, but Neil didn't glance down. His eyes were trained on the diggers clearing the site. Poppyfields, a large garden centre conglomerate, had recently acquired Uptown Craft Centre and intended extending the site by utilising the land to the rear. It was Neil's job to ensure this happened, and soon.

Tony grunted a response that was lost in the noise of clanking digger buckets and rain splashing onto the umbrella. He was used to people bellowing and pushing for him to finish on time. The fact remained that it was a filthy, wet day and even his top-of-the-range machinery and experienced workforce couldn't perform miracles. They'd been able to remove brambles and old shrubs and clear the land, but if the weather carried on like this, it would add a good couple of weeks to the schedule. Laying foundations into sodden ground would prove impossible.

Neil tried to reason with Tony, whose look was more than a little intimidating. 'I'll be honest. There's a little wriggle room in the date, but we can't delay much longer. We need to get this up and running and making money as soon as possible. And I don't need to remind you that the contract definitely states—'

'I know what's stated in the contract.' Tony's voice was a low growl. Fucking contract. He cursed agreeing to the tight deadline. If they didn't meet it, he'd have to forfeit some of the payment – a hefty chunk – and he couldn't afford that. 'We're working, aren't we? It's gone four on a shitty day and we're all working. We'll have it completed on time.'

Neil nodded although his face remained impassive. His phone rang and he excused himself to answer the call, leaving Tony to check on progress. The entire site was eight hectares – some twenty acres – in size, over half of which was already built upon. The remaining acres were to be developed. It was no mean feat, but had the weather been kinder, they'd have been much further along with the project.

There was a sudden commotion with arms flailing and shouts and hails from one of the men who'd been supervising the diggers.

'Whoa! Stop!'

Bob, one of Tony's longest-serving employees, cut his digger's engine and yelled back at the man on the ground. Something serious had happened.

'Fuck!' said Tony. If they'd gone through a buried electric cable, there'd be hell to pay. He stomped forwards, boots sinking in the sucking mud.

The machines had fallen silent and Bob had clambered out from his cab and dropped to the ground to join the men. He spotted Tony and yelled. 'Boss! Here.'

The commotion attracted Neil's attention, and he ended his call and watched as Tony drew up to the workmen and knelt down. The rain pattered on his umbrella as he observed the scenario in front of him. Tony stood up again, shook his head and ran his hand through his hair before patting Bob on the back. He lifted his mobile to his ear. The men retreated from the spot and stood like sentinels, heads bowed, unwilling to look at what they'd uncovered.

Tony jogged back towards Neil, his voice becoming increasingly clear as he approached the man. 'Yes. Immediately. Yes. The old Craft Centre and Farm in Uptown.'

Neil's brow creased as the foreman slowed to a halt. 'Well, what the hell's going on now? Why've you all downed tools? That was my boss on the phone, wanting to know how far you've progressed, and he's not best pleased at all the delay. You understand the importance of this. If you can't meet the target date, we'll have to invoke the clause in your contract.'

Tony threw the man a look of disgust. 'It's out of my hands. Invoke it or whatever you like, but we can't excavate any more. We've unearthed a body. There'll be no more digging, not today.'

*

'I don't care if Ben Lincoln has got a pair, we can't afford them,' said DI Natalie Ward, ignoring the look on her fifteen-year-old son's face. 'It's not your birthday for another three months, and you already have a pair of perfectly good trainers.'

'Da-ad,' Josh whined.

'No good dragging me into this,' said David. 'I'm not the main breadwinner any more.'

His words and the bitter edge that accompanied them cut into Natalie. If she didn't handle this properly, they'd end up bickering – another pointless argument about money and careers – and she couldn't face that again.

'Look, if you still want them come your birthday, I'll think about it then, but you know what you're like, Josh. Nike Air Force or not, you'll be bored of them in a few weeks and want something else. See how you feel in a month or two,' she reasoned, trying to keep her tone light and not glance in her husband's direction. He'd be no support, sitting as he had been for the last ten minutes, arms folded, eyebrows lowered and lip out. *Christ!* Some days, it was like living with three hormonal teenagers. All she needed was for thirteen-year-old Leigh to appear and start moaning about school or friends or the non-vegetarian casserole Natalie was preparing for dinner, and she'd be ready for a stint in the local asylum.

She lifted a hand to signal the end of the conversation and let Josh's killer stare wash over her. It worked. He stomped off upstairs and slammed his bedroom door.

'We could have afforded the trainers,' David began.

She turned on him. 'For crying out loud, David, you know how much debt we're in. We've still got to clear this month's credit card bill and the bloody mortgage.'

His bottom lip folded down further. She shoved the spoon into the casserole and tasted it. She couldn't keep blaming David for the mess they were in; besides, one of them had to be around for the kids, as he often reminded her. She wasn't always available when they needed her. At least he spent most of the time at home.

Josh was the older, tidier of their two offspring, and the one who normally could be relied upon to defuse the volatile situations that occurred more and more frequently since Leigh had turned thirteen. He wasn't a bad kid and she'd love to be able to offer him a new pair of trainers, but facts were facts, and David's work as a freelance translator barely pulled in enough to cover the food bills each week. If it weren't for her job as a detective inspector with Samford Police Force, they'd be up shit creek.

She dropped the lid back on the dish and returned it to the oven. It was passable. Domestic goddess, she was not. 'I could take on some overtime,' she began.

'Oh, for fuck's sake, Natalie. Don't do this to me.' David stood up in one swift movement.

'Do what?' she asked, but she already knew. David losing his position as a translator at the law firm where he'd worked for twenty years had been one of the worst things that could have happened. He'd not been able to find more work like it, and going freelance had been his only option. The problem was, in this digital age, his skills were less in demand, and finding a new position had proved impossible. He resented the fact that Natalie was their only hope of keeping a roof over their heads. His pride had taken a massive knock, and try as she might to tell him otherwise, that it didn't matter, and that he was just as useful being a stay-at-home dad, they both knew the truth: it was eating away at him. David simply wasn't good at taking the back seat.

'Fancy a drink?' she said by way of making peace.

'It's not even six o'clock yet.'

'Go on. There's some wine in the fridge. The casserole can wait. Josh won't want to eat yet, and anyway, he needs to cool off for a bit. We'll get him the bloody trainers as an early birthday present if you think that's what he really wants.'

'It's about street cred, Nat. He needs that. Not easy for him to fit in.'

'Yeah. I know.' Her face softened. Josh was a great kid but one who had issues – he wore braces to straighten his teeth and recently had been getting a rough time from his classmates, who teased him relentlessly. Kids needed kudos to garner respect from friends, and for Josh it was the trendiest clothes, rather than gadgets or the latest smartphone, that gave him a feeling of self-worth. Natalie thought it was a pity he didn't get any esteem for being clever – Josh was a bright lad.

David seemed satisfied with her response.

'You want a glass of wine then?' she asked again.

'Okay. Just the one. I have a script to translate for a client who wanted it by yesterday.' He stretched and yawned. It was the signal that the tension between them had passed.

She threw him a smile. The translation probably wasn't the big deal he made it out to be, but she let David have his moment. He needed to feel he was valued.

She turned towards the fridge and drew out the chilled bottle of Chardonnay. As she did so, her mobile buzzed on the kitchen worktop. It was work.

David's mouth set into a thin line and his expression changed. 'You better get that,' he said and withdrew from the kitchen.

'David,' she called, but it was too late. He'd retreated to his office. A heavy beat started up from Josh's room and vibrated down the stairs. He was listening to his music on full volume. She answered the phone with one finger in her other ear to block out the noise.

'Natalie, it's Aileen.'

The voice was musical with its soft, southern Irish lilt and it was difficult to imagine it belonged to its owner, Superintendent Aileen Melody. Aileen might have a gentle voice but she was one of the toughest policewomen Natalie knew: a ball-busting officer who had risen through the ranks at a meteoric speed thanks to her time with the London Met, working first with the vice squad and then heading units in anti-terrorism. If Aileen was calling her, it was bad news.

'What is it, Aileen?'

'I'm ringing you because you were involved in the Olivia Chester investigation.'

Natalie's veins turned to ice at the mention of the case to which she'd been assigned in 2015. It had ended badly.

'I'd like your expertise on this one.'

'Have you found a body?'

Aileen's silence told Natalie all she needed to know.

'When?' she asked.

'An hour ago. It's not a recent death. Pathologist thinks the body's been in situ a couple of years or so. It's a youngster.'

'How old?'

'Difficult to say at the moment.'

Natalie blinked back the memories of the last time she'd seen the body of a dead child and responded. 'I'll be there. I'm leaving now.'

As she collected her murder bag – the forensic kit she'd need for the crime scene – from the hallway, David wandered out of his office. His forehead was wrinkled with unasked questions and he observed her in silence as she picked up her coat and car keys.

'The casserole will be ready in fifteen minutes.'

He nodded in response and as she opened the door, his lips parted as if he might speak. She slipped outside, mind on what lay ahead of her. Sensing his intention, she turned back briefly but David shut his mouth and closed the door after her. Whatever he'd wanted to say, it was too late now.

Natalie blipped open her car door and slid into the driver's seat. She rested her palms on the cool leather steering wheel. *A child.* She had to get it right this time. It was more than her life was worth, to make the same mistake again.

CHAPTER TWO

TUESDAY, 25 APRIL – EVENING

What had once been Uptown Craft Centre and Farm stood at the far end of a huge parking area – far larger than the car park at the cheap supermarket where Natalie did the weekly shop. The signage had long gone but the façade looked similar to garden centres she'd visited before: a brown brick building with an arched entrance.

The centre was on a busy main road leading from Samford – where Natalie worked – to Uptown, well known for its parks and annual music festival. This was her first visit to the town, and as Natalie drew closer, she became increasingly aware of her heartbeat, which was becoming erratic.

She manoeuvred into a spot close to the entrance, pulled on her wellington boots and strode towards the officers in front of the building, holding her ID out in front of her. They noted her name in the crime scene log and directed her to the side entrance that led through empty yards towards the rear of the centre. The rain was still tumbling from dark, evening skies, making inky black puddles on the concrete floor that Natalie splashed through. The centre had once been a mixture of a garden centre, arts and crafts centre, tearoom and small farm. In addition, there'd been a farm shop that sold local produce and a wide variety of gifts. The new owners, a business consortium, were expanding it and bringing in more farm shops and various attractions, including a blacksmith's shop and a steam railway that would run through the grounds, ferrying passengers to various points on what was going to be more theme park than garden centre. Natalie left the yard and trudged onto the boggy earth behind two greenhouses. A skinny man in his fifties was standing beside the nearest greenhouse, hands pushed deep into the pockets of his hi-vis vest. His grey hair was flattened to his head and his eyes were sunken.

'I'm Neil Linton,' he said, holding out a slender hand. 'Project manager. We found the body.'

She took his hand. It was smooth to the touch. 'Have you given a statement, sir?'

He nodded miserably. 'I have but I can't leave. Not until I know. Officers said it was okay to wait.'

'Know what, sir?'

'That it's human remains we uncovered.'

'There's nothing to be gained by staying here and we won't be releasing any information until we're able to, regardless of what the officers might have told you.'

The man's shoulders slumped. 'They didn't exactly say. I hoped…'

She gave him a tight smile. 'I'm afraid not.'

'Can I wait for a while?'

'I'd rather you went…' His eyes caused her to pause. They were filled with pain; she'd seen the same pain in the eyes of parents – parents whose children she hadn't been able to locate in time to save. 'Stay if you must, but you'll not learn anything tonight,' she said gently. 'You really would be better off returning home. We'll contact you in due course.'

'Just ten minutes. I feel I owe it to whoever is out there,' Neil replied.

Natalie nodded her assent and left the lit grounds. She crossed the field, training her torch on the earth, all the while rain driving into her face and mud sucking her feet into the sticky ground. She didn't care about either. All she wanted to do was get the next few minutes over with. Several officers were standing close to a makeshift tent. Again, she showed her ID to a pale-faced policeman, who opened the tent flap. Crossing the field, she'd tried to calm her thoughts, focusing on tested techniques of imagining a still lake, a sunset, cows chewing cud – each and every one of the things her psychiatrist had advised after the Olivia Chester case. She'd learnt many relaxation techniques and ways of coping, but today they failed her. She was about to witness something she'd hoped she'd never see again in her life: a dead child.

The floodlights shone brightly inside the tent, making her squint for a moment. She blinked and made out Mike Sullivan, in charge of the forensic unit, who was talking to a man she presumed was the pathologist. Natalie had known Mike for most of her career – some twenty years – and he was a close friend of her husband's, having shared digs with him at university. There was nothing Mike enjoyed more than reminiscing about their good old days – all night parties and endless fun. For him the world had since spiralled out of control, and those hedonistic days were a thing of the past. His wife, Nicole, had recently separated from him, taking his young daughter, Thea, with her. On the surface he seemed unaffected by their departure, but Natalie had noticed small changes – weight loss and dark bags under his eyes – that suggested otherwise. Natalie joined the men and fought back a guttural sound that rose involuntarily in her throat.

The body was so small, three feet from crown to heel. It had been wrapped in some material – sackcloth or similar – and was now exposed, a dried-out, tiny corpse with skin tightly stretched over visible bones. The skull was small – no larger than Natalie's cupped hands. The jaw was open, revealing even, white teeth that would never be hidden under a pillow for the Tooth Fairy to discover. The sight was a sucker punch to Natalie's solar plexus and she drew short breaths, trying hard to conceal her dismay from her colleagues. She knew Mike felt the same. He'd be thinking of his own daughter, and the sight of this child had brought out the Papa Bear in him. He clenched his fists like he wanted to do serious harm to whoever had done this. He looked up and threw her a brief smile. It was like an anchor in a storm and she clung to it, returned it and regained composure.

'This is Ben Hargreaves,' said Mike, indicating the pathologist and shifting his position so she could move next to him. She slid beside him, feeling the warmth rise from his solid body. 'He's transferred from Birmingham. Ben, this is DI Natalie Ward.'

'Hi,' said Natalie, glad to have somebody else to focus on rather than the child on the ground. Ben glanced briefly in her direction and gave a mumbled grunt of acknowledgement before returning his attention to the corpse in front of him. Silence fell. Mike threw her a look then shrugged. Maybe the man was as shell-shocked as they were.

'Ben thinks the body's been here for up to two or three years. It might be less time. It's clay soil in this area, so it's probably better preserved than if it had been left in ordinary soil. The clay acts as a barrier against insect activity. That, coupled with the fact it was wrapped in this,' he said, looking at the material underneath the body, 'will have affected the rate of decomposition.'

Ben stood up and adjusted his glasses. He was a good six inches taller than Natalie, who was five foot nine. She noticed a wedding band on his finger. 'That's right. I can't see any obvious marks on the body, no fractured bones, no cracks or holes, and nothing obvious to help me determine cause of death. All I can say is, looking at the eruption of teeth, and size of the skeleton, I'd hazard a guess that the child was between four and seven years old. Those look like milk teeth. I'll be able to be clearer about that once we've had the chance to analyse the bones.'

'Can you tell us the sex?'

Ben shook his head, his long, dark hair glistening wet from the rain. 'Not immediately. It's difficult to ascertain until after puberty because sexual dimorphism – the differences between males and females – is slight in children. Your forensic anthropologist will need to examine bone size and look at the pelvis to identify the sex of this child. I can't give you a definite answer although, as you can see, there are some lengthy strands of blonde hair attached to the remaining skin on the scalp, which could suggest we're looking at the body of a girl.'

'Mike, you got anything else you want to ask before we remove the body?'

Mike shook his head. 'Nah, best get started. I'll put Naomi on it.'

Naomi Singh was a top forensic anthropologist with a no-nonsense approach who shared the lab with her husband Darshan, a specialist in forensic odontology. Mike had nothing but praise for the pair of them. He shifted again. Natalie felt his discomfort.

Ben nodded briefly. 'Okay. Could you arrange the removal, please?'

Natalie moved outside and flicked her Maglite back on. The torch beam stretched across the field, catching the corkscrewing raindrops. Mike joined her and pulled his collar up against his neck.

'You okay?' he asked.

'What do you think?'

'Yeah. Dumb question. Too many shitty memories, eh?'

Natalie couldn't answer. She'd spent so many hours after the Olivia Chester investigation winding back the clock, reliving each moment, and each time trying to will a different outcome, until she had no more to give. The fact was the case had gone wrong. She'd been part of a team investigating the disappearance of the thirteen-year-old in Manchester. Her body had finally been discovered in a disused warehouse. It was Natalie's firm belief they'd reacted to leads too slowly, and not for the first time. There'd been another case, before Olivia – one that had affected her so badly she couldn't bring herself to think about it. She fought back that memory and concentrated on Olivia, who might have been saved if the case had been handled differently. She couldn't give answers to Olivia's parents, but she'd try and find some for the parents of this youngster.

Mike walked her to the buildings. Neil Linton was resting against a wall, eyes trained on the activity now taking place as forensic officers hastened past them, a folded stretcher under one's arm. Neil's eyes rested on Natalie's face as she drew level with him. 'No need to tell me,' he said. 'You wouldn't be here if it were an animal out there. It looked to be a small body…' He left the rest of the sentence hanging.

'Best go home and get some rest, sir,' Mike said.

As they headed back to the car park, Natalie asked, 'What's the story with him? Why's he still here?'

'No big deal. He's under pressure to complete the work here. It'll be held up now. We'll have to check the area in case there are any more bodies and that'll screw up his schedule.'

Natalie shuddered involuntarily. 'You reckon there are more bodies?'

'Who knows? Could be a whole family out there.'

Neither spoke. The thought was sobering. They stood at the entrance to the centre, observing the arrival of more officers. It was going to be a long night and unless the rain ceased, the hunt for more bodies would be impossible. Mike patted the pockets of his coat, extracted a packet of cigarettes, tapped one out and offered it to Natalie.

She shook her head. 'Given up.'

'Really? Since when?'

A vision of the pair of them, sweaty and naked, swam in front of her eyes: plain white duvet on the floor, her legs draped over his muscular thighs, a cigarette between her lips, smoke curling to the ceiling. She'd given up smoking that afternoon – the same afternoon she'd sorted out her shit and promised herself she'd never be so fucking stupid as to cheat on her husband again. 'A while back.'

He pulled a face. 'Good for you. I wish I could. Costs me a sodding fortune, and with Nicole screaming for blood, I'll soon be down to bumming from my colleagues or going cold turkey.'

'She gone for good?'

Mike shrugged. 'She's taken the Volvo, all her and Thea's belongings, and the dog. Go figure.'

'You okay?' Her concern was genuine. Mike adored his daughter.

He dragged on the cigarette. 'I'll survive. You know me.'

She did. She knew Mike very well. He was charming and confident and his eyes crinkled handsomely when he smiled. He was dangerous and cavalier, and he couldn't hold down a relationship. It had been a surprise to both her and David when he'd announced he was going to marry Nicole. Mike had never seemed to be the marrying type. She opened her mouth to speak but he interrupted her by holding up a finger.

'Before you ask, no, she didn't leave me because she found out what happened between you and me. She never knew about that. She left me because I "can't separate work life from real life".' He shoved the cigarette between his lips, then snorted. 'Work life *is* fucking real life.'

Natalie was glad she wasn't the reason for Nicole leaving Mike. The one-night stand they'd shared had been a crazy moment, brought about by booze and despair. David had been gambling again, in spite of his promises, and accrued online debts that had sideswiped her. She'd stood by him when he'd been made redundant and cajoled him into applying for job after job. She'd encouraged him to go it alone as a translator, and all the while, she'd made sure they were fed, that Josh could go on the school trip to Austria, that Leigh could take up drum lessons and that David's ego was stroked. She'd understood he felt a failure but he wasn't. However, when she'd discovered their joint bank account was in the red, and uncovered the truth about his online activity, she'd blown her top.

She should never have reached out to Mike, but he'd been in the office when she'd found out about David's gambling, and asked her what was wrong, and she'd cracked. Later, they'd gone for a drink. Later still, she'd slipped between hotel sheets with him. Four months had passed since then and she didn't intend on making the same mistake again.

They stood shoulder to shoulder, allowing the patter of the rain to fill the silence that now hung between them as more white vans drew up.

'My lot,' Mike said, approaching his crew, issuing loud instructions as Natalie made for her car. She'd gather her own team together for briefing back at the station. It was going to be a long night.

CHAPTER THREE

TUESDAY, 25 APRIL – NIGHT

As well as being home to local officers, Samford Police Headquarters was one of only four investigative hubs across the county, with criminal investigation department, public protection and forensic staff from the north of Staffordshire all based at the new state-of-the-art building. The police station had been two years in construction, completed early in 2016, and was one of the reasons Natalie had been transferred from Kingsville, a more traditional station on the outskirts of Manchester. At least that's what she liked to tell herself.

Truth be told, after the Olivia Chester fiasco, she couldn't face her superiors or colleagues at Kingsville each morning. She could no longer look them in the eye and feel part of a team. So, when she'd learnt about the new headquarters, and heard they were recruiting new investigative squads, she'd requested a position on one. Living where they did, in Castergate, she could just as easily commute to Samford as Kingsville.

Her anxiety about working with officers hitherto unknown to her had proven unfounded. She'd slipped into the role of mentor and team leader as if it had been created for her, and she was more than pleased with the officers chosen to work alongside her, one of whom was standing near the front reception. She ought to have guessed Sergeant Lucy Carmichael would be one of the first to report for duty. The 28-year-old wore a perpetual look of irritation, accentuated by a deep scar across the bridge of her nose that spoiled her otherwise striking looks. With jet-black, short-cropped hair, bushy, strong eyebrows and what Natalie would describe as an ectomorphic body shape, Lucy oozed confidence; if spotted out of uniform, wearing her traditional garb of ripped T-shirt and leather trousers, she could be mistaken for a rock star. Lucy had attitude but she also had tenacity and courage. Natalie had spotted those qualities along with loyalty soon after the team had been formed. They'd hit it off quickly, and as she walked over to her younger colleague, she wasn't surprised to see a shadow of sorrow etched on her features.

'Shit,' was all Lucy could offer.

'I know.'

'I hate it when kids are involved.'

'We all do, Lucy. It's a sad fact that men, women and children die every day. Our job is to get answers and put aside those feelings.' The response came from Sergeant Murray Anderson, three years older than Lucy, round-faced and sandy-haired.

'Yeah. I don't need the lecture, just a chance to get my head around it,' replied Lucy.

Murray ignored the sharp retort. He and Lucy had known each other a number of years and had come from the same station in Stoke-on-Trent to be part of the new team at Samford. It had taken Natalie a while to work out the exact nature of their turbulent relationship, but it transpired they were no more than good friends. Murray was married to one of Lucy's close friends – Yolande – who he'd met through Lucy, and whom he idolised.

'What've we got?' Murray asked Natalie.

'Not a great deal. The body is en route to the pathology lab, and Forensics are still searching the immediate area in case they discover any more corpses, although weather and darkness are hampering efforts at the moment. I think they'll abandon it soon and try again at first light. It's too boggy in the field.'

The trio headed towards the briefing room at the end of the corridor and Natalie snapped on the lights as they trooped in. The cleaners had already been in – the whiteboard was smear-free, the oval table that could seat ten officers had been wiped down, and the entire room smelt of freshly squeezed lemons.

Natalie set up her laptop and clicked on the photographs of the body that had been sent through. Mike had ensured they'd reached her quickly. There were several, taken at different angles: the material with mud in its folds, the body unveiled, two legs out straight and arms folded across the chest, the skull with its grey skin-like parchments stretched fully and the little white teeth. When Josh's first milk tooth had come loose, he'd wriggled it out in bed and not told Natalie. Instead, he'd hidden it under the pillow and been heartbroken when it had still been there in the morning. Natalie explained that he should have sung to the Tooth Fairy, and she made up a silly rhyme on the spot for him:

Tooth Fairy, Tooth Fairy, please come to me.
I want to sell you my tooth for a shiny penny.

That night, they'd sung it together and put the tooth back under the pillow, and the following morning, Josh had been excited to discover fifty pence in its place. After that, the song had to be sung every time he lost a tooth, and then she'd done the same for Leigh when she also began losing her baby teeth.

Natalie looked again at the photograph and was about to speak when the door clattered open and the last member of her team hurtled in, a takeaway cup of coffee in his hand.

'For crying out loud,' said Murray. 'We're all sitting here like lemons, waiting for you, and you stop off on the way to buy a fucking coffee.'

'I was already in the coffee shop when I got the call,' said PC Ian Jarvis. 'Seemed a waste to leave it behind.' He took a deliberate slurp of the drink. At twenty-three, he was the youngest on the team, and although good-natured, he managed to constantly rub Murray up with his slightly cheeky attitude. From the outset, there'd been antagonism between the men when they discovered they supported rival football teams: Murray was an ardent Stoke City fan whereas Ian was mad keen on West Bromwich Albion. It had resulted in some heated discussions. Natalie recognised something in the younger officer – a spark that would drive him on in his career: he was bright, dedicated and unflappable and he'd calm down in time. As for Murray, well, he'd have to get over whatever was eating at him.

'Okay, everyone. Thanks for getting here so promptly. At five p.m. today a body was uncovered at Poppyfields, the new garden centre opening in Uptown.' She twisted the laptop around so she could show the photographs of the body to the team. Murray winced. Lucy glared defiantly at the screen as if she could stare down the images.

'The last few days, developers have been excavating land belonging to the centre for an expansion project. The project manager is Neil Linton, and it was his foreman, Tony Mellows, who rang the police when the body was discovered. Both men were on-site at the time of the discovery of the body.

'There is no doubt that the remains are human: sex unknown, a child aged between four and seven. The cadaver is in a state of decomposition but was wrapped in material that has helped preserve it to some extent. To that end, long blonde strands of hair are visibly attached to the scalp and might indicate the child was a girl although we could equally be looking at a little boy. We're waiting for confirmation from the pathologist and Forensics. Mike's heading up the forensic team and Naomi is the forensic anthropologist working on this investigation. In the meantime, we need to jog things along and look into any missing children cases from the last few years. Drag up all MisPer files.'

Murray scrawled on his notepad, lips pressed tightly together. All the while, his left knee bounced – a nervous habit.

Natalie continued, 'Ben Hargreaves is the pathologist on this case. Anyone know him?'

Lucy shook her head. 'He's a newbie. Came in a couple of weeks ago. Met him in the canteen. Seemed a bit stand-offish.'

'He's okay,' said Ian. 'He just needs time to adjust, get to know everyone.'

'You spoken to him?'

'Yeah. We chatted. He supports West Bromwich Albion too.'

Natalie nodded appreciatively. It was always good when they established a rapport with Forensics or the pathologists. It helped to speed up investigations.

'We've no idea how the child died. It might be natural causes. It's too soon to make that call. Ben didn't spot anything that raised red flags. However, I'd like to run a background check on Neil Linton.' Natalie ignored Ian's sudden raised eyebrows. She'd learnt to her cost that those who seemed to be the most helpful during an investigation were sometimes responsible for the crime. 'Neil's men might have found the body, but he was the one hanging around the place in the dark, awaiting further information, until we insisted he go home.'

'Surely, if he knew about the death of this child, he wouldn't have got involved in the extension project? He'd want to distance himself from it,' Ian said.

'That's actually a very good reason *to* become involved,' said Murray, arms folded. 'If he was on-site, he'd know if the body was discovered. He might even assume, by being there, he'd put himself out of the frame.'

'That's my reasoning too,' said Natalie. 'However, priority is to establish who this child is. Once we've done that, we'll require the pathology report and set about working out what happened and talking to parents. Any questions?' When there were none, she dismissed them and headed upstairs to see if Mike's team had begun work.

Mike wasn't in the lab but Naomi Singh was. Stood over a pristine white desk, she was currently examining photographs of the child in question, the same photographs Natalie had received. She drew herself up to her full five foot three inches and let out a soft sigh. Her eyes, the colour of polished conkers, were full of sadness.

'There are 206 bones in the adult body. A child has more – up to 300, depending on their age, until the bones begin to fuse.'

'Ben thinks the child is between four and seven years old.'

'Then there'll be approximately 213 bones.' Naomi shook her head slowly from side to side. 'I have to wait for the pathologist to finish examining the body. Meanwhile, I'll take a look at the blanket or whatever it was wrapped in.'

'I didn't come to pressure you. I only dropped by to get your initial thoughts.'

'Whatever was wrapped around the body has helped protect it from insects and scavengers,' said Naomi, her eyes again on the photographs. 'We ought to be able to get some results from the strands of hair attached to the scalp and from the teeth to help with identification.'

'Sure. Mike around?' Natalie kept her tone light.

'He's staying on-site for a while in case they find anything else. Anything I can help you with?'

Natalie gave her a brief smile in response. 'Just let me know as soon as you have something.'

'You know I will.' She returned to the photographs, eyes screwed in concentration, Natalie already forgotten.

Natalie joined the others in their glass-fronted office, accessed from the second-floor corridor, outside which stood a crescent-shaped, multicoloured, six-person settee. None of them understood the reason for it being there.

'Who's going to sit on that? It's in the middle of a busy corridor, for fuck's sake,' Murray had grumbled when it had first arrived. Since then, it had become part of the landscape they looked out upon daily, and they no longer discussed it even though it had never been used.

Full-length, double-glazed windows, that overlooked the main road but maintained the occupants' privacy, took up the far side of the office. No need for blinds or window coverings in this modern building. Natalie still found it odd that she could watch the traffic snaking past but none of the occupants of the vehicles would be able to see what was going on inside. The structure was so futuristic in design that drivers would often crane their necks and stare at it while stuck in a jam, oblivious to the officers observing them. The walls had been painted a soft grey, not that much of it was visible, hidden as it was behind tall metal cabinets and shelves of box files. There were two silver-grey tables facing each other, each with four ergonomic chairs, and a third smaller desk with two chairs, set at an adjacent angle. Natalie placed her laptop on the smaller desk, where she usually worked, although nobody had a special place in the room. This was modern policing – they had to be flexible and not mark out a personal territory.

Ian was next to Lucy, both working on individual laptops, while Murray was trawling through cases using the larger fixed computers on the opposite bench. No sooner had Natalie lifted the lid on her own laptop than Murray spoke up.

'Got details of 128 missing youngsters under the age of ten from the area since 2012, but only five are the right age to be our victim: Noah Lawson, Michaela Brown, Dee Horton, Poppy Islington and Ava Sawyer.'

'Okay. We'll concentrate on those five for now.'

'Got something here, Natalie. It's a press release from July 2015,' said Ian.

Natalie scooted across and read out what he'd found:

The start of the school summer holidays saw over 300 locals join the hunt for five-year-old Ava Sawyer who disappeared during a children's birthday party at Uptown Craft Centre and Farm on Friday, 24 July.

Ava was last seen in the Play Barn on-site, at approximately 4.30 p.m., and was wearing a yellow dress and cream shoes. Police are concerned for her welfare and are asking anybody who may have seen Ava, or have any information about her whereabouts, to come forward urgently.

'That's the site. It was Uptown Craft Centre and Farm before it became Poppyfields Garden Centre. Could be our girl,' said Ian. 'Is there a photo of her?'

Natalie scrolled down the article. 'Yes.'

She turned the screen to reveal a picture of a girl in school uniform of white blouse and blue cardigan, with long blonde hair held back in a plait and wearing heavy-framed glasses that seemed too much for her delicate face. Her small fingers were interlocked and her hands were lifted in front of her, almost as if in prayer, but it was the smile that tore at Natalie's heart. The girl looked so happy and full of life.

Lucy's fingers had been flying over her keyboard the entire time Natalie had been reading. 'Got it. She was reported missing in 2015. Never found. Suspected kidnapping.'

'Okay. Let's not get ahead of ourselves. This might be a coincidence. We need confirmation. I'll send this information across to Forensics and we'll wait for confirmation of her identity.'

The house was in complete darkness when Natalie pulled onto her drive and parked behind David's old Nissan. She'd be up and gone before he needed his vehicle to drop off the kids at school. She remained in the driving seat for a while and reflected on the latest development. She'd sent her team home and waited alone for the confirmation that came after midnight. The body was that of Ava Sawyer, the five-year-old who'd attended a birthday party at Uptown Craft Centre and Farm in 2015. The knowledge a child could be taken from such a happy event and turn up in a field had chilled her blood. It was going to be a testing case for her. She stared through the windscreen at her house, a place of sanctuary and safety, and was glad to be back home even if it was only for a few hours. She stepped out of the car, thumbed the torch app on her mobile to light the way, and entered. Josh's school bag was packed and standing ready by the door. He'd never needed cajoling from his bed or encouragement to complete homework. He'd rise at 7.30 a.m. without fail and be ready to leave on time, bright-eyed and alert. Leigh, however, was the complete opposite. She'd sleep through all the alarms set on her mobile, require several shouts to rouse her and then have to be dragged from her bed, eyes thick with sleep. While Josh would be in the car, texting his mates, Leigh would be staggering around her bedroom, hunting for the elusive homework or a sock or a hairband, until either Natalie or David came to her aid and found whatever she needed and swept her out of the house. It was the same most school mornings: the yawn chorus, David called it. The thought made her smile.

She'd been hard on Josh, saying he couldn't have the trainers. He was a good lad. She ought to cut him some slack. The braces had dealt his confidence a severe blow. He was at an awkward age – girls had finally hit his radar – and now, it was a cruel blow that he was unlikely to impress the opposite sex. Coupled with that, he'd been subjected to name-calling: 'metal mouth' and 'Jaws'. The barbs had crept under his skin and Natalie knew they hurt. She'd agree to a pair and watch the smile creep across his handsome features. He'd have the last laugh. Once those braces were removed, every girl in his class would be making eyes at him.

She removed her boots and left them on the mat by the door, walking on tiptoes up the carpeted stairs. As she passed Josh's room, she thought she heard the ping of a text message. She waited, ready to admonish him for texting so late, but heard no more and deduced she'd been mistaken. Leigh's door was slightly ajar. She always slept with it open and a night light plugged into a socket. Leigh had always hated the dark. Natalie pushed the door open a little and peered in. Leigh was flat on her stomach, an arm and pyjama-clad leg hanging over the side of the bed. Natalie slipped in and tucked her arm back under the duvet. Leigh didn't make a sound. She bent and kissed the top of her daughter's head.

David was fast asleep, making light popping noises that would soon develop into seismic snores. She undressed in the bathroom and studied her reflection in the round mirror they'd bought from IKEA. What had Mike seen in her? She was a 43-year-old woman with a prominent nose and a wide mouth. She had nothing special to offer. Mike was far better suited to the Nicoles of the world: breezy, sexy, young women who were fun. Natalie had almost forgotten what fun was. In the bedroom, the snoring had begun. Natalie sighed and closed her eyes.

CHAPTER FOUR

WEDNESDAY, 26 APRIL – MORNING

The next day started with a scream. Natalie sat bolt upright in bed wondering if she'd dreamt it until she heard it again. It wasn't human. It was answered by a high-pitched cry, no doubt from the large tabby cat next door. It was 5.05 a.m. She cursed the crepuscular animals and closed her eyes again in an attempt to drift back to sleep for an hour. The yowling intensified, dramatic sounds that sledgehammered their way through her brain. David shifted next to her, let out a groan and yanked the pillow over his head to muffle the noise.

Eventually the cries ceased, but by then Natalie was too wound up for sleep. She threw back her side of the duvet and got up.

Downstairs, she switched on the kettle, and while she waited for it to boil, she wondered how best to handle the Ava Sawyer investigation. She'd read some of the news items covering the child's disappearance while at the station waiting for the confirmation they had uncovered Ava's body. Ava's parents, Beatrice and Carl Sawyer, had faced every parent's worst nightmare and since 2015 had lived each day wondering if and when their daughter would be found alive. Today, they'd discover the one thing they'd clung onto for the last two years – hope – had finally been extinguished.

'Hey!'

Her head jerked upwards, startled by the voice. David, bare-footed and wearing lounge pyjamas that hung loose on his slender frame, was at the door. *Mike would have filled the doorway*, she thought. He offered a smile that transformed his face from sullen to good-looking in an instant and ran a hand through his unruly hair. He padded towards the kettle and pulled out a tin from the cupboard above it.

'Sodding cats,' he grumbled, tugging the lid from the brown ceramic teapot next to the kettle.

'I'd have had to get up anyway,' she said.

He picked up on her tone. 'Want to talk about it?'

Natalie half-grimaced an apology. 'Not much to say. We found the body of a little girl who went missing a couple of years ago. Have to break the news to her parents and then find out which bastard killed her.' She stood motionless. The words had drained her and made her acknowledge the reality of what she was about to face. He moved towards her and placed warm hands on her shoulders, forcing her to look at him.

'It'll be okay. This is a cold case. You couldn't have done anything two years ago. You weren't working at Samford then. You were in Kingsville.'

She nodded dumbly. He'd understood what was bothering her – a silent telepathy shared by them both. The kettle switched off with a loud click. He squeezed her shoulders and withdrew. She dropped onto a chair and rested her elbows on the pitted wooden table, bought at a half-price sale. It was a solid table and had withstood the test of time: spoons banged by hungry toddlers, toy cars raced at speed with their tiny wheels digging into the surface, and felt pens that had scribbled beyond the edges of the paper they were colouring.

'You were right about Josh. I was too quick to say no. We'll get him those trainers as an early birthday present.'

'Glad you agree. He'll be over the moon.'

He brought two filled mugs over and banged them down. 'Bloody cats. At least I'll get a couple of hours on that translation before the kids get up.'

Natalie gave him a smile and lifted the mug to her lips. The tea was just right.

'Who's the FLO on this?' Murray asked, referring to the family liaison officer who'd be with the officer breaking the news to Ava's parents.

'Tanya Granger. I told her we'd go over later to talk to them. Give them a chance for the news to sink in first.'

Natalie brushed to one side the printed articles they'd retrieved from the Internet, and spoke again. 'DI Howard Franks led the original investigation. He had to retire from the force soon afterwards on account of his wife's health. She's sadly passed away since. He'll be in any minute to take us through it. Has to drop off his daughters at school first.'

On cue, the ex-detective arrived, dressed in jeans, a sweatshirt and a light-coloured bomber jacket.

'This is very modern,' he said, glancing around the office and taking in the layout.

'Behold, the future of policing,' said Murray, his eyebrows lifting high on his forehead. He made a gesture like a magician about to reveal a trick and smiled winningly.

Howard returned it, deep creases forming around his eyes. 'Bit different to the old station, that's for sure. Tiny reception and a blue lamp outside the building.' He extended a hand. Natalie shook it.

'Thanks for coming in.'

Howard's olive eyes studied her face and he held her hand a little longer than necessary. 'I had to find out if it was true,' he said in a soft voice.

'I'm afraid Ava's been identified.'

Howard rubbed a hand across his forehead. 'It's a bastard, eh? You do everything in your power to find them, but it's all too late.'

Natalie completely understood what he was feeling. They'd both been through similar experiences. They'd given their all and failed. 'We'd really appreciate anything you can tell us about Ava. We're all new to this area and not at all familiar with the case.'

He rubbed a pale hand across his chin and held it there before speaking. 'You all know I was in charge of the Ava Sawyer case. Friday, 24 July 2015, Ava Sawyer was one of twenty children attending a birthday party at Uptown Craft Centre and Farm when she went missing. We interviewed every child present at the party, every member of staff, every parent and every visitor who'd been at the centre that afternoon. That is to say, every visitor who came forward following the television appeal and those we spotted on CCTV. There were six operational CCTV cameras at the time: one at the front entrance, two by the tills at the main exit, two covering the interior of the centre and one overlooking the exterior, noticeably the more expensive plant aisles. There were none in what they called the Play Barn, or by the animal enclosures, the stables or to the side of the building where goods were stored in a locked and secured area. We believed Ava had been intercepted and abducted when she went in search of the toilet, but no witnesses came forward. Nobody saw a young girl being taken outside the centre by force, or even willingly. No one spotted a young girl leaving those premises, either with somebody or alone.'

Natalie watched as Howard's face screwed up in concentration. This case was still fresh in his mind. With eyes narrowed, he was able to recollect every person he interviewed as well as the craft centre layout, from the barn where the children had been playing games and the route Ava might have taken to the toilet, to the actual store aisles. He'd searched everywhere for the child and the investigation had pierced his heart. Natalie knew how that felt. He would undoubtedly have run through the case a million times and asked himself over and over if he'd handled it correctly or missed something vital.

'It was surprisingly quiet at the centre that day. We interviewed only thirty-three people. We had teams out for days, hunting for any evidence, but came up with nothing. Ava Sawyer simply vanished.'

He paced the floor for a moment, gathering thoughts, and his words came slowly. 'We interviewed her parents and for a while, we were concerned. Carl Sawyer was at work thirty miles away at the time of the abduction, and Beatrice Sawyer had met up with one of the other mothers in town, so we had no reason to suspect them of any direct involvement.'

'Why were you concerned?' asked Natalie.

'Beatrice Sawyer was receiving treatment for depression and we were unsure if her health had a bearing on Ava's disappearance. Testimonies from her husband, mother and friends confirmed she'd been having a difficult time – mood swings, that sort of thing. You'll find details in the files.'

He nodded to himself and continued, 'We interviewed the employees at the centre and ran background checks on them all, even those who weren't there that day. Again, we came across nothing untoward. Janet Wild, who'd been in charge of some of the children, had been spotted near the toilets around the time Ava wandered off, but she did not see the child, and after further questioning, we had no reason to suspect she'd kidnapped Ava or was involved in her disappearance.

'Ava's parents made an appeal to the public. Nothing came of it although we followed up every claim that the girl had been spotted. We received calls from all over the country and even as far away as Greece, alleging a girl matching her description had been sighted. After three intensive months, the leads and information dried up. We spoke with every one of Ava's family, neighbours and friends. We dragged up every bit of information on her parents and their friends, but we couldn't find her. Then, four months after she was abducted, we received a note claiming Ava had been snatched for her own safety because her mother had become irresponsible and had even threatened the child. With it came a photograph. You'll find it in the files. It's a picture of a blonde-haired girl playing on a beach taken from quite a distance but it isn't clear enough to prove it actually is of Ava, so we put experts onto it. We identified the beach as one in Devon. The team ran face recognition programmes and established it was unlikely to be Ava. We believed it to have come from some crackpot.

'The Sawyers were subjected to a hate campaign for several weeks, aimed largely at Beatrice. Beatrice believed it was started by one of the other mothers, which was possible. One or two of the parents, notably Paula Kilburn and Caroline Briggs, had mentioned during their interviews that Beatrice had seemed in a hurry to drop off Ava and had driven away without waiting to check the youngster had gone inside, or to even acknowledge the parents.'

'But it was a *drop-off* party. My understanding is that parents generally leave their children at that type of party,' said Natalie.

'Yes, that's correct. Beatrice rejected the claims. She'd fully intended accompanying Ava into the centre but the youngster insisted on being let out to join Rainey Kilburn and Audrey Briggs instead. Her mother hadn't wanted an argument, and seeing the girls were next to the entrance, she'd let her have her own way.'

'You didn't think she was involved in her daughter's disappearance?'

'We certainly looked at the possibility. We interviewed Beatrice and her mother at length but couldn't find any evidence to point to them.'

He raised his hands in a submissive gesture. 'We met dead end after dead end. The search for Ava was scaled back and I was left to handle it with only a small team. I spent months searching for Ava Sawyer and got nowhere. I had to resign from the force for personal reasons and, in light of no new evidence, the case went cold.' He shook his head again.

'Would you mind staying here with us while we go through the files?' Natalie asked.

'That's fine. I've nothing else pressing for an hour or two.'

With notes piling up on tables and fingers flying over keyboards, they trawled through the relevant information, piecing together the events of 24 July 2015, the day Ava went missing. As they worked efficiently, examining interviews and checking back through case notes, it became certain they'd never uncover the truth about how Ava disappeared and died unless they could track down whoever had buried her. It was a tall order. Nearly two years had passed and memories had dimmed, but there'd been other cases like this – cold cases – where officers had found the perpetrator after a lengthy period of time. Natalie wouldn't let this go until she had some answers.

'We uncovered fragments of material at the site. Naomi's been examining them and we believe they belonged to a yellow dress. We also retrieved a plastic bracelet,' said Mike Sullivan. His voice sounded distant, broken up by wind.

Natalie looked across at Howard, who was sifting through notes with Lucy. 'Howard, was Ava wearing a bracelet?'

Howard nodded. 'An orange-yellow arm bangle. Used to belong to her mother but she borrowed it for the party.'

Natalie turned her attention back to the phone. 'We think it's hers. Anything else?'

'We identified the material protecting her body. She was wrapped in hessian. It's stopped raining so we're examining the site in more detail and will see what else we can find. No other bodies in the vicinity at the moment. I'll keep you up to speed. Just wanted to give you the heads up on what we have so far.'

'Thanks for that. I'll talk to you later.'

Natalie ended the call and glanced at her watch. It was already gone 11 a.m. Heads turned in her direction as she spoke. 'Ava was wrapped in hessian. Can you find out who uses hessian?'

Lucy checked on the nearest laptop while Natalie continued, 'Looks like Ava was wearing a yellow dress.'

'She wore a yellow dress to the party,' said Howard. He flicked through his notes. 'Yes. Her mother described it as a lemon cotton dress with a wide skirt and puffed short sleeves.'

'Hessian blankets are used to cover animals,' said Lucy.

'And there were animals at the centre,' said Ian.

'No kidding, Einstein,' said Murray.

'Just stating facts,' said Ian. 'It probably came from the centre. It's not the sort of material you normally have hanging about the house, is it?'

Lucy looked up. 'According to Google, builders use it to prevent brickwork from freezing and gardeners use hessian or jute to protect plants from frost.'

'And there were plants at the centre. See, the material might well have come from there,' said Ian.

Murray grunted.

Natalie continued, 'We can't jump to conclusions but it's possible the hessian came from the centre. Howard, did you come across any such material during your searches?'

'If my memory serves me correctly, there was a pile of folded blankets inside one of the stables. They could have been hessian, I suppose.'

'We'll talk to the staff and find out.'

'You okay if I leave you to it? I have to sort out some stuff before the girls come home.'

'Sure. Thanks for helping us out with it.'

His face was earnest. 'Thanks for asking me. I hope you have better success than me. Ring me if you need any other information. Any time.'

'I shall,' she promised. Howard had to see this case through to the bitter end. She could see it written across his anxious features. It was how she felt about the Olivia Chester case. Not knowing who had murdered the girl would haunt her forever.

CHAPTER FIVE

THEN

The baby-blue eyes, fringed by long, brown eyelashes, stare at him with love and trust. Her perfect bow lips are puckered as if waiting for a kiss, and her unblemished arms are outstretched.

'Pick me up.'

He lifts her from the soil. She weighs next to nothing. Her pale hair is shiny and he caresses it, then pulls his hand back sharply in disgust. He imagined it would be like stroking a puppy, or a furry rabbit, but the hair feels scratchy. He doesn't like scratchy and tosses her back on the ground where she lands on her back, legs in the air, displaying cream underwear. Her eyes shut but she makes no sound. Something stirs inside him. He kneels down, examines her again. She's so pretty in her yellow dress and black shiny shoes, like Sherry Hunt, who's in his class but never speaks to him and instead laughs at his fat arms and pudgy legs, and mocks him when he is puffed out from running. He makes soothing noises like his mother does when he's upset, lifts her again, avoiding touching the hair this time, and cradles her in his arms. She opens her eyes and regards him seriously. She looks a lot like Sherry: same blonde hair, same pink lips. He squirms in delight at a sudden thought. She belongs to him now. He found her so he'll keep her.

He slips the doll into his school satchel and scurries off along the path home. He'll hide her in his room so his mother doesn't find her.

He'll have to think of a name for her: not Sindy or Barbie, or anything like that. A secret name that only he will know – Sherry. He begins to whistle. He likes having a secret.

CHAPTER SIX

'She's hardly spoken a word,' said Tanya Granger, the liaison officer. 'I've been here three hours and in that time she's mostly sat and stared into space. I asked if she wanted me to ring anyone for company – a friend or relative – but she refused.'

'What about her husband?' asked Natalie.

'He left her a few weeks ago.'

'We didn't know.'

'Neither did I until about half an hour ago when Beatrice told me. He's at work at the moment.'

'No one's informed him yet?'

'I don't think so. I haven't dared leave her alone. She seems pretty fragile.'

'We'll visit him. She okay to talk, do you think?'

'You can try.'

Beatrice Sawyer no longer resembled the woman from the photographs Natalie had been examining. She'd aged at least ten years since Ava's disappearance and was a shadow of that woman, her face little more than a skull with skin stretched over it, and dark, haunted eyes in sunken hollows. The loss of her daughter had literally eaten her away. She tugged her cream cardigan around her wasted frame and studied Natalie and Murray with a vacant expression. Tanya placed a cup of tea on the stained coffee table in front of her, but she barely acknowledged the act of kindness. Natalie and Murray sat opposite her in the living room, a purely functional space devoid of colour or style, with mismatched pieces of furniture and dusty surfaces. A large photograph of Ava – the very one used in the newspaper article about her disappearance – was hanging on the wall. Natalie noticed other, smaller frames with pictures of the girl and her parents, lined up on a shelf.

The mother's grief was tangible. It seemed to evaporate from every pore and permeate the air but she made no sound: no crying, no questions.

'I'm truly sorry,' said Natalie.

Beatrice nodded dumbly.

'Is there anyone we can contact for you?'

'No.' Beatrice looked at the teacup and spoke to no one in particular. 'She tell you Carl's gone too?'

Natalie took the 'she' to refer to Tanya. 'Yes, I'm sorry to hear that.'

'Some couples pull together in these situations and we did to start with, but with everything that happened – the hate letters, the looks, the graffiti on the door, and the accusations – it's been too much. Carl got it into his head it was my fault Ava was taken.'

'But it wasn't. It was a drop-off party. None of the parents stayed behind that day.' Natalie's voice was quiet and calming. She'd heard similar from her own psychiatrist.

It wasn't your fault Olivia died, Natalie. You did everything you could.

Beatrice shook her head. 'I've said that to myself so often I'm sick of hearing it. Fact is, I shouldn't have taken her to the party. She didn't want to go.'

'Why not?'

'She told me that morning Harriet Downing didn't like her and she didn't want to go to the party. I didn't pay her too much attention. Children always fall out with each other and then make up again. Ava was no different. One day Audrey would be her best friend, and then Harriet, and then somebody else. They were only five years old, for goodness' sake. I figured Harriet had done or said something trivial that had upset Ava and she was sulking because of it. That was my girl all over – she'd go off in a royal huff about the stupidest things. I told her not to be so silly and that Harriet must like her to invite her to her birthday. We'd already bought a party dress for the occasion, and a present for Harriet. She played in her room all morning – school had finished for the year – and about two thirty I helped her get ready then drove her to the party.'

'Ava didn't discuss the party again with you at all that day?' Murray asked.

'I mentioned it a few times at lunch. Said it would be fun to see the animals. She loved animals. We talked about the pony rides. She needed cajoling, that was all. Ava often needed encouragement to do things. She had trouble mixing with the other children.'

When interviewed, six-year-old Harriet Downing had said Ava was always going off on her own and didn't like playing with the others. Their class teacher, Margaret Goffrey, had confirmed Ava would often argue with friends and storm off in a temper, and that she could be a drama queen. Based on this information, Natalie and her team had discussed the possibility Ava had deliberately wandered off and concluded she might have done so.

'Was there any reason for that?' Natalie asked.

'Ava was Ava. She could be lovable one minute and difficult the next. If she didn't get her own way, she'd throw a tantrum. If she was happy, she was a perfect child. I wasn't in the mood to put up with any nonsense from her that day and I didn't let her have much say about it. That's why she went off to her bedroom – to sulk. Now, of course, I wish I'd let her have her own way. I can't help but wonder if she left the barn because of Harriet. I should have been a better mother and listened to her.'

Natalie offered a sympathetic smile. 'I don't think you should punish yourself over that. Ava left the games because she needed the toilet. None of the children noticed anything going on between her and Harriet, or anyone else for that matter.'

'They were only five and six years old. They might not have realised.' Beatrice's voice was flat.

'According to their statements, Ava was quiet that day, that's all. There were no arguments, tantrums or fall-outs,' said Natalie.

'But as a mother, you do worry. You can't help it. You think over and over about how you should have handled things differently and what would have happened if only you'd listened.' Silence dropped and Beatrice stared into space, unable to speak. Tanya glanced at Natalie and pushed the tea towards the woman, who ignored the drink. Instead, she looked directly at Natalie and asked, 'Do you have children?'

'A boy and a girl. Fifteen and thirteen.'

'Then you understand what I'm saying. You have a responsibility to them, and when something goes wrong – whether they have an accident or are upset or go missing – you feel you're accountable in some way. It's something you can't shake off. I felt badly enough about it all, but Carl made it worse. He didn't say anything at the time. We were waiting for a ransom demand that never came, and caught up in the speed of events – searches, the television appeal – and every minute was taken up with the desperate desire to know she was safe and would come home. It was all-consuming. Then, we suffered the hateful people who made our life even more of a living hell. Why did people do that? Couldn't they see we were hurting enough?'

Natalie had no answers. People could be horrendously cruel.

'They accused me of neglect, of deliberately planning to sell my child and pretend she'd been kidnapped, and even of us both doing away with our own daughter. As if we would. We loved her with every bone in our bodies. It all got too much. Carl turned against me too. He began to pick… pick… pick at it all. He'd go over the events of the day like he was some sort of prosecutor in court: remind me that when Ava received the party invite, he told me to turn it down, but I didn't. *I* insisted she go. I had to explain over and over that I didn't want her to be the only child in the class not to go. Carl disagreed. Said that was a stupid reason. He didn't like the Downings. Thought they were snobby – Carl thinks most people who speak nicely are snobs – and kept repeating I shouldn't have dropped her off. I should have gone inside and waited in case she wanted to go home. He wouldn't stop dragging it up, like he could change events by talking about them. But he couldn't. Nothing can ever change what happened.'

'When did Carl leave you?' Murray asked quietly.

'Only a few weeks ago. I was relieved he went. There's only so much guilt you can take.'

She lifted the teacup and sipped, then looked Natalie in the eye. 'What happened to Ava?'

'We're trying to establish that. We'll do everything we can.'

'When can she…?' Beatrice's voice cracked. 'I want to say goodbye properly to her.'

'We'll let you know so you can make arrangements.'

Tanya put a reassuring hand on the woman's shoulder.

Beatrice blinked a few times as if trying to comprehend what was happening. 'I want my mum to come. She lives in Sheffield.'

Tanya picked up her mobile. 'Shall I ring her for you?'

She nodded.

Natalie and Murray stood to go. 'We'll be in contact again. In the meantime, I'll leave you with PC Granger. She'll stay as long as you want. Please accept our sincerest condolences.' The words sounded so empty, yet Natalie meant them with complete sincerity.

'Thank you.' Her eyes flicked towards one of the photographs of a smiling girl on a swing, legs outstretched in front of her, hands gripping the ropes tightly as she soared into the sky. It was a simple picture of a happy child – a child who'd never again feel the breeze on her face.

Carl Sawyer lifted the wheel as if it weighed nothing and rolled it across the floor towards the truck resting on the ramp. His huge hands were stained black with rubber from the tyres. His two work colleagues were out delivering a vehicle. Natalie and Murray waited for some reaction to the news they'd found his daughter.

The workshop was empty apart from one lorry, and it was this vehicle Carl was working on. He grunted as he slotted the wheel into place and set about tightening the wheel nuts on it. The high-pitched airgun sounded like a dentist's drill and made Natalie flinch.

'Carl, maybe you could spare a couple of minutes,' she shouted, above the noise.

He stiffened at her voice. 'What's the point? You found her and she's dead.'

She'd have thought him unfeeling had she not seen the look of anguish on his face. He was a man at breaking point. The noise stopped. 'Carl,' she said, gently. 'Come into the office for a while.'

He stared at her and replaced the airgun onto a work bench. His hands fell to his sides and he walked towards the door marked *Private*. Natalie and Murray trailed behind his lumbering frame. He slumped onto one of the plastic chairs haphazardly strewn about the room and rested his elbows on the Formica table, a mess of unwashed mugs and empty wrappers.

'I knew it,' he said. 'I knew she was dead. I could *feel* it. Beatrice always thought she was alive. She was always seeing her in shops or playing in the park, or on television, or spotting her every fucking time we went out. It did my head in some days.'

'It often happens in these cases.'

'I know. I just couldn't handle it any more. You have told Beatrice, haven't you?'

'Yes. She told us where to find you. There's an officer with her, and her mum's on her way to the house. What about you? Is there anyone we can contact for you?'

'Me?' He half-laughed. 'No. I'm beyond grief. I've been living in a sort of hell for the last two years. I suppose at least I really know the truth now. She's gone. My little girl really has gone. How… I mean… what… happened?'

Natalie understood what he was trying to ask. 'We haven't established the cause of death yet. The pathologist is still examining her.'

'She was murdered though?'

'We can't be certain although we are treating her death as suspicious.'

He shook his head, dark eyes now sparking. 'No. She was killed. You get that straight. My baby girl was murdered and you'd better find the bastard who did it. I want him put away forever.'

Natalie spoke calmly to the distressed man. 'We're running a full investigation into the cause of her death. I have the statement you made back in 2015. You were concerned about your wife's mental health at the time. Is that correct?'

'Beatrice was suffering from depression. It'd been going on for a couple of years. I mentioned it to the officer in charge. I couldn't get my head around why she'd taken Ava to the bloody party. Ava had been adamant in the morning that she didn't want to go. Next thing I knew, not only had Beatrice taken her, my daughter had disappeared. She insisted Ava had changed her mind, but I didn't believe her. I think Beatrice forced her to go. She could be manipulative when she wanted to be. Part of me suspected she wanted Ava to go to the party for her own reasons.'

'What sort of reasons?' Murray asked.

He shrugged. 'I don't know for sure. I half-thought she might be having an affair. You know, drop Ava off, have an hour with her man, and then pick Ava back up. I was pretty messed up at the time – all sorts of crazy ideas going on. I didn't know what I was thinking. When the hate mail started, that made it worse. I couldn't think straight.

'I actually accused her of deliberately wanting Ava out of the way. I'd had a few drinks that time and just wanted to understand – get an idea of what the fuck happened. Beatrice broke down and

I felt like a proper shit afterwards. I had no right to hurl that sort of accusation. She's been in bits over this. You've seen her. She's not eaten properly since the day Ava went. It's like she's punishing herself.'

Natalie pushed him on the subject. 'You feel your wife was in some way responsible for your daughter's disappearance?'

'Felt. I don't *feel* that any more. Look, I'm not proud of myself. I've said some terrible things to Beatrice since that day. I should have been more supportive. She was wrecked by what had happened, and instead of easing her guilt, I heaped on a whole lot more. Trouble was, no matter how I tried, I couldn't shake off the feeling she was at fault. If she'd only kept Ava at home, this wouldn't have happened. She'd still be with us.' His fists clenched and he raised one to his forehead, resting his head on it and squeezing his eyes shut. His words were little more than whispers. 'My sweet little girl.'

'Carl, would you like the sergeant here to drive you home?'

He untightened his fingers and looked up. 'No. I have work to do. This changes nothing. My relationship with Beatrice is over. Ava's gone. Tell me when you catch her murderer. I want to put a name to the piece of shit who killed her.'

Natalie turned away, Murray by her side, and walked to the door. Behind her the airgun had begun again.

'Where next?' asked Murray.

'Could we get hold of the previous owner of Uptown Craft Centre and Farm – Elsa Townsend?'

Murray shook his head. 'She's living in Spain now. It would have to be a phone call or via Skype.'

'Who else was working at the centre at the time?'

Murray scanned his notebook. 'Guy Noble, Janet Wild, Kristin Jónsson and Ted Marshall.'

'We'll start with Guy.'

'He's now employed at Sudbury Wildlife Centre, a small sanctuary about half an hour away.'

'Okay, let's go and talk to him.'

As they pulled away from the workshop, Natalie caught a glimpse of Carl in the wing mirror. He'd stopped working and was sat on a tyre, head in his heads, shoulders shaking. She continued watching until he became little more than a speck, and they turned to join the busy line of traffic.

CHAPTER SEVEN

WEDNESDAY, 26 APRIL – LATE AFTERNOON

According to the green sign fronting the building, Sudbury Wildlife Centre was a small sanctuary housing mostly exotic animals and birds of prey. Guy Noble was standing behind the front desk to welcome any visitors. He flashed them a broad smile that faded slightly when Natalie held up her ID card.

'Are you Guy Noble?'

'Yes, I am. What's this about?' Guy's face scrunched up in puzzlement.

'Ava Sawyer.'

His eyes narrowed further. 'I remember Ava. She was the little girl who went missing at the birthday party where I used to work. She disappeared from under our noses. Why? What's happened?'

'We've uncovered her body.'

His eyes clouded with concern. 'Oh, crap! Hang on. I need to get someone to take over here.'

He disappeared through a door only to return almost immediately. 'Sorry, we have to man the desk. It gets more popular after school when it's decent weather, like today, and we've got a birthday party group coming in at about four o'clock. You found Ava Sawyer?'

'Yes.'

'Where?'

'Buried behind the garden centre.'

'Really? Oh no. That's dreadful. She was at the centre the whole time we were searching for her?'

'We're not sure about that, yet. I'd like to ask you about the party. We were hoping you might remember something, anything, that would help us with our enquiries. Did you notice any strange activity at the Craft Centre and Farm in the days before Ava's disappearance?'

'Nothing springs to mind. I gave a full statement at the time,' he said, heavy eyebrows furrowed deeply.

'I know but this is no longer a missing person enquiry and we have to look at it with fresh eyes.'

'Of course.'

'What can you tell me about Elsa Townsend and Alistair Fulcher, the owners of the centre? Did you notice anything unusual about their behaviour around that time?'

His forehead creased in concentration. 'Not really. They didn't get along easily so there were always disagreements. Erm… let me think. I might have overheard them arguing on a few occasions and Elsa shouting. She shouted a lot. After Barney, her husband, left her and the business, she got shoutier, if that's a word.'

'But Alistair and Elsa co-owned the place?'

'That's right. Barney and Elsa used to run the place but they split up and he sold his half of the centre to his friend Alistair. Elsa had to go along with it because I don't think she could have run the place without a partner. Mostly, they stayed out of each other's way; Alistair dealt with the craft and garden side and Elsa stuck to the parties and animals.'

'Alistair didn't get involved in those?'

'No. It was more Elsa's thing, although once Barney had gone, she backed off and left the running of the events to Donna, Janet and me. I think she found the kids a bit much some days. They could be a handful.'

'How was Elsa that day?' Natalie asked, wondering if the kidnapping had been a deliberate act against Elsa, to discredit her business.

'Majorly stressed. Alistair went off at the last minute, leaving her to run both the craft and garden centre side of things and the party. There were only four employees at work that day, so we were all stretched to the limit. Ted Marshall and Kristin Jónsson were working the craft centre side and Janet Wild and I were helping Elsa with the party. Elsa stomped about a lot, barking orders and nitpicking: the games in the barn hadn't been set up properly, the horses didn't look like unicorns – stuff like that.'

'Was that normal behaviour for her?'

'When she was hassled, she could be a right bitch.'

'And how did you feel about that?'

Guy gave a half-laugh. 'I took the crap she dealt out with a smile. I was already making plans to leave and had applied for a job at this place. I wanted to get into falconry and wildlife. Plants are okay and I enjoyed working on the farm side there, but it got a bit too heavy sometimes.'

'Heavy?'

'Yeah, when she was like that, it wasn't much fun. She'd upset people and that ruined the atmosphere. It's difficult to be upbeat with a bunch of children when the boss is staring daggers at you.'

'You told officers at the time you didn't see Ava Sawyer at any point that day.'

'That's true. Donna Swanson was supposed to be in charge of the birthday party, but something got screwed up and Donna took the day off, leaving Elsa to deal with it last minute. Normally, whoever was in charge would hold a quick briefing so we'd all know how many children were coming and whose birthday it was, but not that day. Elsa handled the meet-and-greet, which is something we usually all got involved in, and then conducted the party games alone. I was supposed to help out at those, but I went to check on the animals and one of the rabbits had nibbled through some wire netting and escaped, so I had to find it, and then repair the netting. By the time I arrived at the barn, the games were over and Elsa was in a fluster. She told me to take the kids to the petting zoo. She shot off, leaving me with the children. I joined Janet, who was already waiting at the animal enclosures, and together we sorted them out. It was only when Elsa met up with us at the stables much later, we knew a child was missing.'

'None of the children mentioned Ava was missing?'

'There was loads going on. I was telling them all about the animals and letting them pet or feed them. We went all around the yard, stopping at various points. There wouldn't have been time to register that one of their friends was missing. I expect everyone in each group thought Ava was with the others in the other group.'

'Can we go back a minute? You said you checked on the animals. What did you do exactly?'

'I made sure they'd got food and water, that there was clean straw in the lamb enclosure and some milk ready for the children to feed him. That sort of thing.'

'The animal enclosures were near the barn, weren't they?'

'That's right.'

'You didn't spot anyone, staff or visitors, in the vicinity?'

'I didn't.'

'You looked after the ponies too, didn't you?'

'That was mostly Janet's area. I dealt with the other animals.'

'Did you ever use hessian blankets to keep them warm?'

'Not that I'm aware of. They were kept inside. Not much call for blankets.'

'What about the ponies?'

'They had blankets. You'd have to ask Janet whether or not they were hessian.'

'What about the plants? Did you ever need to protect them from frost?'

'They were mostly under cover or, if they were fragile, we over-wintered them in greenhouses.'

'Did you sell hessian as frost-protecting material?'

'I don't know. I didn't work on the sales side of things. That's something you'd have to ask the other staff.'

'Okay. Thank you for your time.'

As they walked back towards the car, Natalie glanced across at Murray. 'Not much help regarding the hessian, then. We'll ask Janet Wild. By the way, did you read Donna Swanson's statement?'

'Yes. She was at a hotel with Alistair Fulcher at the time of the disappearance.'

'I wonder if Elsa knew about their tryst?'

'Even if she did, how would it have any bearing on the case?'

'I don't know if it does. I just think it's jolly convenient that on the day Ava Sawyer disappeared, the woman who was supposed to be in charge of the party suddenly took the day off to shag her boss, who should also have been at work. We really need to talk to Elsa about this. Can you find a number for her as soon as we get back to the station? I want a quick chat with Janet Wild first. She lives about ten miles away from Uptown in Axmouth. I'll give her a ring to let her know we're on our way.'

Axmouth was a small village consisting of two antique shops, a pub, a primary school, a church and a village hall. The village green was bordered by a mishmash of houses, an eclectic mix of white-and-black timbered properties, thatched cottages, three-storey properties and renovated Victorian residences.

The house they were looking for was towards the end of a narrow lane, one of a line of terraced cottages facing the church. Murray parked the car in the church car park and they walked across to number 4 Elm Tree Road. Natalie rang the bell and was greeted by a volley of yaps. The door opened and an eager snout emerged before a hand grabbed the animal's collar and hauled it back inside. 'Come in. Bart, no. Sit!'

Janet Wild was in her thirties, with deep auburn hair and ruddy cheeks. The dog, a cheerful mongrel, sat obediently, wagging its tail all the while.

'He doesn't bite but I don't like him jumping up at people.' She produced a bone-shaped biscuit from her jeans pocket, which the dog immediately took to another room to consume. 'Okay, want to come into the kitchen?'

They followed her and crammed into the tiny, utilitarian kitchen.

'As I told you on the phone, we would like to run back over the events surrounding Ava Sawyer's disappearance.'

'It was a terrible thing. I couldn't sleep for days after she went missing. I kept seeing the look on her mother's face when she found out Ava had disappeared. I can only imagine what she was going through.'

Natalie had clocked the photograph of two toddlers in the hallway when they'd entered.

'You have children?'

'Oh, you saw the photo, didn't you? They're my nieces, my sister's kids. Love them to bits. I don't have any children. I'm not in any serious relationship so probably won't have any for a while yet. Bart's my baby at the moment.'

'I'd like to go back over the statement you gave at the time of Ava's disappearance. You told DI Franks you were by the animal enclosures when Guy arrived with a group of children. You took nine of them with you.'

'That's right. We divided up the group willy-nilly. They weren't the quietest group of children we'd dealt with and some became quite excitable when they spotted the animals, lots of squealing and so on, so we set about the animal experience pretty quickly.'

'What does that entail exactly?'

'Basically, taking the kids around to each pen and telling them about the animals inside it, then letting them stroke or pet the animal. There were gerbils and floppy-eared rabbits in addition to pot-bellied pigs, and a few sheep. We had a lamb at the time. He was a big success. The children loved him. We let the birthday girl or boy feed him. Harriet, the birthday girl, was in my group so she got to give him a bottle of milk.'

'Did any of the children mention Ava at any stage?'

'I don't think so. Like I told the detective at the time, it was difficult to register what they were saying, given they all talked at the same time, and Harriet was especially demanding and quite vocal. If any of the children said anything about Ava, I missed it.' She chewed momentarily on her bottom lip. 'When I was first interviewed I tried really hard to think back at what was said but I really couldn't remember. Your mind plays tricks on you, doesn't it? Since then I've talked myself into believing one of the boys said something about her being outside, but I must have imagined it. I'd have remembered at the time, wouldn't I?'

'In these sorts of cases, after so much time has passed, it's unlikely your memory would be as accurate as it was at the time of the event.'

'That's what I figured. I wish I could help more. You still searching for her?'

'I'm afraid not. Her body was recovered yesterday afternoon.'

'Oh no. That's dreadful news. Her poor parents.' Janet shook her head sadly.

'Janet, I understand Elsa was in charge of the party that day. Did she seem okay to you?'

'As okay as she ever was. She was quite bossy at times, especially when she got stressed. I'd worked with her for five years so I knew her moods. I remember she wasn't happy with Donna for leaving her in the lurch. I saw her in the office an hour before the party. She wasn't looking on form. I asked if she was okay. She replied she had a "bit of a headache". I volunteered to take over for her but she insisted she was fine and she'd do it. Apparently, Harriet's mother was well-connected and Elsa wanted to keep her sweet. She took Ava's disappearance really badly.'

'Did she ever confide in you?'

Janet shook her head. 'She didn't confide in anybody at work to my knowledge. She kept her private life private, especially after she and Barney split up.'

'You gave up your job at the centre soon after Ava disappeared.'

'We lost all the party bookings overnight and it wasn't the same place. We all felt extremely responsible. Elsa was the worst. She stopped coming into work and then Alistair got rid of the farm and the animals, so I felt it was best to move on. It came as no surprise Elsa and Alistair sold out to Poppyfields. I don't think she and Alistair could actually bear the sight of each other towards the end.'

'What makes you think that?'

'Arguments, snide remarks, angry words. She made it quite clear how she felt about Alistair. It was no secret they didn't get along.'

'You looked after the ponies, didn't you?'

'Yes, that was one of my jobs. I cleaned out their stables and decorated them for the parties.'

'Did you ever use hessian blankets?'

'We used to but we got rid of them in favour of fleece blankets, which were warmer.'

'Did you retain the hessian blankets?'

'Yes. Elsa didn't like waste. I think they got stored in one of the stables. Can I ask why?'

'I'm sorry, I can't comment,' said Natalie. 'I think that's everything for now. Thank you for your time.'

Janet chewed again at her bottom lip. 'I'm truly sorry about Ava. Every parent's worst nightmare.'

'It is.' Natalie handed over a card. 'If you remember anything, however insignificant it may seem, give me a call.'

She and Murray crossed the road to the church once more. Natalie hesitated by the car, puzzling over what she'd discovered. Murray waited for her to voice her thoughts.

'We've not got much, have we? So far, all we've ascertained is that there might have been some hessian blankets in one of the stables and that Elsa and Alistair had issues and didn't get along too well.'

'Do you think Elsa had something to do with Ava's disappearance?' Murray asked.

'If I'm to believe what I read in the case files earlier, then no. DI Franks examined every aspect of this investigation, down to the last detail, and followed up every lead. He checked out Elsa thoroughly and could not come up with a motive as to why she'd take the child or how she'd manage to do so without being spotted. Yet, there's a question mark over her whereabouts that afternoon. We only have her word she was in the office trying to shake off a headache.'

'Elsa knew about the hessian blankets too,' said Murray.

Natalie nodded. 'I agree. We must talk to her. Uncovering Ava's body at the centre has cast fresh light onto this case. Why there? Why the centre? And surely somebody must have noticed something suspicious that day.' She scratched her head, perplexed.

Her thoughts were interrupted by ringing from her mobile. It was Lucy.

'Natalie, we've just received information regarding another missing child. It's one of Ava's friends from the birthday party that day – Audrey Briggs. She's been found dead in Queen's Park.'

CHAPTER EIGHT

WEDNESDAY, 26 APRIL – NIGHT

Mike, who'd also been called to Queen's Park, stood in quiet conversation with Natalie on the pavement outside 75 Queen's Avenue, home to the Briggs family. Officers were keeping a small group of journalists, photographers and neighbours at bay. Mike had already told them to back off but still they waited behind the police cordon that now stretched across the Briggs' front garden. Police had blocked the road at both ends, preventing all vehicles other than emergency services from entering. Blue lights strobed across the darkening sky as Natalie spoke to her colleague.

'What do we know?' asked Natalie.

'Audrey's mother collected her from school at three twenty this afternoon and took her directly to the Little Stars Dance Academy in Uptown for a class. The class finished at four thirty and they returned home from school at approximately four forty-five. Soon after, she cycled to the local convenience store situated at the bottom of Queen's Avenue to buy a bottle of cola. Apparently, it's a very safe neighbourhood and Audrey had cycled to the store before on a few occasions,' he said, catching the look of surprise on Natalie's face. 'When she hadn't returned by five thirty, her mother, Caroline Briggs, went in search of her. The shop manager,

Rod Bunting, hadn't set eyes on the girl. On learning her daughter hadn't even reached the shop, Caroline alerted us.'

Natalie squinted into the distance. By the entrance to Queen's Park, adjacent to the road, the K9 unit was loading eager German Shepherds into their van. She dragged herself back to the conversation. 'What about her friends?'

'None of them saw her after school. Her mother was the last person to see her.'

'Audrey was missing for about three and a half hours,' said Natalie, glancing at her watch.

'That's right. Initially, officers spoke to Caroline Briggs and then called it in to the missing person's team. Due to the nature of Audrey's sudden, unexplained disappearance and her mother's obvious distress, we decided to act immediately and began the search.'

'Where was her father during the search?'

'Stephen Briggs works for a marketing company and is currently away on business in Glasgow. He was notified of Audrey's disappearance and arranged to drive back to Samford without delay. We didn't want to break the news that we'd found her body over the phone, especially while he was driving. Understandably, Mrs Briggs is in a bad state. She's got a liaison officer with her until her husband returns – Tanya Granger.'

'I was with her earlier today,' said Natalie. 'She was with Beatrice Sawyer, Ava's mother.'

'Yes, she didn't want to leave Beatrice, but there was no one else free and Beatrice's mother was on her way to stay with her.'

'Officers came across Audrey's body at eight twenty-five p.m. and I got dragged away from the lab. I hear you're heading the enquiry into her death.'

'That's right. We think that case might be related to this one.'

'That's a tough gig.' His eyes rested on hers for a moment and he offered a kindly smile. 'I'll take you to her if you're ready.'

Natalie couldn't reply. She really didn't want to look but what option had she got? To keep morbid thoughts at bay, she kept talking as they first crossed the road and then took the footpath beside the park's high railings. An unmarked police Audi pulled up ahead of them, and Lucy and Ian emerged from it.

'I know she's only an eight-year-old but did Audrey own a mobile phone?'

'Yes, but she didn't take it with her to the shop. We checked it but we didn't find anything of relevance on it. She used it mostly to play games and stay in contact with her mum. I was going send to the lab to double-check but if you want to look at it...'

'No, it's okay. Send it across.'

They passed an ambulance with its back door open and a white forensic van. Both pulled up onto the verge and reached the entrance to the park, which was flanked by two officers.

'How many entrances to the park are there?'

'There's the main entrance, accessed from the town centre, and this one.'

A noticeboard adjacent to the open gate showed a map of the park layout. The more commonly used walkways, playground and bowling green were located closer to the main entrance. The path in front of her forked approximately fifty metres ahead – one way leading to the river, the other to the bandstand and beyond to the formal gardens. A small cough behind her alerted her to the presence of her team. Together they entered the park.

Queen's Park was more of a formal garden than a park, with walks around raised beds, floral displays and monuments to fallen heroes plus fine statues of people Natalie had never heard of. It was a popular attraction with grassy banks that flanked the River Blithe, frequented by flotillas of ducks observed by large numbers of picnicking locals during summer months. The park provided the usual recreational facilities for families, along with a multi-play area for toddlers. The team's route took them past massive dark trees, each bearing a wooden nameplate explaining their origin, and thick vegetation. At the fork, they turned right onto a narrower path marked, 'Gardens and Playground'.

Judging by the activity ahead, they'd almost reached the spot. Natalie steeled herself. She recognised one of Mike's team immediately. He was in a crouched position, his back hiding whatever was in front of him. He rose as they approached and shifted to one side. Natalie released the breath she'd been unknowingly holding. A pink bike was on its side in the grass.

His eyes acknowledged her presence. Mike spoke again. 'It's a Bridgford Rainbow Girls Classic Heritage bike in pale pink with a front wicker basket. I think they're quite popular. Thea has the exact same one.'

'Audrey's?' she asked.

'We believe so. It's about a hundred metres from her body. We're checking it over for prints. Looking at the tyre marks in the grass, I'd say she braked hurriedly and threw the bike down. It's not been laid down with care, more likely cast aside. You can see traces of dirt on the right handlebar where it struck the soft grass and mud first.' He shone a torch onto the area in question.

Natalie wiped sweaty palms against her trousers. Darkness had now fallen and only the pathways in the grounds were lit. Behind them were dark bushes, shadowy sinister forms that could conceal a person. Murray, closest to her, voiced her own thoughts.

'Audrey might have been frightened by something or somebody hiding in the undergrowth, dumped the bike and run away,' he said.

Natalie nodded.

Ian added his own thoughts. 'I still don't understand why she was here. She was supposed to be going to the shop, which is in the opposite direction.'

'She got waylaid?' Lucy offered. 'Maybe a friend met her as she was coming out of her house and called her over to the park.'

'Then why was she alone? What happened to her friend?'

Lucy shrugged. 'Got me there. I don't know. Maybe it's some-thing we should consider though.'

'Is there any CCTV in this park?' Natalie directed her question to Mike.

'Only on the main gate, near the greenhouse and overlooking the children's play area. Nothing here. There are none along the street where she lived either.'

Natalie tutted. 'That's a pain. We'll need all CCTV footage regardless. See if we can trace her movements or indeed identify anyone in the park at the time of her disappearance. Ian, can you arrange that?'

'Will do.'

Following Mike, they moved away from the bike, across the damp lawns of springy grass towards artificial lights. Natalie slowed her pace, her ears drumming. Fifty metres ahead, white-suited officers were at work close to a large chestnut tree, whose wide branches spread like protective arms over some bushy evergreen shrubs, which were about two metres in height and fifty in length.

'What a fucking nightmare for her parents,' Lucy whispered. Natalie could only agree. She balled her hands to stop them from shaking.

Natalie lifted a hand. 'Stay here,' she said to Lucy and Ian. 'Don't want us all tramping over the crime scene.' She beckoned for Murray and, slipping on plastic gloves and overshoe protectors, took a deep breath.

The sight of the slight figure flat on her back was heartbreaking. There'd been no attempt to bury the child. Her legs, in pale-pink tights, stuck out straight in front of her, feet in flat, pink dance pumps, and her arms were limp by her sides, palms face up. Her pageboy hair had fallen away from her sweet face with its upturned nose. Her pale-violet eyelids were closed, her head tilted to one side, as if she were asleep.

'We haven't moved her but you can see a mark on her neck,' said Mike.

Natalie looked at the red ligature across the girl's throat. It was difficult to work out what had caused it. She knew better than to assume. The mark could have been caused after death or be unrelated to her death. Policing taught you to never jump to conclusions.

'Didn't you say she came in from the class and went straight out to the shop?' Natalie asked.

'That's right.'

'I doubt she was dressed like this for a dance class.' Audrey was wearing a lemon chiffon dress that had been spread out neatly to show off its pleats and the large yellow bow around her midriff.

Natalie looked the child up and down, all the while wishing she could lift her and breathe life back into her still body. She blocked such thoughts. 'There are grubby stains on both knees and on her palms. Could be grass stains. She might have fallen off her bike and stained them then, or tried to crawl away from her assailant. Her tights are dirty and I think there's mud or dirt on the soles of her shoes. The dress, however, looks new.'

Murray's voice was barely audible. 'Ava Sawyer was wearing a yellow dress when she disappeared.'

Natalie's stomach churned like a washing machine. Her words forced their way between her lips. 'I know. That's what really bothers me. Somebody has dressed Audrey up for a party. Her dress has been arranged. Not only is she in a party dress, her lips are unusually red. I think she's wearing lipstick – reddish lipstick.' Natalie bent closer to study the child's face, trying hard not to focus too much on the angry ligature around the child's neck.

'Is it normal for an eight-year-old to be wearing lipstick?' asked Murray.

'I'm sure girls of all ages try out make-up. Leigh used to when she was this age. Maybe she put some on at the dance school. We'll talk to her mother and discuss this further at the station,' said Natalie, suddenly keen to move away from the little girl. 'Would you video the scene, please? And when the pathologist arrives, get his initial thoughts on cause of death. I also want to know if anyone interfered with her sexually.' She repressed a shudder at her words and rejoined the rest of the team.

'Ian, continue with door-to-door enquiries. Obviously, we need to secure the park too.'

Ian nodded. 'Of course. I'll sort it.'

'I wonder if the clothes she was wearing are missing. I'm hoping they're somewhere nearby and we can get them tested for DNA. Mike, will you let us know if you unearth them?'

'Sure, I'll get back to my team and see what we can find.' He strode away into the darkness.

'We have the more pressing task of talking to Caroline Briggs, Audrey's mum. You okay with that?' she asked Lucy, who nodded her assent.

They trudged back the way they'd come. Outside on the road, activity had intensified with police vehicles departing and forensic teams arriving. Drawing closer to the house, Natalie spotted a curtain twitch at a neighbour's downstairs window and sighed. News was spreading fast. More people had gathered and the first flowers – a bunch of daffodils – had been left near the police cordon. Soon the media circus would begin and Caroline and Stephen would be faced with more than just the nightmare of their daughter's death. Ian was making his way towards the nearest group, arms motioning for them to move away. It was only natural everyone would want to know what was going on, but Natalie only had thoughts for the grieving mother. She tapped on the door and was greeted by Tanya, who ushered them inside and shut the door immediately behind them.

The house, an unexceptional semi-detached residence with a plain carpeted entrance, somehow felt homely with a pink *Frozen* school bag hanging from a banister, shoes kicked off haphazardly by the door and coats hanging from gaily coloured pegs, each with a name above it: Caroline, Audrey, Libby and Stephen. It was dreadful that such tragedy had entered these people's lives.

Caroline Briggs was a petite woman with elfin features. She seemed dwarfed by the settee she sat on, knees drawn to her stomach, arms clasped around them, her cheeks stained with tears. Tanya sat beside her. Natalie introduced herself and Lucy and offered her sincerest condolences. Caroline couldn't look at her.

'I told them she'd been taken,' said Caroline, hugging her knees more tightly. 'I knew it the moment she didn't come back from the shop. It wasn't like her.'

'Are you feeling up to talking to us?'

Caroline looked at her, eyes glassy with tears, and nodded.

'If you could go through everything that happened when you got home again, that would be really helpful,' said Natalie, quietly.

Caroline sniffed back tears. 'I picked Audrey up from school at the usual time – three twenty. She has a ballet class at the dance academy in town every Wednesday so I dropped her off and collected her again at four thirty. It's about fifteen minutes from here. As soon as she got in, Audrey went straight to the fridge. Said she was thirsty after all the dancing. We'd run out of cola. That's her favourite drink.' She stopped, caught unaware by her words. She lifted wet eyes and whispered. '*Was* her favourite drink.'

She studied a spot on the ceiling for a moment and then picked up where she'd left off. 'The baby was screaming and needed changing so I told Audrey to wait and we'd go get some, or to drink some juice instead, but she insisted on cola and asked if she could go and buy some herself. There's a convenience store we use regularly at the bottom of the street and it isn't far away. I wasn't too keen to agree. I get nervous when she's out of sight, especially after what happened to Ava Sawyer, but it really wasn't far away and I've let her go once or twice before. I gave her the money – two one-pound coins – for the drink and went upstairs to change Libby and put her down for a nap, but she was really grouchy – she's teething at the moment – so it took a long time to get her to settle. When I came downstairs, it was twenty past five and Audrey still hadn't returned. I thought at first there might have been a queue at the shop. There's only one till and sometimes Rod chats a long time to the customers he's serving. Then another ten minutes passed and I wondered what was keeping her. I collected Libby and went to the shop. It's only a ten-minute walk. There was no sign of her so I asked Rod if she'd been in, but he hadn't seen her. I knew straight away something had happened to her.' She began to rock, a slow steady rhythm.

'You didn't assume she might have stopped off to chat to friends or gone off with them?'

Caroline's answer was hampered by attempts to prevent herself from crying. 'No. She wouldn't do that. Not after what happened to Ava. I told her she was never to talk to strangers and always make sure I knew where she was. Ava didn't tell anyone where she was going and she disappeared. Audrey was terribly upset and frightened after that party. She would never, ever go off without telling me where she was. No way.' Her final words were barely audible. She pressed her lips together tightly until they turned white, and rocked again.

'Did she often go to the park?'

Fresh tears rolled over her cheeks. 'Now and again but she wouldn't have gone without telling me.'

'But if a friend had happened to call her from over the road, maybe?'

'There's quite a bit of traffic that uses this road and she isn't allowed to cross it alone.' Again Caroline shook her head and pointed out a photo of Audrey holding onto a furry black puppy licking her chin. 'That was Muffin. He was Audrey's puppy. She absolutely adored him. Dog daft, she is… was. She'd been desperate for a dog and eventually we gave in and bought Muffin for her. He escaped from our front garden six months ago, belted across that road and was struck by a car. It was horrible. We both saw it happen but couldn't save him. Audrey was completely cut up about it, but she knew to never cross that road unless she used the pelican crossing near the shop, or she was with me.'

A baby began wailing upstairs. Caroline shifted uncomfortably at the sound. She wiped her stained cheeks with the back of her hand and unfurled from the settee. 'That's Libby. I have to get her.'

As soon as she'd left the room, Natalie looked across at Tanya. 'Any news from her husband?'

'He ought to be home soon. He hasn't rung. Last he heard his daughter was missing.'

'Shit,' whispered Lucy. 'He doesn't know yet?'

Tanya shook her head.

Caroline returned with a red-faced baby, who stopped crying when she saw there were visitors. Caroline sat down again and held the child on her knee. Libby stuffed a fist into her mouth and stared at Natalie with wide eyes.

Natalie spoke again. 'Caroline, what was Audrey wearing when she went out?'

'Her ballet outfit: black leotard, pale-pink tights and pink dance pumps, and her favourite pink cardigan. That one.' She pointed at a picture of Audrey beaming a gap-toothed grin. The cardigan was bright pink and hung down her skinny frame almost reaching her knees. Audrey's hands were stuffed in the pockets and she had half-opened it to show off her T-shirt bearing her name written out in glitter.

'Was she wearing any lipstick?'

Caroline shook her head. 'She sat in the passenger seat in the car and we chatted about her lesson. I'd have noticed if she'd been wearing lipstick.'

'Might she have borrowed yours when you went upstairs to change the baby?'

'I don't see how or why. She left straight away with the money. Why are you asking?'

'We think she might have been wearing lipstick,' said Natalie.

Creases formed in Caroline's forehead. 'She wasn't when I last saw her. Where would she have got it? I'll check to make sure she didn't take mine.'

'Want me to hold her?' Tanya held out her arms for the baby.

Caroline passed the infant across and stood up. Her handbag was on a nearby table. She rummaged through it and extracted a silver container. 'It's here.'

'You have others?'

'No. I only wear the one shade. I buy a new one when it runs out.' She pulled the top off to reveal a pale-pink lipstick.

The front door opened and shut with a bang and a voice called out, 'Caroline.'

More tears filled her eyes.

A man appeared in the doorway, his suit rumpled and his tie undone.

'Oh, Stephen!' she said, her head shaking from side to side.

He rushed towards her and scooped her into his arms. His voice cracked. 'I know. I know. As soon as I saw the police cars, I knew.'

Natalie rose to leave. She'd not be able to talk to Caroline again for the time being.

Stephen swivelled his upper body in her direction and spoke, his voice tremulous. 'I need some time alone with my wife.'

'Of course you do. PC Granger will wait outside and I'll return tomorrow. I'd like to add we're truly sorry for your loss.'

His lips quivered and he turned his attention back to Caroline, wrapping his arms around her more tightly and resting his forehead against the top of her head.

CHAPTER NINE

THEN

His mother blows her nose with one of the monogrammed handkerchiefs she received as a Christmas gift from Granny. It has small, purple flowers embroidered in one corner: violets, his mother had told him, on account of her name. He likes the thought of his mother being named after a flower even if she looks nothing like one. He'd wondered what scent a violet would have. After she'd put the hankies away in her drawer, he'd hunted one out and studied the stitching, tracing the raised flowers with his chubby fingers. He'd held it to his nose but there was no perfume.

The nose-blowing stops and he is brought back to the present. He's in the headmaster's office, his mother in one of the two voluminous chairs opposite the headmaster. He, however, is standing upright, hands behind his back. He's guilty of a crime.

'I can't think what got into him,' says his mother, as if he weren't in the room. 'He's normally very gentle. A gentle giant,' she adds and tries to smile at Mr Gordon. Mr Gordon never smiles and he isn't about to start now.

'If Miss Tideswell hadn't heard the commotion, heaven knows what would have happened.'

His mother shakes her head. 'That's ridiculous. He's only ten years old. He isn't likely to have caused much damage. The girl is exaggerating the entire affair out of all proportion. He's not got a malicious bone in his body.'

'Nobody is saying that. I'm merely suggesting the boy doesn't know his own strength and it will be best if he keeps right away from the girls in his class. It will be better if he stays in the classroom during playtime for a couple of weeks at least, and then we'll reassess the situation.'

'That's outrageous. You can't keep him cooped up like a prisoner. He's a little boy. He needs to go outside and enjoy fresh air. Besides, it'll ostracise him further from his classmates if you single him out and keep him inside every day.'

The headmaster considers the logic of what the boy's mother is saying, and although the boy doesn't understand what 'ostracise' means, he knows she's on his side. He never meant to hurt Sherry. He'd wanted to check if her hair felt the same as the doll's hair, and when he'd spotted her sitting alone on one of the benches in the class cloakroom, in front of a row of duffel coats, he'd never meant to frighten her. He'd crept up behind her, intending only to briefly stroke the golden curtain that hung to her hips, but she'd sensed his presence, leapt to her feet and started screaming. Miss Tideswell had rushed in, followed by half the class and Sherry's friends who'd stared at him with big googly eyes, hiding behind each other while Sherry had sobbed.

He might have got away with it had her friends, Gail Shore and Kitty Francis, not told Miss Tideswell he'd been watching all of them doing handstands from behind the wall. They said he was always staring at Sherry, especially on the school bus going home, and it was beginning to scare her.

He'd been questioned but refused to respond. What could he say? He wouldn't hurt Sherry. He just wanted her to like him. He couldn't tell them he had a doll that looked just like her and he wanted to know if her hair felt like the doll's hair. Everyone would laugh at him. Better to let them think he was scary. Then, the teasing wouldn't happen.

'Why?' His mother is speaking to him.

'I only wanted to be friendly,' he says, letting crocodile tears fall down his cheeks. His mother sighs heavily. 'See. He's a lonely boy and keeping him inside at playtimes won't help.'

The headmaster seems surprised by the crying and confession and reluctantly agrees to let him keep his playtimes as long as he promises not to go near the girls' area and never to sneak up on a girl again.

He nods, letting the tears dampen his cheeks. His mother lends him a clean handkerchief – one with violets on – and he blows his nose on it noisily, all the while thinking about Sherry's face. She was so scared of him. It made him feel powerful.

CHAPTER TEN

WEDNESDAY, 26 APRIL – LATE NIGHT

Lucy stretched languidly and attempted to stifle a yawn. Natalie, bent over paperwork, noticed the act and glanced at her watch. It was coming up to eleven. It had been a harrowing night. They'd examined the video footage Murray had filmed at the crime scene. The sight of Audrey's body in the party dress had stunned them all into silence for quite some time.

At the moment, Lucy was concentrating on CCTV footage in and around the park, checking movements of individuals there at the time and trying to establish identities, while Murray searched through ANPR cameras, noting registrations and owner details for each vehicle that passed the park entrance at around the time of Audrey's disappearance. Natalie and Ian were digging through the pile of statements they'd acquired and were attempting to piece together the route Audrey had taken after she left the house at 4.50 p.m. Using a map of Queen's Avenue on her laptop, they worked their way through the possibilities.

'There are ninety houses on Queen's Avenue and seventy-four of them are located between number 75, where the Briggses live, and the local shop. Out of those, how many residents were at home at the time she disappeared?' asked Natalie.

Ian ran through the list. 'Only fifteen houses in total were occupied and nobody saw Audrey ride past in the direction of the shop.' He pointed out the convenience store situated at a junction between Queen's Avenue and Jackson's Road. 'The only witness who can confirm any movements is an unemployed woman, Denise Roberts, who lives at number 73, two doors down from the Briggses. She remembered seeing Caroline's car pull up at about quarter or ten to five, and heard the car doors slamming. Said the baby was screaming its head off. She was at her kitchen sink at the time. Shortly after that, she received a phone call and moved into the sitting room to take it and didn't see Audrey go past on her bike.'

'If Audrey headed in that direction somebody ought to have seen her. What about if she turned left and not right out of her house?'

'She'd have passed fifteen houses and ended up at a junction leading onto a dual carriageway. Again, we have no sightings of her.'

'How many houses actually face the park entrance?'

'The road curves at that point, so only numbers 91, 92 and 93 have frontages that actually overlook that part of the park. Out of those houses, only one of the residents, Ned Coleman, who lives at number 91, was at home at the time. I spoke to him. He's sixty-eight years old and slightly deaf. He was watching television and doesn't recall looking out of his window. He knows the Briggs family and was quite upset to learn about Audrey. Said she was an engaging girl who sometimes spoke to him and made a big fuss of his dog if she saw him out walking it.'

'She was obsessed with dogs. Her own got knocked down in that road. How well did Ned know the family?'

'Difficult to say for sure, but I don't think he knew them too well.'

'Okay. Run a check on him all the same. Nothing else useful from the statements you got?'

He pulled a face and rubbed a hand across his five o'clock shadow. 'Pretty much all say the same thing. Nobody saw Audrey.

Many didn't even know the Briggs family.' He opened his palms. 'For goodness' sake, this is a street occupied by God knows how many people. How can nobody have seen a thing? It's a real sign of our times, isn't it? People simply don't know who their own neighbours are any more, or care. Doesn't make this job any easier, does it?'

'We've got technology on our side,' said Natalie with a gentle smile. 'We'll track down the owners of all the cars passing the park at around that time and question them about what they saw. There'll be a television appeal and the press will be supportive. You saw the increasing number of floral tributes outside the Briggs' home. The public will be behind them on this and will want to help track down whoever is responsible.'

Her mobile buzzed, piercing the quiet of the office. It was Ben Hargreaves, the pathologist. He sounded weary.

'Thought you should know I passed Ava Sawyer on to Naomi for examination earlier today. There's far too much tissue damage and deterioration for me to establish cause of death. Naomi might be able to fare better.'

'You couldn't determine if cause of death was natural or not?'

'I'm afraid not.'

There was a brief pause and rustling before he spoke again. 'We've just completed the autopsy on Audrey Briggs. Firstly, there appears to have been no sexual interference. For the record, she was wearing a black ballet leotard and pink tights under the dress. They don't appear to have been touched. There is no DNA or fluids in or on her body. There are no defence wounds on her hands or face but there is slight grazing on her knees and hands and light scratch marks on the inside of her arms. There are also patches of discolouration around her neck along with a distinctive ligature mark across her throat. More importantly, there are signs of mechanical violence: bruising to the tissues and a fracture of her larynx. There is no sign of a struggle: no fingernail marks where she might have attempted to remove any restraint, or other markings usually associated with struggling to escape, suggesting she was rendered unconscious very quickly. I would therefore assume she was either taken unawares or attacked with such strength she didn't know what was happening and unable to offer any resistance. To conclude, Audrey Briggs died of asphyxiation caused by strangulation. We had to eliminate other causes of asphyxia death before we could be certain but there's no doubt she was strangled.'

'Any idea what was used to strangle her?'

'It's not my field of expertise. Again, I'd bow to Naomi's judgement on this. I'll pass the body across to her. Sorry I couldn't be of more help.'

'You've been very helpful. Thank you, Ben.'

Ben seemed surprised at the praise. 'You're welcome,' he blurted before hanging up.

Natalie faced her team. 'Right, we know for sure Audrey was murdered and we'll continue to treat Ava's death as suspicious. Bearing that in mind, I think we ought to look at any connections between Audrey and Ava, and examine the lives of these two girls. Something or somebody connects them and we need to ascertain who or what that is. I propose we start with the most obvious – the birthday party at Uptown Craft Centre in July 2015. Both girls attended it and Audrey was aware Ava left the games to go to the toilet. There's a lot to consider and I don't think we should purely focus on the party at this stage. I want to make sure we examine all avenues. For now, I'm going to call it a night and suggest we reconvene at eight a.m.'

She shuffled her paperwork into order and smiled her thanks at each of her team as they trooped towards the door.

David was still awake in bed when Natalie got in. He removed his glasses and put aside the book he'd been reading.

'It's very late,' she said as she peeled off her clothes and removed her lenses. 'You should be asleep.'

'I wasn't tired. Besides, I wanted to see if you were okay. There was a report about a missing girl on the late news.'

She came out of the bathroom and flopped onto the side of the bed. 'Audrey Briggs. Her body's been found now. She was friends with Ava Sawyer and was at the party in 2015 when Ava went missing.'

'Oh, I'm really sorry. Is that relevant?'

'I think it might be… I don't know. It's all… pretty crap.'

'Come here.'

'I haven't cleaned my teeth yet.'

'Come here,' he urged, throwing back the duvet.

She slid into the cool sheets and he drew her to his chest, arms around her. His body was warm and he smelt of citrus fruits. She allowed him to hold her, knowing she ought to draw comfort from his concern. She should feel affection and even love at such a tender act, but all she could think of was Mike and his team, still searching around the body of a little girl in a party dress.

CHAPTER ELEVEN

THURSDAY, 27 APRIL – MORNING

Morning couldn't come quickly enough for Natalie. What little sleep she got had been punctuated with visions of a young girl tied to a chair, alone in an abandoned warehouse. The nightmares associated with Olivia Chester's murder had plagued her every night for months and had only gradually withdrawn to the recesses of her brain, thanks to the intense therapy she'd undergone. Now they were back. She had to shrug off the dire feeling that accompanied them. She wouldn't be able to function properly if she dwelled on the failures of the past.

At the first sign of light, she'd propped herself up on one elbow and studied her sleeping husband on his back, mouth slightly open. He'd woken several times thanks to her restlessness but hadn't complained. It wasn't easy being married to a detective. She resolved to take some leave after this case to work on their marriage. It required more effort on her part if it was to survive.

The urge to escape her thoughts became overwhelming. Some days they closed in on her so much she wanted to hide from the world…

'What frightens you most about these nightmares?'

'The silence. Olivia looks at me, accusingly, yet says nothing. I beg her to forgive me but she continues to stare as if I'm the person solely responsible for her death.'

'We both know your superiors made the decisions that resulted in the death of Olivia Chester. You were not culpable.'

'I was part of that investigation and the team. I thought they were handling it incorrectly and I ought to have been more vocal. I might have dissuaded them from their decisions.'

'You can't spend your life blaming yourself, Natalie.'

'But I do. Answer me this: how can I prevent myself from feeling such guilt? Some days it's unbearable. I wake up after one of these dreams and can't breathe. Last night, I ran a bath. I was so tired I dozed off in the water and suddenly her face appeared, drifting in front of my eyes. I woke with a start and found myself fully submerged underwater, and surprisingly, it felt right. I didn't want to surface. I wanted to rest there and allow the real world to drift away. I remained underwater, relishing the tranquillity and becoming comfortably numb. It was a heaven-sent release. I stayed like that until I ran out of breath and some animal instinct took over and I came up for air.'

'How did you feel when you emerged?'

'Better. Calmer. For a short while.'

'You might benefit from some breathing techniques that will help de-stress you. We'll schedule you an appointment and go through some with you.'

She crept from the bedroom to the landing and into the bathroom, where she ran the taps, staring at her reflection while she waited for the tub to fill. Her eyes didn't see the woman in the mirror. Instead they saw two little girls in yellow dresses. There was a significant connection between Audrey and Ava. It was far too great a coincidence that the day after they'd uncovered Ava's body, another girl who'd attended the birthday party at Uptown Craft Centre had turned up dead. The dress was a major clue. She'd pursue that angle and also go back over the Ava Sawyer files.

She climbed into the bath, allowing the heat to soothe the tension in her muscles. She wasn't a shower person. David was. He much preferred to use the shower cubicle in their en-suite than soak in a bath. She shared the bathroom with the children and there were reminders of them everywhere she looked: toothbrushes in mugs, Leigh's collection of shampoo and bath gels in multicoloured bottles that completely covered the table by the sink, and Josh's Manchester United football towel, now a faded pink rather than red, hanging from a peg on the back of the door. She thought again of the named coat pegs in the Briggs' house. She'd have to talk to the parents again today. She sighed at the daunting prospect and ducked further into the water until she was fully immersed and such thoughts no longer plagued her, trying to hold her breath as long as possible and listening only to her heartbeat.

When she finally emerged from the bathroom, she felt better prepared for the day. David was no longer in bed. She dried her hair quickly and scraped it back into a functional short ponytail. She pulled on the same trousers from the day before and a clean white shirt, and then applied a minimum amount of make-up, enough to look pleasant. Her mother had taught her the 'less is more' principle, a fact she'd taken to heart. She'd always been the plain Jane in the family, and while her sister had applied false eyelashes and spent hours painting her toenails and going out clubbing, Natalie had buried herself in her books. She shook away thoughts of Frances, her estranged sister. She was relegated to the past.

Downstairs, Josh, still in pyjamas, was shovelling cereal into his mouth and simultaneously staring at his phone. He acknowledged her presence with a grunt. David had made the tea and was spreading marmalade on his toast.

'Fancy a piece?' he asked.

'Not hungry,' she replied, emptying the teapot into her mug and adding milk.

'How's school, Josh?' she asked.

He rolled his eyes. 'Same old,' he mumbled.

'Dad and I had another talk about those trainers you want. If your grades are decent again at the end of this term, we'll buy them for you.'

'Really?' He looked up from the screen, abandoning the purple balls he was chasing.

'Yeah, why not?' she replied.

'Cool. Thanks.' He stood up, stuck his bowl in the sink and sauntered off.

'One happy son,' she said over the rim of her mug.

'Happiest I've seen him look for a few days. Any sign of Leigh?'

'Nothing when I came downstairs. Want me to go shake her?'

'I'll do it. What time are you going in?'

'Eight.'

'And you're still here?'

'I thought I owed you at least five minutes before I disappeared. Don't know what time I'll be back.'

He shrugged a reply and ate his toast in silence. He'd been in this situation before, many times. 'I'll cope,' he said eventually.

'I'll wake Leigh and get off.'

'Leave her. I'll do it,' he said again, a note of sharpness creeping into his voice. She took it as her cue to depart, and placing the empty mug next to Josh's bowl, pecked David on the cheek and headed off.

The station doors swished back and the heavy scent of pine forests rose to greet her. She circumnavigated the wet floor sign directly in front of her and headed to her office. Mike was slumped on the round settee in the corridor.

'You're probably the first person to ever sit on that,' she said cheerfully. She'd been too offhand with him recently. What had happened between them was over. It had only been one night. They were now no more than work colleagues who rubbed along okay together.

'It might look good in my new flat,' he said with a half-smile.

'Sure it would. You got multicoloured walls or just neon yellow?'

He chuckled and patted the seat. 'It is a bit on the gaudy side, isn't it?'

She raised her eyebrows in reply. 'You waiting for me?'

'Yes. Thought I'd come give a quick update in person. Got some news for you.'

She swiped the keypad with her pass and opened the door wide for him. He remained on the settee. She left the door open and stood in front of him.

'Go on. What is it?'

'It'll keep until your team gets in. I need all the rest I can before I start again.' Mike yawned and shook his head to wake himself up.

'What time you get home?'

'Home? That's an interesting word: a place where one lives permanently as a member of a family; where the heart is.' He paused for a second and shrugged nonchalantly. 'Nicole is demanding the house, so I've moved to a motel for a few days until the apartment I'm about to rent comes free. When I say *moved to a motel*, I mean *will move*. I spent last night on the back seat of my car. There was little point going anywhere by the time I'd finished.'

'She returned?'

'Yesterday afternoon. Only to kick me out.'

'You really are moving into a flat. I thought you were kidding earlier when you mentioned the settee. Was Thea with her?'

His face softened. 'Yeah. Managed to take her out for a quick burger and chips before I was called to the crime scene at the park. Nicole hates her eating crap food but Thea loves it, so what the heck?'

'How's Thea taking the split?'

'Not sure it's registered with her yet. I told her I'd see her most weekends. She's used to me working stupid hours anyway. I don't suppose she'll miss me being around too much.'

'Tough, all the same,' she said.

'What about you?'

'Me?'

'You and David?'

'Fine. He's sorting himself out.' She was saved from further conversation about her marriage by the arrival of Lucy and Murray.

'You want any coffee before we start? I could nip out and get some,' Natalie offered.

'Nah. I might need a hand getting off this settee though. I seem to have run out of energy.'

'Come on, you'll be fine once you get going.'

No sooner had they gone into the office than Ian appeared. Natalie began the briefing immediately.

'Okay, we've got a busy day. I want occupants of all vehicles passing that park entrance between four fifty p.m. and five thirty p.m. interviewed, along with everyone we can identify on those park CCTV cameras. Ian, ensure noticeboards calling for witnesses are placed by entrances. Murray, I'd like you to talk to the neighbour, Ned Coleman, who lives opposite the park entrance. I know he said he saw nothing but see if you can jog his memory or confirm his statement. He might have witnessed activity over the road and not registered it. While you're in the vicinity, double-check the shop manager, Rod Bunting, didn't see Audrey, even for a second, outside the shop. Find out who went into the shop at about that time and talk to them too. They might have spotted Audrey. Have we run background checks on Rod?'

'I did,' said Ian. 'He seems sound enough. He lives above the shop. It used to belong to his parents. He took over the running of it after they passed away. He's fifty-two, unmarried, and a member of the local birdwatching club. No previous convictions.'

'Do you think she went to the park instead of the shop?' Lucy asked.

'At the moment, I'm leaving all options open until we find a witness. It's reasonable to assume she didn't go in the direction of the shop given nobody saw her cycle down the road. However, her mum said she'd never cross the road alone without using the pelican crossing, and that's near the shop.'

Murray was next to speak. 'What about the parents?'

'We'll talk to Mr and Mrs Briggs and Mr and Mrs Sawyer again. We really need to gather as much information as possible on these two girls. I believe the cases are related. Did you track down Elsa Townsend, the woman in charge of Ava Sawyer's birthday party?'

Murray shook his head. 'She was living in the Marbella area but she left her last known address and has fallen off the radar.'

'Somebody must know where she is. How about her ex-husband?'

'Barney Townsend. Want me to track him down?'

'Can you handle that along with tracking down witnesses who might have spotted Audrey?'

'Yep.'

She paused. There were no other questions. She nodded across to Mike. 'Over to you.'

Mike, who'd been resting against the glass wall, cleared his throat. 'As you know, we are yet to find the cardigan Audrey was wearing. I've got officers currently sweeping the whole area but it's a thirty-acre park, and it could take some time. Given the sniffer dogs didn't pick up on it yesterday, we're not convinced the clothing is in situ. There's no identifying label or washing instructions on the dress she's wearing, so we don't know where it was purchased.'

'It might be home-made,' said Lucy.

'Indeed.' Mike pushed himself away from the wall and moved across to Natalie's desk, where he perched on the edge.

'On to the child's pushbike. We found rubber tyre marks we're certain came from the bike near where it was dumped. Further examination leads us to believe Audrey was riding quickly and came to a sudden halt. The bike is clean with only three sets of fingerprints on it: hers and two larger partials, belonging to her parents. Her attacker either wore gloves or didn't touch the bike. Given the way it's been cast aside, it appears Audrey dismounted in haste and ran over the grass in the direction of the shrubs where we finally found her. We've uncovered two footprints that match the soles of her shoes. She was running on the balls of her feet, indicating a sprint.'

'I thought she might be running from somebody who was hidden in the shrubs and who frightened her,' said Natalie.

'It appears to be the opposite. She ran *towards* the bushes. We've located fibres we believe might be from the missing cardigan caught in the branches, and there are scuffed-up areas of earth around and under the shrub where Audrey was found. It seems she was scrabbling about on all fours. I'd imagine to hide from whoever was pursuing her.'

'Poor little soul,' said Ian. 'She must have been terrified.'

'Any DNA?' Lucy asked.

'No, we haven't found any. There is some news though. I received confirmation first thing this morning that the scraps of material we found on Ava's body were made of cotton fibres and presumably came from the dress she wore that day.'

'Like the dress Audrey wore?'

'Similar. Audrey's dress is made of a completely different material, a lemon-yellow chiffon.'

'Too much of a coincidence, though, isn't it?' said Natalie. 'Both in yellow party dresses – one in lemon chiffon with a pleated skirt and a bow, another in yellow cotton with puffed short sleeves.'

'That's for you to investigate. I can only offer forensic evidence. I'll get back to the park and let you know as soon as there's more.'

'One last thing, Mike. Audrey was headed to the shops with some money – two pounds – did you find the coins near or on her body?'

'No money at all.'

'She might have dropped it somewhere, unless it's in her cardigan pocket.'

'We'll keep an eye out for it.' He gave a mock salute to Natalie and headed to the door.

She caught him up. 'Thanks for coming over in person.'

'I wanted to,' he said, letting his eyes rest on hers a second longer than was necessary. 'Needed to check you were okay.'

'Yeah. I'll be fine. Just have to nail the bastard behind this and I'll feel a whole lot better.'

'You'll get him.'

Natalie watched as he strode confidently down the corridor and disappeared down the far staircase; she hoped fervently he was right. The Olivia Chester investigation had fallen apart because they hadn't explored every avenue. They'd concentrated on one suspect, dragging him into custody and interrogating him at length, only to discover at the eleventh hour that he was innocent. By then, the little girl had been murdered. Natalie wasn't going to allow that to happen again. If the deaths of Ava and Audrey were somehow connected other than the birthday party, she needed to establish how quickly, and that meant looking at every possible shred of evidence and acting on every hunch.

The office had turned into a hive of activity, the desire to capture the perpetrator almost tangible and etched on the faces and in the quick movements of her officers, each focused on a task. Natalie squared her shoulders and joined them, thoughts now on tracking Audrey's movements the afternoon before. The lipstick bothered her. If Audrey hadn't been wearing it when she'd left home, she'd either applied it after she'd left the house, or her killer had painted it on her lips. The latter seemed logical in light of the fact the girl had been dressed for a party. Could Audrey have made an excuse of going to the shop, and planned to meet somebody? It was an unlikely possibility that nevertheless required ruling out.

Natalie dragged up the details of Little Stars Dance Academy. Owned by Carlton and Bruce Kennedy, a married couple who'd opened the academy in 2006, it boasted a range of classes including hip-hop, tap and ballet, all of which were aimed at girls and boys aged three to sixteen years. She dialled the number for the school and asked for the names of the other children in Audrey's class, only to be told she would have to turn up in person to discuss the matter with one of the owners because such information couldn't be given out over the phone. She made an appointment for 11 a.m.

Casting an eye around the busy room, she decided she'd go it alone and talk to Audrey's parents again. It was time to try and make connections between her and Ava.

'Lucy, can you arrange to talk to the class teacher who taught both Ava and Audrey in 2015? If I'm not back in time, interview her yourself. We need to find out how friendly the girls were. Ava had trouble getting on with her classmates. See where Audrey fitted in. And, while you're at it, find out anything else you can about their classmates.'

'Will do.' Lucy kept her eyes glued to her computer as she spoke, concentrating on scrolling through images of yellow dresses. 'There are literally hundreds of thousands of yellow dresses for sale. I wouldn't have thought it possible to sell that many.'

'It might not have come from a shop.'

'I know. Thought it worth a look online. Can't see one like this though.' She tapped the photograph of Audrey's dress on her desk with her forefinger.

'We could do with a picture of the dress Ava was wearing when she disappeared just for comparison's sake. We'll ask her mother when we speak to her next.'

'Planning on doing that today?'

Natalie checked her watch. She should reach the Briggs' before nine thirty. She'd maybe have time to interview Beatrice before going to the dance academy. Looking up to respond, she quickly pulled herself up short. She had to delegate tasks even though the desire to follow up everything herself was overpowering.

'It would make sense if you and Murray could talk to her.'

Lucy's head bobbed up and down. 'Sure. We'll sort that.'

'Cheers. Okay, stay in touch, everyone.'

With that, she hurried towards the stairs and exit, hoping she'd made the right decision. A lot was riding on her management skills. There was no room for screw-ups.

CHAPTER TWELVE

THURSDAY, 27 APRIL – MORNING

Caroline and Steven Briggs sat as one on the settee, hip to hip and fingers entwined as if to anchor them to the real world. Their faces showed the greatest strain. Caroline's eyelids were swollen from crying, and Stephen's forehead was a web of lines.

'We were told she'd been strangled,' said Stephen.

'It appears that way.' Natalie looked across at Tanya Granger, who was once again with the couple. She or one of her colleagues would stay with them and help them through the whole process of the coming days. The journalists from the evening before had been sent away but television crews were now by the railings, reporting on the search currently taking place inside the park.

Stephen swallowed heavily. 'And she wasn't raped.'

'No. She wasn't.'

He blinked back tears and fell silent.

'I understand this is a very difficult time for you but I'd really appreciate your help. Can you tell me how friendly Audrey and Ava Sawyer were? Did Ava ever come back here to play? Did Audrey ever mention her?'

'Our daughter is dead and you're asking about Ava Sawyer?' Stephen's face was incredulous.

Caroline squeezed his hand. 'Stephen, no. She wouldn't ask if it weren't important.'

'That's right. I wouldn't upset you. Not at such a terrible time. I'm trying to establish connections between the girls.'

'You think our daughter's death has something to do with Ava's disappearance?'

'It might have. Ava's body was found two days ago, Mr Briggs. I'm afraid I can't discuss details of the investigation with you but trust me, it's relevant.'

Caroline's face crumpled again. Stephen's lips trembled but his head bobbed up and down as if on a spring. Seeing his wife in tears again, he took over. 'They were friends and in the same class at school. Ava came here quite a few times.'

'What did Audrey tell you about Harriet Downing's birthday party?'

'We went over and over this when Ava disappeared. The police questioned her. Audrey was the last person to see Ava. They were playing party games in the barn. Ava was in a funny mood and hadn't been joining in much. While the woman in charge was sorting out an argument between two boys, Ava announced she was going to the toilet. Audrey reminded her they'd been told to ask if they wanted the toilet. Ava replied she was old enough to go to the toilets on her own and she knew where they were, and then walked off. Audrey became involved in a game and then they all were sent outside to the animal enclosure where they were split into two groups. She thought Ava had returned and joined the second group of children. When they reached the stables, it was discovered she hadn't and Audrey told them what had happened.' He heaved a sigh at the end of his monologue.

'And Audrey saw no more of her friend after she went to the toilets?'

'No.'

'I heard Ava was prone to moodiness and would sometimes walk off on her own. Did she exhibit that sort of behaviour at any time during one of her visits here?'

Stephen shrugged. 'I wasn't here.'

'Once,' said Caroline, blowing her nose before continuing. 'She came home for tea after a dance class. Beatrice and I were going through a phase of play dates. Audrey would go to their house one week and Ava to ours the next. She was a huffy little madam at times and I could tell she was in a mood when I picked her up. Audrey was trying very hard to be friendly, bless her. They were both going to be in a small dance production and Ava had been relegated to the back row. I think that's what needled her most, that and the fact Audrey had been chosen as lead dancer. While I was preparing the food, I overheard the girls arguing about a television programme. Shortly afterwards, Audrey came into the kitchen to fetch me. She was worried because Ava had stormed off and she'd searched the house but Ava wasn't anywhere to be found. We both looked and shouted for her, and then I spotted her coat had gone from the coat pegs by the front door. I became really concerned she'd run off and was going to search for her in the car. I was on the way through the side door to the garage to collect the car when I noticed the back door was slightly ajar. We found her hiding in the garden shed in a dreadful sulk. When I asked her what was wrong, she replied she was angry with Audrey for changing the television programme when she was watching it, and was teaching her a lesson.'

'She didn't do it again?'

'No, although I believe she pulled similar stunts at school from what Audrey said.'

'Did they fall out?'

'No. Audrey was a loyal friend. She put up with Ava to the end. I think she felt sorry for her. That was Audrey. Kind-hearted.'

'You said Audrey and Ava attended the same dance class. Was that here in Uptown?'

'Yes, at the Little Stars Dance Academy. Audrey still goes. Went. Audrey went there.' She blinked several times and the tears began again. 'Sorry. I can't...' She pulled her hand away from her husband's and ran from the room.

Stephen dropped his head into his hands. Tanya jumped to her feet. 'I'll go check she's okay.'

Natalie stood too. 'I'm truly sorry. Look, I'll leave you again until you feel more able to talk to me.'

He lifted damp eyes. 'I don't think there'll ever be a right time but thank you.'

Little Stars Dance Academy was situated inside a one-time grain warehouse that was four storeys high. Built in the early 1900s, it retained the original brickwork with stone dressings and nine small windows on each floor. On the ground floor there were only four windows, flanked to the left and right by what had once been two cart openings, now entrances fitted with oak doors.

Natalie chose the door marked *Reception* and found herself in a modern, airy office with cream seating and a water cooler, where she was greeted by the woman who'd answered her earlier phone call. Natalie offered up her credentials and was issued again with an apology.

'We're not allowed to release any information over the phone; after all, we're dealing with minors. We have to be careful who we talk to,' said the young woman.

Natalie passed the time reading the glossy brochure for the academy that not only offered a range of exciting courses but boasted several success stories, now renowned names in film and theatre.

Her concentration was broken by the arrival of Carlton Kennedy, whose dark, wavy hair created an impression of a man in his thirties rather than forties, and whose outfit of pale-yellow shirt, dark jeans and deck shoes with no socks was distinctly continental, as was his light French accent. He stood erect with shoulders back and chin up, and oozed confidence even though the top of his head only reached Natalie's chin. He extended a slim hand.

'DI Ward, would you like to come to the office? Bruce is already there.'

He tripped lightly to a hallway that opened out into a wide, empty studio with floor to ceiling mirrors on three sides. The place was eerily quiet and her footsteps rang across the wooden floor. 'Haven't you any classes to teach?'

'Most of the classes and courses are run at weekends, during holidays and after school. We let out the top floor to individuals wishing to hold adult dance classes, but we don't have anything to do with the running of those.'

He stopped by a door marked *Private*, resting his hand on the door handle, and swallowed hard. 'I'm truly sorry about Audrey. She was such a sweetie. She's been coming here since she was five and she was such a pleasure to teach. It's been a huge shock to learn what's happened. It's like losing one of a special little family.' He squared his shoulders and opened the door. 'Come in,' he said.

Bruce, working at one of the two desks placed back-to-back in the centre of the room, was bent over some figures. He lifted his head, his pale-blue eyes flicking over Natalie, weighing her up, before sitting back in his seat and folding his arms. They were opposites: stocky Bruce, sandy-haired with neatly trimmed facial hair that barely disguised his full cheeks, and Carlton, hair coiffed in a wave above an expressive face.

Carlton pulled a chair over for Natalie. 'Please sit down,' he said, dropping nimbly onto his own chair and looking at her with dark, anxious eyes. 'Such a terrible thing to happen.'

'I understand Audrey was at one of your classes yesterday afternoon.'

'She was, but I don't see what bearing that has on her death,' said Bruce, picking up a pen and studying it. 'She didn't disappear from our school. Her mother collected her from here.' He turned his cool gaze onto Natalie.

'That is absolutely correct but in these situations, we like to interview everyone connected to the victim. It helps us gain a fuller picture as to what might have taken place.'

'I really don't see how.'

'Bruce,' hissed Carlton. 'That's enough. Excuse him. He's very upset about what has happened. We all are. Poor little Audrey.'

'Was she a good dancer?'

'Very promising,' said Carlton, his full lips turning down. 'And she was serious about dancing. Many children come for a few lessons and then give up, or show no ability whatsoever, but Audrey was enthusiastic from the first time she came. She took part in quite a few of our academy performances.'

'Were there many in the class?'

'Only five in that particular class. It's what we call level four, so only those who have been through our grade system are able to take part in it.'

'Did you take the class, Carlton?'

'I take all the ballet classes.'

'And you, Bruce? Are you a ballet dancer too?'

'I mostly work on the admin side.'

'His background is musicals. He provides classes for the older children – works through routines with them. He's very accomplished,' said Carlton, giving his husband a smile.

'What did you do with the children yesterday?' Natalie asked, mindful that whatever they'd done had made Audrey thirsty.

'We started with stretching on the floor, then pliés and went on to work across the floor work: chassés, sautés, passés and grands jetés. We did a lot of those jumps. They love them. So much energy. We then tried a simple combination from the "Sugar Plum Fairy".'

'That's quite demanding.'

'Demanding no, tiring yes.'

'Did the children change from their school uniforms here?'

'Yes, we have changing rooms beside the studio.'

'And what was Audrey wearing?'

'Same as all the girls: black leotard, pink tights and pink ballet pumps.'

'Do the girls wear make-up, maybe lipstick, during lessons?'

Carlton's eyebrows lifted. 'Not at this age. Unless it is for a performance.'

'Was Audrey wearing any lipstick?'

He shook his head. 'I don't think she was. Bruce, was she?'

'You saw her too?'

'In reception. I was there when the class ended. I saw her leave with her mother. I wouldn't know if she was or wasn't wearing any lipstick.'

'What about the other girls? Were any of them wearing lipstick?'

'Again, I wouldn't know,' said Bruce.

'Would you give me their names and contact details so I can speak to them?'

'I'll arrange that,' said Bruce. 'You finished with me? I have some work to get on with.'

'Actually, I have another question. Ava Sawyer used to come here, didn't she? She was in the same class as Audrey.'

Bruce put down his pen and pushed away from his desk with both hands before standing up. 'Look, I really don't have much to do with the ballet classes. You're best off talking to Carlton about this. I have to attend an important meeting in Samford to sort out the programme of events for the festival next month. I must leave or I'll be late.'

Carlton's eyebrows shot upwards. 'Of course. I'd forgotten about that. You get off. I can talk to DI Ward.'

'I'll make sure those contact details are in reception for you when you leave,' he said, picking up the jacket on the back of the chair.

As soon as he'd left, Carlton shook his head. 'He was really sad when Ava disappeared.'

'But he didn't teach her.'

'No, but he often talked to her. She was a funny little thing. She really wanted to be the best in the ballet class but she wasn't cut out for it. Sometimes, she'd walk out of class if it was going wrong and she couldn't keep up, and sit downstairs in reception. Bruce was invariably on duty and would keep her company. They got on. I think he liked the rebel in her. She was only five but she knew her own mind, that one. Reminded him of his little sister.'

'Were Audrey and Ava close?'

He lifted his shoulders high and pouted. 'You mean sticking together like glue, best friends? No, not really close. Sometimes Ava would get a little jealous of Audrey and give her such a look it almost made me want to laugh. She would do this.' He pulled a sulky face. 'I find such things amusing.'

'When was the last time you saw Ava?'

'The day before she disappeared. She wasn't herself that day. She made no effort in class and was distracted. In the end, she asked to sit in reception. I said she could. The door only opens from the inside if someone on reception presses a buzzer to release it, so I knew she would be safe there; and besides, Bruce was there.

'When we learned about her disappearance, we headed straight over to Uptown Craft Centre and joined the search parties. Bruce was especially upset, partly because he liked Ava, but also because he'd stopped off at the centre that same afternoon to collect a plant for his mother's birthday.'

'Did he come forward when the police were asking for witnesses?'

'There was no need. He was there before the party started. He didn't see Ava or any of the children.'

'What time was he there?'

'About two thirty. He left soon afterwards and headed into town to buy a birthday card.'

Natalie pushed her business card across to Carlton. 'I know he doesn't want to talk, but please ask him to. I'd really like to hear what he and Ava chatted about. Will you get him to ring me?'

'I'll try. He can be quite stubborn some days.'

'Try hard. I'm investigating a child's murder, and if he doesn't willingly talk to me, I'll be forced to make him come to the station. I want to speak to him today. As soon as he finishes his meeting.'

CHAPTER THIRTEEN

THURSDAY, 27 APRIL – MORNING

While Natalie was talking to Caroline and Stephen Briggs, back in the office, Lucy was doing her best to track down the yellow dress with no luck. The frustration was mounting and she hated it when she couldn't come up trumps. She raked her hands through her hair. With Murray out of the office, Ian had been working quietly. It was better when they weren't bickering. Not that it bothered her; she was well used to such behaviour. She'd spent much of her younger life fielding jibes and taunts, and learning to make quick retorts. It was just more productive when everyone was concentrating on work rather than settling scores. Ian had seemed more relaxed and offered a smile of encouragement as he departed to interview several vehicle owners, leaving her alone in the office.

She'd not been able to get hold of Beatrice Sawyer but had made an appointment to talk to Ava's form teacher, Miss Margaret Goffrey, during school break at 11 a.m. Ignoring the page of yellow dresses on her computer screen, she scribbled a few questions in her notebook for the teacher. She wanted to do this right. Natalie was relying on her.

Lucy admired Natalie. She'd liked her from the off when she'd first stood in front of them and introduced herself as their new DI. Murray would no doubt tell her it was some stupid girl crush she was experiencing, but it wasn't; after all, Bethany was now in Lucy's life. Natalie was everything Lucy wanted to become: a no-nonsense detective, committed to her job, but who also managed to remain human. She'd begun modelling her own approach to cases on Natalie's. One day, she hoped to rise up the ranks. She could do it with the right guidance and luck. She believed in herself. Bethany believed in her. Lucy might have been a right little troublemaker when she was a teenager but she'd got the bug now – she was going to be one of the police force's best officers. Murray knew she'd do anything to climb that ladder and prove herself. He knew what it meant to her. That's why he'd suggested she move from Stoke-on-Trent with him and join the new team at Samford. 'Better opportunities, for us both,' he'd said and he had been right. Murray had good instincts and understood her. He got who she really was, and still liked her. She liked him too. He wasn't a back-stabbing shit like some other officers. He put up with her strops and, like her, was as determined as hell to make it as a detective.

Murray appeared out of nowhere, face set in a scowl, and threw his car keys on the desk.

'No go?' she said, picking up on his mood.

'Ned Coleman definitely didn't see Audrey and there were only two customers at the convenience store at the time, neither of whom saw Audrey. I've drawn a blank and I'm now majorly pissed off.'

'Want to come and interview Miss Goffrey with me?'

'You guys find anything useful?' Murray asked, ignoring Lucy's question.

'Not yet. Ian's out interviewing potential witnesses. He also checked out those guys who found Ava's body at the garden centre site. They're squeaky clean. Tony Mellows, the foreman, was working in Dubai in 2015, and Neil Linton, the project manager, was overseeing the development of a new golf course in Scotland, so neither was in the area at the time of Ava's disappearance. Come on. I'm sick of looking at sodding party dresses. They're all starting to look the same to me.'

'Have you been looking at dresses for the last couple of hours?'

'No. I just started again. I went to the lab earlier to see if they'd found anything suspicious on Audrey's mobile phone.'

'Had they?'

'It was clean. She genuinely only used it for playing games, taking photographs, messaging family members. Seems her parents had tight rules about what she could and couldn't do on it. I went through all the pictures just in case there was anything relevant but couldn't spot anything odd – they're mostly photos of her family, friends and some random dog pictures. Natalie said she liked dogs.'

'She really did go out to get a bottle of cola then and not meet up with somebody.'

'Seems that way. She hadn't sent or received any messages that suggested otherwise and she wasn't on Snapchat or WhatsApp.'

'Bit too young to be on those.'

'You'd be surprised how many kids actually use those apps even though they're aimed at older children. Thought it sensible to make sure she wasn't. Well, you coming to interview the teacher or sit about looking pissed off?'

Murray heaved himself up. 'It's tough being a parent, isn't it?' he said, continuing to ignore her offer.

'It's tough being an adult but we cope with that. You're not getting cold feet, are you?'

He picked up his keys again. 'No. You do understand what you'll be putting yourselves through, don't you?'

'Bethany is determined, Murray. She's thirty-nine. She knows her own mind and she's dead set on a baby. It's the right time for her and us both.'

'What about you? You have your career to think about. You definitely sure you want to go through with it?'

She gave him a serious look, her dark eyes fixed on his face. 'If Bethany's happy, I'm happy. I'm ready for the responsibility. It's not like we *suddenly* decided to do this. We've been through it a gazillion times. Bethany desperately wants to be a stay-at-home mum and she understands my needs too. Look, if you want to back out, we'll both understand. You only have to say.'

'Nah. I'm good.' He gave her a winning smile. 'What time you seeing the teacher?'

'Twenty minutes. Let's go.'

Uptown Primary School was located off a housing estate next to a sports leisure complex. Sole access was through a gated entrance via a street from the main road. Lucy had to press an intercom button to gain entry and wait for the gates to automatically open.

They followed the signs to the staff parking and pulled up outside an attractive, red-brick, one-storey building that appeared to be divided into three sections, the front flanked by square columns and bearing a large, multi-pane window, above which was an ornate carving of two unicorns, while the side sections contained twelve smaller windowpanes. The roof was a matching reddish-brown slate, from which rose two tall brick chimneys at the front and two smaller ones at the rear.

'Pretty grand for a school,' Murray commented. 'Far cry from the Portakabins we were taught in.'

They rounded the building to the entrance secreted in the side of the building and spotted a smaller, less ornate structure, surrounded by a fence.

Lucy pointed out, 'They take five- to eleven-year-olds but the youngest are taught separately. No doubt that's the infant school.'

The secretary's office was close to the main entrance. There they were met by a plump, matronly type and escorted along a dimly lit corridor to the staffroom, the size of a small kitchen, into which was stuffed a table, cupboards and eight plastic chairs.

'Miss Goffrey will be across any minute.'

'Not much space in here,' said Murray, examining the mugs lined up on the worktop. He ducked down and opened a fridge, staring at the Tupperware containers marked with names. 'Looks like they bring in their own food. I guess school lunches are still as dreadful as I remember them being.'

Lucy gave a wry smile.

A bell rang out shrilly and no sooner had its piercing peals ended than the general commotion associated with the start of a school break began: doors crashing open; the clattering of footsteps down the corridor; the clamour of voices gradually fading into the distance. The staffroom door opened and a woman in her fifties, petite, black-haired, neatly dressed and clutching a file to her chest, burst in.

'Miss Margaret Goffrey?'

'That's me. How can I help you? The school secretary told me you wanted to ask about Ava Sawyer.'

'It is really more in connection with Audrey Briggs.'

'That poor child. Such a shock. Terrible news. The head teacher said a few words about her at morning assembly. Some of her class are going to have to undergo counselling to help come to terms with her death.'

'She and Ava were in the same class in 2015.'

'They were. I was their form teacher that year.'

'Were they good friends?'

'They were *sometimes* good friends. Young children form allegiances and break them on a regular basis. Ava was actually close friends with Harriet Downing. It was an unlikely pairing given Harriet was extremely gregarious and Ava awfully withdrawn, but they were definitely best friends for most of that year.'

'What about Audrey?'

'Audrey was a drifter. That's to say, she got on with everyone, and would flit from one group of friends to another. The last two weeks of term, Audrey and Ava started sitting together and Harriet had moved next to Rainey Kilburn.'

'You think Ava fell out with Harriet?'

'I'd say that was most certainly the case. Ava was a little on the volatile side at times. If she didn't like something or someone she wouldn't hide her feelings. She was a bright little girl but she could lose her temper.'

'We read through your statement you gave at the time and understand she was prone to walking off and hiding. Can you expand on that?'

'When I gave the statement, I was trying to assist the police. Ava had disappeared and I explained that she had, on the odd occasion, taken it into her head to walk off. She once hid in the staff toilets for an entire lesson because she said the teacher had told her off for talking when she hadn't said a word. I thought it would be helpful to know she might have been deliberately hiding, but as it happened, they never found her. And now we've lost Audrey too. We appear to be blighted as a school.'

'Did you see much of Audrey?'

'Not after she moved up into the main building. I tend to stick to the infants, which means I'm usually at the other building.'

'What about the other members of that class? Can you remember how they interacted, who they played with and, more importantly, how they got on with Ava?'

'There was nothing that stood out. I can give you a list of the children in the class if you want, although they were all at the party when Ava disappeared, so you might already have their names. There were no real standouts in the group. Harriet had oodles of confidence and was an attention seeker, and used to getting her own way. Ava was her number-one fan. Without Harriet, I imagine Ava would have found it difficult to mix with the others. Harriet got along with everyone and Ava naturally became accepted by them. I never fully worked her out. She was polite and enjoyed schoolwork but during form times she'd sometimes simply stare into space, and the look on her face – it was dreadfully sad, as if something was troubling her.'

'You didn't ever ask her about what might be bothering her?'

'I did try on more than one occasion. She became defensive and said nothing was wrong.'

'Did you press the issue?'

'It's difficult to stay on top of a class of five- and six-year-olds. They throw tantrums. They make noise. They all want your attention. They need supervision all the time. Ava wasn't a troublemaker. She didn't suddenly burst into tears or need a cuddle. She was a reserved child and I let her be.'

'You ever suspect she might be being abused?'

'It crossed my mind. You come across it, now and again, but there were no obvious marks on her body or any of the other signs we look out for. I broached the subject of her withdrawing with her mother, and she said it was typical of Ava. She often retreated into herself. She believed it was because Ava was an only child and this was her first experience of mixing with other children. We talked about ways of engaging her further, and we had hoped she'd grow out of it.'

'And Audrey?'

'Quite the opposite. An easy-going, likeable, delightful girl.'

The staffroom door opened again and two women entered, heading directly to the kettle on the worktop.

Margaret lowered her tone. 'I don't really have anything new to add to my statement. I'm sorry I can't be of more help.'

'Thank you for your time. If you can think of anything else, please would you let us know?'

'I shall.'

'Should I have asked her anything else?' Lucy said as they marched back to the car.

'I can't think of anything. We know Ava was reserved and would go off if she felt like it. She and Harriet fell out sometime before the party. Audrey was popular with her classmates. I think that's everything.'

'None of it helps, does it?' Lucy's dark eyebrows drew together. 'We've got shit all to go on.'

'I don't know. Maybe if you slot that information into place with everything else we get, it'll be useful. Maybe Ava wandered off at the party and wasn't abducted. That would explain why nobody saw anything. What if she intended hiding somewhere, had an accident and died? Or hid so well she couldn't be found, and then got frightened, got into trouble? Oh, I don't know… something happened to her. We haven't established she was murdered yet, have we?'

Lucy put her hands on her hips and stared at him. 'I did a crap job in there. Why are you being ultra nice?'

'That's me all over, isn't it? Mr Nice.'

She barked a laugh. 'Fuck off. That's not why Bethany and I chose you to be the father of our child.'

'What was it, then? My good looks and fantastic genes?'

'We didn't know who else to ask,' she said and grinned.

CHAPTER FOURTEEN

THEN

His mother is out at the shops and he's been ordered to stay inside. No sooner has she gone than he extracts the old cardboard box from the bottom of his wardrobe and pulls the doll from under the boxes of games and comics. She looks pleased to see him.

'Hello, Sherry. Do you want to play a game?'

He walks her along the floor to his bed, fingers circling her cool, plastic legs.

'I don't know any boys' games. I only know how to skip, do hand-stands and play chase,' he says in a silly voice.

'We could play cowboys. You can be captured by Indians and tied up to the table leg and then I can come and rescue you.'

'I don't like that game.'

He stares at the doll and wonders what to do with her next. She is of no real use to him. She can't turn somersaults like his wind-up dog, or move at all without assistance. Only her eyes open and close, depending on if she's upright or lying down. She can't do anything, but she's pretty and he doesn't want to get rid of her. He pokes one of the eyes and she doesn't scream. She merely smiles her gentle smile. He lifts her skirt and pulls at the cream knickers, wondering what's under them, and is disappointed to find only round plastic. He hoists them back up.

The day before, Sherry and her friends had been doing handstands on the 'girls only' grassed area, and he had observed them from close to the playground wall. He'd marvelled as they kicked and lunged and balanced on their hands, giggling whenever they tumbled over. Their movements seemed impossible for he could never imagine getting his huge frame upside down like that. Sherry was a natural gymnast. With her hair tied in a ponytail, she'd shimmied her shoulders then raised her hands and spun effortlessly onto them, immediately pushing her arms and legs straight into the air. In the process, her pleated skirt had fallen over her shoulders, exposing her navy-blue school knickers. What had caught his eye most were her long, pale legs in short, white socks, just like his doll's. Sherry had spotted him lurking and stood up, patting her skirt back into place, and yelled at him to clear off. He had sloped away, embarrassed at having been caught staring. Back in the classroom, he'd heard one of her friends whisper he was a fat pervert, and Sherry sniggered.

In his bedroom, his cheeks heat up at the memory and he lifts Sherry the doll by her hair.

'Why did you laugh at me?' he asks. 'I only wanted to be your friend.'

The doll doesn't respond, and as he recalls the look Sherry gave him in the classroom, he begins to twist the doll's head round and round until it comes off in his hand. He's disappointed. There's no sense of pleasure or elation at having yanked off the head. He holds the expressionless head in the palm of his hand and hurls it across the room, where it strikes the wardrobe door and rolls away. The eyes shut. Now he peers into her body cavity. The doll is completely empty. He wonders what Sherry Hunt would look like if her head twisted off; a giggle erupts from nowhere and explodes into the air, and he falls back onto the bed, laughing loudly at the thought.

Then the laughter turns to silent tears and he retrieves the doll's head, presses it back into the neck hole. It resists and won't pop back into place. His hands become sweaty and the head slips in his palms. His pulse quickens. He didn't mean to break the doll. He doesn't want her to be broken. He pushes the head again, this time with more force, and is relieved when it finally pops back into place.

'Sorry, Sherry,' he says.

'It's okay. You're my friend.'

CHAPTER FIFTEEN

Natalie left Little Stars Dance Academy with the feeling she was onto something although she could not fathom out its significance. She needed to talk to Bruce again, and soon.

Ian had messaged across an address and phone number for Barney Townsend, who together with his ex-wife, Elsa, had owned Uptown Craft Centre, and who now lived only ten miles from Uptown, on the outskirts of Bablington, a village renowned for its gardens that were open annually to the public. Given Natalie was not far away, she decided to visit rather than ring. She preferred eye contact with people when asking them questions. It was harder for them to be more evasive. He might have an idea of where Elsa was and could maybe tell her more about the woman.

Barney Townsend was toiling in his garden, a cornucopia of colours and enormous blooms, when she arrived. He removed his gardening gloves and left them on the handle of a wheelbarrow, approaching her with a smile. His face was weathered, and his thick arms, sticking out from a short-sleeved shirt, were lightly tanned from exposure to the spring sunshine.

'Can I help you?'

'I'm DI Ward. I've been trying to locate your ex-wife, Elsa, but we can't find a contact number or address for her. It's regarding an incident that took place in 2015.'

'The little girl that disappeared,' he said, face screwing up.

'Ava Sawyer.'

'I remember her name. Won't ever forget it. Elsa took it badly, really badly.'

'We've uncovered her body.'

Barney let out a groan. 'The only way Elsa could live with herself was to believe Ava was alive.'

'She confided in you?'

'We had divorced by the time Ava disappeared but we stayed in touch. After the child went missing, Elsa came to visit me. She was in a dreadful state. In the wake of what happened, the party bookings had stopped and the business began to nosedive. The garden centre side of it was just managing to stay afloat but the animals, parties and so forth were what had kept it profitable. She was depressed about everything: Ava disappearing, the business sliding, and she hated working with Alistair. She wanted to get away from it all. She asked if I'd buy her share at a discounted rate. I refused. I'd done my time there and I was happy taking early retirement. I'd already bought this place and I get pleasure out of looking after it. It's enough for me.'

'Why did you sell to Alistair Fulcher?'

He gave a tight smile. 'He made me an offer I couldn't refuse.'

'Were you aware at the time that Elsa wouldn't get along with him?'

'No, no. You're barking up the wrong tree. I sold out to Alistair because he offered me sufficient money to be free of both the business and of Elsa. Working and living together drove us apart. We stopped being a couple. Every conversation became about the business. All the problems followed us home and we never switched off. It drove a wedge between us.'

'What did Elsa tell you about the day Ava went missing?'

'Only that she'd had one of her migraines. She was so desperate for some relief, she passed the children to Guy as soon as she could and went to the office to get some painkillers. It took a while for them to take effect, and as soon as they did, she met up with Guy and Janet, only to find out Ava had gone.'

'You weren't at the centre that day?'

'After I sold my shares, I didn't set foot in the place again. There was no need.'

'Have you spoken to Elsa since she went to Spain?'

'Last time I saw her was when she told me she and Alistair had decided to cut their losses and sell to Poppyfields. She didn't care about the money. She wanted to get as far away from the memories as possible. It wasn't only the business that changed and suffered after that terrible day. Elsa did too.'

'Do you have any idea where your ex-wife might be?'

'As it happens, I don't. I do, however, have an email address for her. She emailed me a couple of weeks ago, on my birthday. I'll write it down for you.'

He strode towards the door and a black cat ambled outside, plonking itself down on a low wall to bask in the sunshine. Natalie chewed over what she'd learnt. Elsa had wanted to get away from the centre soon after Ava's disappearance. Had it been because she'd felt guilty? Had she somehow been involved in the girl's death or in hiding her body?

Barney returned, a scrap of paper in his hand. 'If she contacts me, I'll let you know.' He paused, his eyes resting a moment on a clump of late-flowering narcissus. 'Can I ask – where did you find Ava Sawyer?'

'Behind the centre. Have you not seen the news recently?'

He shook his head. 'I don't own a television any more. I got rid of it when I moved here. I wanted tranquillity and to be cut off from the world. I work in my garden most days and I prefer to read of an evening. Behind the centre. That's dreadful. That means Ava was there all the time.'

'Possibly so. I'd appreciate it if you hear from Elsa, to let us know. We need to talk to her about all of this again.'

'I understand.'

She withdrew to the lane where her car was parked and climbed inside. Her mobile rang, revealing an unknown number. It was Carlton from the dance academy.

'I've persuaded Bruce he must talk to you. He's going to stop off at Samford Police Station on his way home from his meeting. He ought to be there in an hour.'

'Thank you, Carlton. I'll make sure I'm back to talk to him.'

Natalie reached the station with half an hour to spare before Bruce's arrival and raced to the office to gather as much information about the man as she could ahead of the interview. The team was back, with not much news and glum faces. Ian was first to speak as soon as Natalie threw her handbag on the floor.

'I've interviewed the entire list of registered vehicle owners who were in the vicinity at the time Audrey vanished, and not one of them saw her, or anyone else for that matter, around the park entrance or on the street.'

'Damn. I really hoped somebody would have seen her,' said Natalie.

'I hate it when investigations stall like this. Are people so blinkered they see nothing? Two girls vanish and no one notices.'

'It hasn't stalled, Ian. It's ongoing and we're still processing information. We'll find something. There'll be something. Check out Bruce Kennedy for me. He co-owns the Little Stars Dance Academy. He'll be here soon for an interview. Apparently, he had a few chats with Ava. Sometimes she'd drift off and sit in reception and chat with him. Murray, you can come in on the interview. Help me extract some information from him. Okay, what else have we established so far?'

'Not a great deal. We couldn't get hold of Beatrice Sawyer, Ava's mum. I rang her and we tried her house but she wasn't in. All we found out was that Ava would sometimes wander off and hide,' said Lucy. 'That's pretty much all we've ascertained.'

'That corresponds to what I've been hearing. It's increasingly likely she strolled off the day of the birthday party, though I can't guess what happened to her afterwards. I'm concerned Elsa Townsend was keen to dispose of her share of the business soon after the event. It smacks of a guilty conscience, but whether that was because she knew Ava was dead or she had some part in disposing of her body, or she killed Ava, or she felt responsible, we won't know until we speak to her. Here's her email address. Can you see if the tech guys can trace it?'

'I'll do it when you're interviewing Bruce,' said Ian.

'Lucy, look into Barney Townsend for me. He was married to Elsa. Check there's nothing untoward.'

'Any reason?'

'Eliminating him and making sure we look at everyone who was possibly connected. That's all. Talking of which: Murray, how did you get on with Ned Coleman, the gentleman who lives opposite the park in Uptown?'

'Nah. He didn't hear or see anything outside yesterday. He was glued to *Heartbeat* at the time.'

'Nothing in the police database about him?'

'Nothing at all.' Murray looked away, his focus once more on his screen.

Lucy swivelled around in her seat to speak. 'By the way, Ian found nothing on those workmen who uncovered Ava. They're clean. Weren't in the vicinity when Ava went missing.' Ian acknowledged her comment with a nod.

'Another blank.' Natalie scrolled through the police general database for information regarding Bruce. The office fell silent apart from the clicking of keyboards. Bruce had obtained a degree from a drama school in London and had had minor roles in several musicals. In 1999, he joined an entertainment team on board the *Queen Nefertiti* that cruised regularly around the Red Sea. In 2006, he and Carlton set up the academy. He married Carlton in 2016. Natalie's phone rang shrilly. She snatched it from the desk, eyes still on the screen. Mike was on the other end.

'We have some important news for you. Naomi completed her examination of Ava's bones. There were no evident injuries to the skull or breakages to the limbs, but there was sufficient damage to the hyoid bone to identify the cause of death. Children's bones may be less brittle than adults' bones, but should sufficient pressure be exerted, they can break just the same. It's her belief that Ava was strangled.'

'And the pathologist confirmed strangulation was most likely the cause of Audrey's death,' said Natalie, resting her elbows on her desk. 'We're either looking for a copycat murderer or one person who was responsible for both deaths.'

'It would appear so.'

Lucy looked up and made a gesture. Natalie ended her call.

'I think I might have just found where Audrey's dress came from. There's one like it on Etsy in the USA.'

Natalie scooted across and looked at the picture. It was a copy of the one Audrey had been wearing.

'I'll contact the seller,' said Lucy.

The internal phone blipped and Natalie answered it. Bruce Kennedy was in reception.

'Ian, you got anything on Bruce?'

'I've uncovered something about him you'll find interesting.'

'Fill me in quickly. He's here.'

CHAPTER SIXTEEN

THURSDAY, 27 APRIL – AFTERNOON

Bruce wouldn't meet Natalie's eyes when they entered the interview room. He shuffled in his seat uncomfortably. Natalie slipped into a seat opposite and introduced Murray, who drew up a third seat and set it next to Natalie.

'Carlton said I had to talk to you. I really didn't want to. I have nothing to say that will further your investigations.'

'It's probably best if we decide that.' Natalie wasn't in the mood to be messed about. 'Two young girls are dead. Both attended your dance school. Consequently, you're a person of interest. I'd like to hear what you have to say. You have a younger sister, Josephine, don't you?'

'Yes. What's that got to do with this?'

'Carlton said something about you getting along with Ava because she reminded you of your sister.'

He heaved a sigh and raised his chin. 'Carlton was right. Ava was like Josephine.'

'He also told me Ava would sometimes come and talk to you rather than continue with her ballet class. Why was that?'

'She'd lose patience with dancing. The second it became too difficult for her, she'd get so angry with herself she had to walk out to calm down. Some people thought she was sulking or moody but it was more a cry for help. Ava struggled to be herself.'

Murray snorted. 'That's quite an analysis. You're not a child psychiatrist and she was only five years old. Lots of kids that age get huffy at times. What made you think she had such issues?'

Startled by the sudden hostility, Bruce faced Murray. 'Because she behaved exactly like Jo. Every time Jo couldn't manage something – her spellings, to perform a somersault, to sing, anything that she felt she should be able to do but couldn't – she'd race off and shut herself away in her bedroom and cry. Ava didn't cry. She hid.'

'I find it odd you'd know so much about a little girl who wasn't a relative. It seems to me you *assumed* Ava was like your sister.' Murray looked steadily at Bruce.

'You misunderstand me. I didn't *know* her. I didn't try and analyse her. The first time she and I met, she was hiding under my desk. I was about to take a class of teenagers and had returned to the office to pick up a CD I needed. Ava was sat there, legs crossed, arms folded and refusing to speak. I had to scrabble under the table and join her before she'd tell me what was wrong. That's how she reminded me of Josephine. I'd been under the table with her many times, helping to sort out her problems and listening to her. I was her big brother. Turned out somebody in the changing room had been spiteful about Ava's dancing and she'd run off to hide. I managed to coax her to the class before she was missed.'

'What a good brother you must have been. Didn't your sister have friends to talk to or your mum?' Murray maintained his sneer.

'My mother didn't have time for tantrums or histrionics. I helped Jo and yes, I'd like to think I was and still am a decent brother.' Bruce spoke less confidently. Murray's bad cop routine was working. He was gradually unnerving the man into saying more.

'Ava developed a trust in you,' Natalie said, offering a smile, playing her role of the more understanding cop. 'She must have looked at you as a big brother figure.'

He nodded. 'Maybe. Beatrice was quite often late collecting her daughter and she'd be the last one to leave so I'd often chat to her.

She was quite inquisitive and asked about a postcard I had from Russia, from my sister. I told her about Jo and how she'd struggled to learn to dance but became a top ballerina with the Royal Ballet and now travels all over the world. Ava became really interested in her. She wanted to be a ballerina one day too. She asked lots of questions about Jo and I was happy to talk about her.'

'You were close to your sister, then?' asked Murray, folding his arms.

'Yes.'

Murray glowered. 'Do you speak to her much now?'

'She's away a lot and I'm occupied with the dance school. We don't get to see much of each other.'

'I understand you spoke to Ava the day before she disappeared. What about?' Natalie asked.

'She was upset and didn't want to go to class that day. Beatrice dropped her off as usual and left her there, but Ava asked Carlton to be excused and stayed in reception with me instead. She sat and kicked the chair legs for ages, staring at the wall. In the end, I asked if she wanted to talk about it. Told her Jo would often confide in me and I wouldn't tell anyone.'

Murray let out a snort.

'It seemed the right thing to say,' Bruce said, looking towards Natalie for approval. She gave another smile of encouragement.

'Ava told me her best friend, Harriet, had said some stuff about her at school and everyone in her class was laughing at her. She was glad it was the holidays but she was going to have to face them at a party she didn't want to attend.'

'Did she say what stuff?' Natalie asked.

'She didn't, only that she'd told Harriet something in secret but she'd blurted it to everyone in the class and now Ava couldn't face them. She had to go to Harriet's party and she didn't want to.'

'What advice did you give?' Natalie asked.

'To go to the party and face up to them, to lift her head high and ignore any jibes. They'd get bored if they couldn't upset her.'

Murray spoke. 'You were at Uptown Craft Centre and Farm the day she disappeared.'

'I didn't see her. I left before the party started.'

'How do you know that?' Murray persisted. 'How do you know what time the party began?'

'I found out afterwards. When I was searching for her with all the others. I overheard them talking about it.'

Natalie took over. 'Carlton said you went to collect a plant, then into town to buy a card.'

Bruce looked at his nails, avoiding her gaze.

'Didn't they sell cards at the shop there? It was a craft centre. Surely they sold birthday cards there?' she said.

Bruce's eyelids fluttered. 'I couldn't find one I liked.'

'So you left the centre immediately after purchasing a plant and went into Uptown itself. Is that correct?'

'Yes.' Again he would not meet her eyes.

'Bruce, I'm going to ask you again. This time, think carefully before you respond and remember a little girl was snatched from the centre, taken and killed.' She let her words sink in. 'What time did you leave the centre?'

His words tumbled out. 'I don't know exactly. I was looking around the card section and ran into one of the employees, who I knew. It was his day off. We had a coffee in the café there and then I left.'

'You didn't tell Carlton about this meeting. Why would you keep it secret?'

'Carlton's prone to jealousy. Of course, he asked me if I was at the centre at the time Ava vanished, but I wasn't. I'd left by then. The fact was, I had nothing to do with Ava's disappearance. I was as horrified as anyone about what happened. I was one of the volunteers who helped search for her, all night and the following day. I wish I *had* been at the centre when it happened. I might have spotted her or whoever snatched her. I didn't come forward because I had nothing of use to tell the police at the time, and I have nothing new to tell you. I'm not responsible for what happened.'

'And yesterday afternoon, after Audrey left the class, what did you do?' Natalie's questions came faster now.

'I remained at the dance school. I was working on the set for the Lichfield performance. I didn't finish until late.'

'Did anyone see you?'

'Carlton. He dropped by while I was painting it.'

'What time?'

'I don't know. I wasn't clock-watching. He dropped by a few times, three or four, in between his classes, to see how I was getting along. He finished at eight p.m. and we went out for a curry then home.'

'This man you had coffee with, what's his name?'

'Mark Randle. He worked in the greenhouses. He lives in Uptown.'

'Have you got a number for him?'

'No. I deleted his contact details. I haven't seen him for about a year. Not since Carlton and I got married.'

Natalie nodded again and sat back in her seat. It was Murray's cue. He pushed up from his chair, hands on the table, until he was in Bruce's face, only inches away.

'Bull. Shit. Why would you delete his contact details?'

'I had no reason to hang onto them. I didn't see him much afterwards. He left the craft centre.'

Murray smiled a predator's smile. 'I know something about you, Bruce. Something you haven't mentioned here today. I know about your addiction. And I asked myself why would a man with a sex addiction be friends with a five-year-old girl and, more importantly, why wouldn't he admit to being at the craft centre and farm when that same little girl went missing? You're holding back on us, and if you don't come clean, we'll charge you with perverting the course of justice or worse, and rest assured, your time in prison will be most uncomfortable.' He sat back on his chair again.

'Shit! No! For crying out loud. I'm not a deviant. I don't have an addiction.'

'You went to a sexual addiction recovery centre twice – once in 2000 and again in 2004 – and are a member of TSAHG, The Sex Addiction Help Group. So, answer me this: why were you at the centre that afternoon if not to wait for Ava to turn up to a party you encouraged her to go to? You knew if she got upset there, she'd run off. The chances were, she would get upset. She'd already told you about Harriet. Did she tell you where the party was, Bruce? Were you waiting for that very scenario so you could attack her?'

'Jesus, no!' Bruce ran a hand over his face, dragging it over his beard. 'No way. I've never laid a finger on a child. I want children! Carlton and I want to be parents. I would never…' His voice broke into a sob as he began to tear up.

Murray folded his arms again, his job done.

Bruce drew several breaths then spoke. 'I *had* a sexual addiction. I've always been attracted to men not children, to adult men. When I was younger I had a ferocious sexual appetite. I knew I had to curb it. TSAHG helped me. I lapsed in 2004 but I'd just met Carlton and I wanted to get over it, for good. I checked into the clinic in 2004, followed the programme and made a full recovery. I began dating Carlton and gradually got better. I am no longer addicted. I wanted to help others who go through the same thing. Not many people understand what it's like to have such an addiction. I signed up to be a sponsor. I was Mark Randle's sponsor. I met him for a coffee and chat that afternoon. It was imperative nobody knew about his condition, so I didn't tell anyone, not even Carlton. He doesn't even know about my dependence, or about me becoming a sponsor. Look, Mark rang me that morning because he was struggling. I agreed to a quick meeting and we chose the craft centre because I had to go there that afternoon to collect a plant for my mother. That's it. The truth.'

Natalie stared at Bruce, trying to decide if she should retain him for further questioning before deciding she had no grounds to keep him. She'd check out his alibi for Wednesday and talk to Mark Randle before she pursued this line of enquiry. She looked at Murray and raised her eyebrows. He nodded, indicating he had no further questions.

'I think that'll be all for the moment. You're free to leave,' she said.

Bruce stood immediately. 'I absolutely had nothing to do with either death. I swear it.'

'We'll be in touch if we need to talk to you again.'

Back in the office, Natalie slapped her desk with the flat of her hand. 'Crap! I thought we were onto something with him. Pull everything we can on this Mark Randle and get him here. See what he has to say for himself.'

'I'll do that. I've already done some background on The Sex Addiction Help Group,' said Ian.

'I've emailed that Etsy address and I'm waiting for a reply,' said Lucy.

'Good. Any news on Elsa Townsend?' Natalie asked.

'Nothing yet,' Lucy replied.

'Then we'll have to stick at what we do have and that's Mark. Talk to his co-workers about him. See what they thought about him. We have to interview Ava's parents. Murray, head over to Carl Sawyer's workshop with Lucy. There's half an hour before closing time; you might just catch him there. I'll try Beatrice again.'

As she marched towards the exit her phone buzzed. It was David. 'Hey.'

'Hi. You want me to order takeaway for later?' His voice had a petulant edge to it.

'If you and the kids want it, go ahead. I don't think I'll be back again until really late.'

'Any idea what time?'

'No. I told you this morning I'd be late.'

'Rich rang to invite me out for a pint at the Golden Cup.'

'Well, go then. The pub's only down the road. They're not babies. They'll be fine for a couple of hours.'

'Sure, just walk out and leave them to their own devices. Not exactly good parenting, is it?'

'They're teenagers, David.'

'Exactly.' He ended the call, leaving Natalie reeling. What was his problem? She shoved the phone back in her pocket and ignored the voice in her head that reminded her Olivia had been a teenager too.

CHAPTER SEVENTEEN

THURSDAY, 27 APRIL – LATE AFTERNOON

Beatrice Sawyer opened the door and looked blankly at Natalie. Natalie had seen the same thousand-yard stare before on the faces of uncomprehending parents or loved ones who'd been given terrible news.

'I came to see how you were bearing up,' said Natalie.

'Come in.' Beatrice moved from the door, waiting for Natalie to enter before peering out and shutting the door. 'There was a journalist came earlier. She wanted to know how I felt about Ava's body being discovered at the craft centre. Dumbest question ever. I told her to fuck off.'

'Has Tanya been back to see you?'

'She was here yesterday for a long while. She's coming back today. She's nice. I like her. My mum's here too. She went out to the shops half an hour ago. I didn't want to go with her. I don't want to see anyone.' Beatrice slumped onto the settee. The television set was on, an American sitcom lighting up the screen.

'I have some news for you regarding your daughter's death. It's not good. I'm very sorry to tell you that we believe Ava was strangled.' There was no sound and then the sudden burst of canned laughter. Beatrice stared at the set, eyes unfocused.

'We're going back over all the statements and witnesses from when she disappeared.'

'They didn't find the person who took her then. What makes you think you can?'

'There's been an unfortunate development. Audrey Briggs was murdered yesterday afternoon. She was also strangled. There's a possibility the same person who killed your daughter also murdered Audrey.'

'I see.'

'Is there anything else you can tell me, Beatrice? Ava and Audrey were friends. Did they share any secrets?'

'None they shared with me, but I wasn't the most attentive mother. Why would they confide in me? I was facing my own demons. I couldn't exit the black hole I'd fallen into.'

'Do you have a picture of the dress Ava was wearing when she went missing?'

'I had one but it was on an old phone. I didn't transfer it when I upgraded my phone. I snapped it the afternoon of the party. She didn't look happy in it. Every time I looked at it, I was reminded of how I forced her to go to that wretched party and how I lost her forever. Is it important?'

'I just wanted to get an idea of what it looked like. Did you buy or make her dress?'

'I bought it. It came from a children's boutique, ChicKids, in Uptown.'

'What was it like?'

Beatrice made a motion with one hand curving over her left shoulder. 'It had these little puffed sleeves that stopped about here.' She held her hand near the top of her arm. 'It was more of a lemon colour than bright yellow, and flouncy.'

'Flouncy?'

She swept her arms down her body and threw her hands outwards at her hips. 'Like a ballerina skirt.'

'Did it have a bow?'

Beatrice frowned in concentration. 'It had a tiny bow at the base of each sleeve.'

'Not anywhere else?'

'No.'

Natalie made a note of the name of the shop where it had been purchased. The dress Audrey was wearing might have also come from there. 'You had Audrey over for play dates. What did you think of her?'

Beatrice breathed in and considered the question. 'I liked her. She smiled a lot and didn't get upset with Ava even when she was being difficult. I'm genuinely sorry this has happened to her. It'll be such a shock for Caroline.'

The words were without emotion. Natalie couldn't work out if it was because Beatrice didn't care what Caroline and her husband were going through or simply because she had no more sorrow left to share.

'Did Caroline spend much time with you after Ava vanished?'

'They all made a fuss of us both to start with, but once the rumours about me being an unfit mother began, she and all the others withdrew their support. Caroline was one of the first to stop visiting.'

'That must have been hard for you.'

'I was never one of their crowd. I wasn't party to the coffee mornings, cosy chats outside the school gates or car-share schemes. It came as no big surprise when they began avoiding me as if by associating with me, their own children might also suddenly go missing. Caroline stopped coming around to visit shortly after Ava went. I'm sorry this has happened to them but now they'll understand what it's like to lose a child.'

A car pulled up on the driveway. Beatrice rose to see who it was. 'It's my mother. If that's everything, I'd like you to leave now.'

'Certainly and thank you for talking to me again.' Natalie edged towards the door and passed a silver-haired woman with sharp features in the drive. The woman shook her head.

'You police?'

'Yes. DI Ward.'

'She's in a bad way. I'm taking her back home to Sheffield with me. I thought we'd leave this afternoon after the liaison officer has visited. Beatrice needs to get away from here for a few days at least. Is that okay?'

'Yes. It might be better. Make sure you leave Tanya all your contact details.'

The woman gave a brief smile in acknowledgement and returned to the boot of the car to offload a couple of bags of shopping.

Before she headed back to the station, Natalie decided to drop by the ChicKids boutique. The shop was situated off a cobbled market square, the front window still dressed for Easter with fluffy chicks, rabbits and multicoloured eggs positioned between plastic coats and open umbrellas in green, orange and yellow, bearing prancing unicorns.

A bell tinkled over the door as she entered, almost knocking into a rail of party dresses immediately to her left, next to which were shelves of coloured T-shirts stacked in separate compartments according to colour. The back wall of the shop held rails of colour-coordinated tops, trousers and skirts, and beyond that, a changing room. To her right was a half-moon counter, behind which stood a young woman.

'Can I help you?'

Natalie showed her ID. 'Is this your shop?'

'Yes.'

'This is a long shot, but I wondered if you recall selling a lemon-yellow, chiffon dress with puffed short sleeves and a ballerina skirt to a woman called Mrs Sawyer, two years ago. Her daughter, Ava, wore it to a birthday at Uptown Craft Centre and Farm. You might remember Ava. She went missing that day.'

'I couldn't forget. The whole community was affected. I was one of the volunteers who helped look for her. I remember the dress too. It was in our sale at the time. We'd had trouble selling that model. Mrs Sawyer chose it. Ava was with her and she expressed a preference for a pink dress we had in the window, and to be honest, I think she'd have looked better in the pink one, but it was full price. Her mother put her foot down and said she didn't want to spend a fortune on a dress that'd get worn once or twice, and the yellow one was within her budget.'

'Do you have a photograph of it anywhere?'

'Gosh, no. Sorry. That model went out of fashion quite some time ago and we'd had it for well over a year.'

'How about this dress?'

Natalie had cropped the photograph of Audrey and showed the woman just the dress.

'Definitely not had anything like that and I don't recall seeing that style in the collections this year.'

'Thank you anyway. If you happen across anything that looks like it, would you give me a call?'

Natalie backed out of the shop, the overhead bell tinkling as she shut the door. Her eyes fell on the umbrellas in the window. Leigh had loved unicorns. She was less into them nowadays. Now she was into gadgets, music, jewellery and make-up. *Thirteen going on nineteen.* Her thoughts jumped swiftly to Olivia. She'd had a toy unicorn too. Natalie brushed the memory away. She had a job to do.

Ian called with news that Mark Randle was refusing to come to the station.

'He says he has nothing to do with Ava Sawyer and doesn't wish to discuss why he was at the craft centre the day she went missing.'

'Does he indeed? Give me his address and ask Murray to meet me at his house. We'll tackle him there. If he's still reluctant, we'll bring him in.'

'He's at work. B&Q in Uptown.'

'We'll meet there, then.'

The B&Q store stood at the far end of a retail park on the edge of Uptown. The car park was fairly empty with most cars parked outside the supermarket at the opposite end. Natalie strode towards the store, Murray keeping pace with her as she filled him in on her intentions. 'He's on the late shift. Doesn't finish until seven. It doesn't seem too busy so I'm sure we'll be able to get five minutes of his time. If he kicks up a fuss, we'll take him in.'

'Understood.'

The automatic doors opened with a swish and they walked into a blast of cool air, easy-listening music and row after row of aisles. Natalie hated DIY stores. It was never a simple process to purchase goods. Signage might indicate the aisle's contents but each lane seemed endless and contained floor to ceiling shelving all packed with merchandise. David wasn't a fan either and certainly no DIY enthusiast. If anything required repairing in their house, it was invariably David's father who they rang.

There were no operatives at the checkout and the store appeared unmanned until they moved deeper into the cavernous space and spotted an employee stacking large bags of gravel.

'We're looking for Mark Randle,' said Murray.

'Garden section,' came the reply. 'Through the double doors at the end of the building.'

A man in his thirties with a goatee beard, eyebrow stud and a large, black, circular earring in his left ear that distended the lobe was holding a length of coiled hosepipe, aiming the spray over a group of large shrubs in pots, and yawning. He started when he spotted Murray's police uniform, dropping the hose which continued to gush water over the floor and his feet. His head turned towards the exit behind him and he made a quick movement in that direction only to be brought to a standstill by Murray's shout.

'Stay where you are, Mr Randle.'

The man pivoted 180 degrees.

'We want to ask you a few questions,' said Natalie, holding her ID card in the air. 'We can do it here or at the station. Either way, we're going to talk to you.'

Mark looked sullen.

'Okay. Let me turn this off.' He sidestepped to the tap and turned it clockwise. The hose sputtered and released a final dribble of water.

'We have reason to believe you were at Uptown Craft Centre and Farm on 24 July 2015, the day Ava Sawyer went missing.'

'I can't remember where I was that far back.'

'Don't be obstinate. It'll do you no favours. Were you there on that date?'

His shoulders slumped. 'Yes. I was there that day.'

'Why were you there? It was your day off so why did you go to the centre?'

'I fancied a cup of tea.'

'Come, come, Mr Randle. You surely could have made a cup of tea at home.' Natalie kept her voice pleasant although it was a struggle.

'I honestly went for a cup of tea,' he repeated.

'Okay, I've had enough,' she suddenly snapped. 'Bring him in.'

Murray withdrew handcuffs from his back pocket and launched at the man, who backed off, hands up in the air.

'Whoa! Okay, okay. I met a friend for a cup of tea and a chat and then went home.'

'Would this friend have been Bruce Kennedy?' Natalie asked.

He looked at his feet. 'You've spoken to him, haven't you?'

'We have and now we'd like your version of events.'

'What did he say?'

'I'm not prepared to discuss that. I want you to tell me why you were there with Bruce and what happened after he left.'

'He's already told you, hasn't he? You know why we met up.' He let out a lengthy sigh. 'Okay. Truth is I had a serious problem – a dependence. I was on a programme to get better and was given a sponsor, Bruce. I phoned him that morning because I'd lapsed. Bruce was going to the centre that afternoon and we agreed to meet there. We chose the farm café because there was a private alcove where we could talk without being overheard. He explained it was normal to have setbacks and not to be so hard on myself. He didn't stay long. In fact, he didn't even finish his tea.'

'What did you do afterwards?'

'I went home, via the greenhouse. I'd planted out some delphinium seeds that week and wanted to check they weren't drying out. I left soon after that.'

'What time would that have been?'

'I really have no idea. I went for a ride afterwards.'

'Ride?'

'I own a motorbike. That's how I get about.'

'You didn't see a child or anyone about or near the greenhouses, did you?'

'If I had, I'd have told the police at the time.' He folded his arms and glowered at Natalie.

'Where were you on Wednesday afternoon at about five p.m.?'

'At home.'

'Can you prove your whereabouts?'

'What's this about?'

'Can anyone confirm you were at home on Wednesday?'

'No. I live alone.'

'What time did you leave work?'

'At four. I walked that day because the weather was nice and I needed the exercise. Takes about three quarters of an hour on foot.'

'Did you happen to go past Queen's Park?'

His eyebrows drew together. 'This is about the girl who was killed in the park, isn't it?'

'Answer the question, please.'

He unfolded his arms and rubbed a hand behind his neck. 'I went into the park for a short while but I absolutely didn't see that girl. I was in and out in a flash.'

'Why did you go in the park?'

'I was walking home, spotted a friend, or someone I thought was a friend, and I followed them into the park. When I caught up with them, I found out it wasn't who I thought it was.' He blinked several times, eyes darting as he spoke.

'That sounds a very muddled explanation.'

'Hand on heart, it's the absolute truth.' He wet his lips and tensed up. He was clearly keeping something back.

'Would you care to elaborate?'

'No, I wouldn't. I've told you enough. And I have work to do. I don't want to lose my job.' With that he spun around and dashed for the exit, knocking over tubs behind him. Murray launched after him, scrabbling in his wake. Mark didn't make it to the door. In spite of the obstacles, Murray caught him before he could reach it, and placing a heavy hand on his shoulder, wheeled him back towards Natalie. Natalie, who'd been watching the events unfold, had spotted another quick movement. Mark had tossed his mobile phone into a pot as he'd scarpered past it. She shook her head and crossed to the large green pot, reached in, extracted the mobile and tutted.

'Good try. Now why would you throw this away?'

Mark did not reply.

'Have it your way. We're going to take you to the station to assist us with our enquiries. You are now under investigation.'

Mark began to protest then clamped his mouth shut and glowered at her.

'Take him in.'

CHAPTER EIGHTEEN

THURSDAY, 27 APRIL – EVENING

Natalie left Mark in an interview room under Murray's watchful eye and deposited the mobile at the tech lab before stopping off at the office. Ian sidled up to her immediately and passed over a manila file.

'There's a restraining order out on Mark Randle. He's not allowed to contact or approach Justine Woodman of 19 Stumpy Lane, Uptown. It's been in place for a year.'

She opened the file and read through the document. 'How come this didn't show up when you were running checks on him?'

'I missed it. I was focused on his sex addiction and past employment record.'

'You missed it?'

'Sorry.'

Natalie bit back an acerbic retort. She was cranky and frustrated like they all were. They'd been working flat out since Ava's body had been discovered and had all pulled their weight. It was an error but mistakes happened. At least he had the information now.

'Okay. Anything else I should be aware of?'

'Not that I've discovered.'

'As soon as the tech department find whatever he doesn't want us to see on his phone, let me know.'

*

Natalie threw the file onto the desk and strode around the room before coming to rest in front of the table. Murray, with his back against the wall, said nothing.

'No more pissing about, Mark. You could be in serious bother. You have no convincing alibi for yesterday afternoon and were in Queen's Park around the time Audrey Briggs was killed. You were also at Uptown Craft Centre and Farm on 24 July 2015, at around the time Ava Sawyer was snatched. You have no one who can confirm your whereabouts on either occasion. Ava's body was uncovered at the garden centre in an area not far from the greenhouses. I'd say that makes you a likely suspect. Unless you come up with something that can extricate you from this mess you've got yourself into, I might have to suggest you call a lawyer.'

Mark looked ahead, eyes on a spot above Natalie's head.

'Have you any idea how serious this is?'

Mark maintained his silence.

Natalie kept her eyes on him, waiting for him to crack and speak but he said nothing.

'This isn't going to help. The longer you remain silent, the worse this will be for you. Say you have nothing to do with either girl's death; you can still be charged for perverting the course of justice. Do you want to go to prison?'

Mark shifted slightly in his chair.

Natalie tapped the file. 'Justine Woodman.'

Mark blinked and looked away.

'You were issued with a restraining order that prevents you from approaching or contacting her. You harassed her repeatedly, and according to that file, waited outside her work and threatened her. She claimed she was terrified of what you might do to her and her daughter.' She paused to drive home her point. 'She has a ten-year-old daughter. The way I see it, there's a connection.'

No response. Natalie thumped the table, making him look up in surprise. 'Mr Randle, I am investigating the murder of two young girls. If you won't answer me, I *am* going to charge you.'

A knock interrupted her. Murray opened the door to Ian.

'Can I have a word, ma'am?'

Natalie pointed a finger at Mark's chest. 'If you don't speak to me on my return, you'll be spending the night in the cells.'

Outside in the corridor with the door shut, she released a long expulsion of air. 'Bastard. He's clammed up.'

'I visited the tech lab. Told them it was urgent. They looked at his mobile while I was there and came across these straight away. They were secreted in a coded file.'

He handed over copies of explicit photographs of naked adults in various sexual positions.

'He's got videos on there too; adult hardcore porn. None of it's illegal but gives you an idea of what he's hiding. Probably still has a sex addiction. These are the photos you might find more interesting.'

She glanced at the three pictures of a young girl smiling up at the camera. 'Thanks, Ian.'

'Thought it might help. Stuffed up on the restraining order.'

She gave a tight smile. 'We all stuff up at times,' she said.

'You ready to talk to me yet?'

Mark looked at his hands now resting in his lap.

'I don't know what television cop shows you watch but rest assured, keeping silent doesn't work in the real world. We've searched through your phone and found your sex videos and photographs. I have to say it doesn't look good for you.'

'I didn't know either of the girls who died. I'd never set eyes on either of them. It's only a coincidence I was at Uptown Craft Centre the day Ava went missing and was in Queen's Park for only a few minutes yesterday.' He lifted his eyes to look directly at Natalie. 'I know what you've found on my phone, but those photographs have nothing to do with the murders. I was in the park because of Justine.'

Natalie waited while he knotted his fingers together and attempted to gather his thoughts.

'I'd like to explain what happened between us. So you get the real picture. I first met Justine at a café that bikers use, outside Samford. We went out together. I really liked her and I got on fine with Boo, her daughter. We started seeing each other regularly then, without warning, she dropped me. It happened suddenly and without any reason. One minute we were going out; the next, she stopped responding to my calls. Whenever I rang or texted, she ignored me; froze me out. I went around to her place to ask why, and she wouldn't open the door. I tried her workplace and next thing I knew, she made an official complaint about me to the police. I was angry and confused. I sent emails asking why she was treating me so badly. She didn't respond. Instead she called the police again and said I was harassing her. While I was walking home from work yesterday, I saw Justine going into the park with another man and I was jealous, okay? I ran after them but before I caught them up, I stopped and hung back.'

'Why didn't you say something earlier?'

'I was breaking the injunction. You could send me to jail.'

Natalie's eyes grew big. 'You have more to be concerned about than breaking an injunction. It would've been better if you had just told us the truth and if you hadn't tried to hide your phone.'

'I don't know why I did that. Moment of panic. I wasn't thinking straight. I guess I didn't want you to see the porn on it even though it's adult porn. No kiddie stuff. I'm not a paedo.'

'There are other photographs on your phone of a young girl, a girl wearing a yellow dress. Who is she?'

'That's Boo. I took them before Justine blocked me.'

'Why did you put them into an encrypted file?'

'It wasn't deliberate. I transferred all the explicit pictures across in case my phone ever got stolen. I accidentally sent those across at the same time.'

'Why not delete them? It's weird you should keep pictures of a young girl you hardly know on your mobile.'

'There are photos of Justine on there too. You must have seen them. I didn't just hang onto the pictures of Boo. I kept all the photos I'd taken. I simply couldn't delete them. They meant too much to me. I'd really hoped we'd become a family. I couldn't let go of that dream.'

Natalie sat opposite Mark and studied his face. In spite of his protestations, facts were facts. He had a weak alibi for the days in question, there were photographs of a girl in a yellow dress on his phone and he had worked at Uptown Craft Centre. Still, she knew she shouldn't get fixated on one suspect when there were potential holes in the case against him. She'd release him until further information came to light.

'I'm going to allow you to go home,' she said.

Mark's shoulders slumped with relief.

'However, if we don't find evidence of you only being in the park briefly as you've claimed, and if we're forced to bring you back in for whatever reason, I shan't be so lenient next time.'

She called Murray into the corridor. 'Have somebody in the tech lab go through the CCTV camera footage outside the park and see if what Mark says bears up, and then go home. I have to admit I can't think of any motive or reason as to why he'd kill Audrey or Ava.'

'Me neither but I think these cases are related to the birthday party back in 2015.'

'I do too. It seems too much of a coincidence that Ava's body was discovered on Tuesday, and then her friend Audrey was killed the following day.'

'Audrey was the only person who knew Ava had left for the toilet that day but said nothing about it until after the visit to the petting zoo. Do you think somebody might be angry about that?'

'You mean they might blame Audrey for not speaking up?'

Murray nodded.

'Maybe so. It's worth considering. Of course, that would lead us to consider Ava's parents. They'd be the most likely suspects. We'll think it over again tomorrow. You best get off. It's knocking on and I need everyone back at the station and feeling alert, first thing in the morning.'

'Best go get some sleep then. I'll arrange for the tech boys to check the CCTV footage before I scoot off. See you tomorrow.'

It was coming up to nine. She ought to call it a day. The office was empty apart from Ian. 'You still here?'

'Been talking to Justine Woodman. She's coming in. Should be here any minute.'

'I'm waiting for CCTV footage to confirm Mark entered and left the park on Wednesday before I talk to him again. Want to interview Justine with me?'

'Sure.' Ian gave her a smile.

Justine Woodman was slight, slender and nervous. She stared at them with huge eyes and clutched her handbag on her knee all the time she spoke to them.

'Mark seemed really nice to start with but after a few dates, I started to think he was too weird for me. He was into sex games and experimental stuff that I wasn't up for. I tried to let him down gently but he wouldn't take no for an answer. I decided the best way was to cut him out of our lives. I was a bit scared of him. He could be really domineering in the bedroom and I was frightened he could be like that all the time. I had my daughter to think of too.'

'You complained about him harassing you?'

'He'd text me and text me and text me – one text after another – all night. I'd turn my phone off and when I turned it on again there'd be hundreds of text messages from him asking me why I wasn't replying. He'd do the same with emails. I had to block his name from my list. Then, when I didn't reply, he came to my flat and would wait outside for us to come home and keep asking me why I was freezing him out. That was when I got really scared. He wouldn't leave us alone. I was frightened he'd start hounding my daughter too. I told the police then.'

'I understand he followed you into Queen's Park yesterday afternoon.'

Her mouth dropped open, lips forming a perfect 'O'. 'Did he? I didn't see him.'

'Who were you with?'

'Just a guy from work – Fraser Lyons. He's just a good friend. He invited me to go with him to pick up his son from the playground. The lad was skateboarding there with a friend. We went to Nando's afterwards.'

'Your daughter Boo wasn't with you?'

'She was with her dad. He has her midweek and every other weekend.'

'Did you happen to spot a girl on a pink bike when you were in the park?'

Justine's eyebrows knitted together. 'No. There weren't any girls about. In fact, there was only Toby, Fraser's son, and his friend near the playground. Are you asking about the little girl who got killed? I heard about it this morning. Fraser and I discussed it earlier, but neither of us saw anything. Fraser even asked his son if he'd seen anything when he was skateboarding, but he hadn't seen her, nor had his friend.'

'What time did you leave the park?'

'We were only there long enough to collect Toby and then leave. In total, we'd have only been ten minutes or so.'

'Did you leave by the same entrance?'

'We did.'

Natalie put her hands flat on the table. 'Thank you for your time. We appreciate you coming in at this late hour.'

'He wasn't following me, was he?'

'Mark? No. He spotted you going into the park and was going to catch you up, then he remembered what would happen to him if he got too close to you. I don't think you need to be concerned about him. He is more worried about that restraining order than trying to approach you.'

Justine nibbled her bottom lip and clung onto her bag even more tightly. 'I thought this sort of thing might happen. Uptown is too small a place and it's difficult to hide away from somebody like Mark. I'm moving away in a week and I've changed my phone number and email address. I've got a transfer to a branch in Stoke-on-Trent. Mark will be less likely to bump into me if I leave Uptown.'

'It'll certainly help ease your mind,' Natalie replied and earned a small smile.

With Justine now gone, it was time to leave. She'd asked Ian to look out for Justine and her friend on CCTV when he was searching for Mark. He stood obediently, like an enthusiastic sheepdog, eyes lifted for more commands.

'Good work on getting Justine in at this late hour. It's good to have somebody who's so thorough on the team. Now, go home.'

The house was silent when Natalie got in. No sound of the television or any music. She headed upstairs. Leigh, in pyjamas and headphones, was watching YouTube videos on her iPad. She removed the headset when she saw her mum. 'Hey. You missed pizza.'

'What did you choose?'

'Margherita. Dad and Josh had pepperoni.' She pulled a face.

'You leave me any?'

'Dad said you'd get something at work. He's at the pub.'

'He rang me. So, what have I missed apart from pizza?'

'Nothing. Oh, I've been invited to a party next weekend. Kelly's fourteenth. It's a sleepover. Dad said to check with you.'

'Kelly's parents going to be there?'

Leigh's mouth dragged downwards. 'Mu-um,' she said, dragging it into two syllables.

'Okay, but only if her parents are there.'

'Her mum's going to be in.'

'You know I'll check, don't you?'

'I hate having a cop for a mother.'

'You don't mean that,' said Natalie, grinning at the exaggerated look on her daughter's face. 'I'm going to say hello to Josh. If you want to watch some television for half an hour with me downstairs…'

'It's a school night. I usually have to be in bed by nine.'

'It's a one-off offer.'

Leigh grinned. 'Okay.'

Natalie tapped on Josh's door. There was no answer so she didn't go in. Fifteen-year-old boys might not appreciate a late-evening visit from their mothers. Her children were rapidly turning into adults and soon she wouldn't be able to guide or protect them any longer. The thought depressed her. She hoped she'd equipped them enough for their future. That's all a parent could do.

Downstairs, she dropped onto the settee and tuned into a sitcom. Tiredness flooded her limbs, making them heavy, but she fought it. Leigh curled up on the chair next to her and for a while Natalie was lost in thought as she studied her daughter's profile. A surge of love washed over her, so powerful it almost winded her. *The maternal instinct.* If anyone harmed either of her children, what lengths would she go to for revenge? Would she want to kill those responsible or hurt somebody she blamed? Could Beatrice Sawyer or her husband be capable of such an act? Leigh laughed out loud and the thought evaporated. For now, she wasn't a cop. For the moment, she was a mother.

CHAPTER NINETEEN

THURSDAY, 27 APRIL – AFTERNOON

RAINEY KILBURN

Rainey Kilburn tucks her hair behind her ear and hoists her school bag onto her shoulder, mindful of the fragile contents inside. The day ended with art – her favourite subject – and she'd put the finishing touches to the clay cat she'd been making for the last few lessons. She's pleased with the result and can't wait to show it to her mother.

The art lesson cheered her up immensely. Up until then, she'd been feeling down. Ever since the news about Audrey Briggs, there'd been a sad feeling in the air and some of the girls had spent all day crying. Rainey was really sorry about Audrey but she'd never been especially close to her. She was best friends with Harriet Downing and two other girls, and had been for the last two years. Audrey was okay to talk to and quite nice, but Rainey didn't know her well enough to feel she had the right to weep so openly.

Harriet, however, had been truly upset. She and Paige Hamilton had cried so much they'd been sent home, which was a nuisance because Rainey's mum had issued her with strict instructions she wasn't to walk home alone. She was to stick with Harriet, who only lived a street away, or wait for Tyler, her older brother, and come home with him.

Rainey's mother had given a long speech about not talking to strangers and the dangers of being alone. She'd reminded her about Ava Sawyer, who'd gone off at Harriet's party, never to be seen again. Rainey had nodded and promised not to walk home alone even though she didn't want to accompany her brother. He and his friends were annoying and dragged out the walk for as long as possible. She hated bringing up the rear while they messed about.

She searches the sea of bodies surging from the main building but there's no sign of Tyler, who usually towers over everyone. She spots his friends Mason and Abe racing after another couple of boys she doesn't recognise. Tyler isn't with them. He's probably in trouble again. He's often kept behind after school for playing up. She loves her brother but he can be a total idiot at times. She waits in case he emerges, watching as the teenagers spread in all directions and jump into cars or buses, or wander away. Within a few minutes there's only a trickle of pupils hanging about the gates and still no sign of her brother. Most likely he is in detention. Mum will be furious. It'll be the third time this month.

She isn't going to wait any longer. It isn't far to her house and there's a quicker route – a grass path – that runs past the school fields and allotments she can take. If she chooses that way, she'll be unlikely to meet anyone.

Her thoughts turn to Ava. She can't remember the events of Harriet's party at Uptown Craft Centre, not clearly. Two years was forever. She can't really even remember Ava, only that she would sometimes give you a funny look, like she was weighing you up. Truth be told, she was a bit put off by Ava. Harriet didn't talk about her. No one talked about her. In fact, until her mother mentioned it, she hadn't thought about the girl.

She passes the allotments, patches of earth divided up into sections. The year before, her brother and his friends stole vegetables, including a giant marrow, from a couple of the plots there. They drew faces on all the produce and then took photos of them with their phones. Mum saw the pictures and clipped Tyler around the ear for doing it, but he only laughed and said it was a bit of fun.

She hears someone calling her name and turns around in case it's Tyler. She recognises the man waving at her. He's one of her mum's friends. She's going to stop to say hello, then she remembers she made a promise not to talk to anyone, and instead of responding, she keeps walking. It isn't far to Monks Walk and home.

She tugs the straps of the school bag more firmly to make sure it rests on her shoulders. She doesn't want the pottery cat to break.

Monks Walk, once part of a Franciscan friary, is a pathway through a pleasant green space, restored by a group of volunteers to its former glory. One side of the path is flanked by a tall brick wall covered in Virginia creeper, and large flower beds full of eighteenth-century garden favourites such as hibiscus, honeysuckle, iris, lily, sage, lilacs and blue passion flowers. The other side of the path consists of a few widely spaced beech trees and grass. Although wooden benches had been dotted about for people to enjoy the solitude of the garden, it is rarely visited.

Rainey draws level with the sculpture positioned halfway down the path – open palms from which a bird flies. She loves the copper bird with its wings wide open, flying upwards, that today shines in the afternoon light. Her mind turns to the art lesson and the pottery they'd been making. She'd really enjoyed scraping away at the clay, transforming a shapeless piece into a recognisable animal. Maybe one day, she'll be good enough to make fabulous sculptures like the one here. Her mind drifts into the realms of fantasy and she doesn't hear the heavy breathing of somebody slowing behind her. Rainey's thoughts are elsewhere until a sudden weight falls on her left shoulder, making her gasp and bringing her to a sudden halt.

'Why did you run away?'

The man is behind her holding a plastic bag in one gloved hand. The other rests on her shoulder, his fingers squeezing her collarbone.

'I didn't. I'm not supposed to talk to anyone.'

'*But you know me. You can talk to me. It's rude not to say something when somebody speaks to you.*' *The man looks displeased.*

She clamps her mouth shut and hopes he'll leave her alone. His face suddenly changes and although he doesn't remove his hand, he gives her a smile.

'*I've got something for you. A present,*' *he says, holding the bag aloft.*

'*Why?*'

'*Because you're a very pretty girl.*'

Rainey doesn't like the way he's speaking. He's being artificially jolly like the fake Santa Claus she visited at the shopping centre in December.

'*I don't want it,*' *she says, attempting to wriggle from his grip.*

'*Now, now. Don't be ungrateful. Why not see what it is first?*' *He pushes the bag towards her. She takes it reluctantly, peers inside and spots what looks like a yellow dress. She doesn't like yellow clothes. She doesn't much like dresses, preferring trousers or jeans. She hands the bag back to him but he doesn't accept it.*

'*Don't you like it?*'

She shakes her head.

'*But it's very pretty.*'

'*I want to go now,*' *she says, trying once more to get away. She shrugs her shoulders and shimmies to escape but his grip tightens. His eyes bore into hers.*

'*It's very pretty. Try it on.*'

'*I don't want it,*' *she says again. She lets the bag drop to the floor.*

He doesn't bend to retrieve it. Instead he stares hard at her, and his other hand snaps around the back of her neck. He pulls her face closer to his and smiles a terrifying smile before speaking again.

'*And I said, try… it… on.*'

CHAPTER TWENTY

FRIDAY, 28 APRIL – MORNING

'What time did you get in?' asked Natalie, lightly.

'Dunno. Twelve-ish,' David muttered. 'Why?'

She tried not to sigh. She wasn't trying to start an argument; she only wanted some semblance of normality, an easy, relaxed conversation of the type they used to enjoy.

'How's Rich?'

'Fine.'

She made another attempt. 'I tried to wait up for you but couldn't stay awake much past ten. Sorry.'

'Not a biggie. I was too pissed anyway.'

'You feeling okay now?'

He gave a half-hearted smile. 'Rough as the proverbial badger's arse.' The ice had been broken.

'Got some paracetamol if you'd like to take a couple of them.'

'I'll be fine. I'll go for a run after I take the kids to school. By the way, Josh was awake when I came in. His door was slightly ajar and I think he was using his phone. Probably talking to all his school chums on WhatsApp. That's the sort of thing they all do nowadays, isn't it? Beats me. I was going to tell him to go to sleep but didn't want him to see me in a state.'

'Leave it be for the moment. As long as he gets up in the morning and his grades don't suffer, it can't be doing too much harm.'

'I'm not sure I like our children being online late at night.'

'It's the way of the modern world,' she said, pecking his cheek. 'We have to try and keep up with our own offspring. Catch you later. Hope your hangover improves.'

She pondered his words as she drove to work. It was difficult to know how much slack to cut the children. She was fully aware of online dangers and had spoken to both Leigh and Josh about them at length. She and David vetted all apps prior to download, and since all such purchases were made through her account, neither child could buy one without permission. She didn't want to give them an online curfew or make them leave their devices downstairs overnight. However, if it came to it, then that's what she'd do. Monitoring youngsters' online activity was yet another responsibility parents had to bear and, after all the precautions taken, there was nothing to stop them looking at friends' mobiles or laptops. Josh was sensible. If he was online, it was probably to talk to his friends, or maybe he had a girlfriend he hadn't yet mentioned. She'd cut him some slack. No teenagers wanted their parents breathing down their neck all the time.

She was on the outskirts of Samford when her phone rang.

Superintendent Aileen Melody's voice was grave. 'Natalie, another girl from Uptown Primary School went missing yesterday afternoon. Name of Rainey Kilburn. I've just received word her body's been located in Uptown at Monks Walk. Mike and his team have been dispatched.'

Natalie released a low growl of disapproval. 'I ought to have been notified as soon the girl disappeared.'

'Miscommunication. I've already expressed my anger.' Aileen sounded as riled as Natalie felt. 'Natalie, I'll level with you. I'm extremely concerned for the safety of all young girls in the Uptown area, especially those that attend the same school. I'm going to have to call a press conference for later today and issue a statement to calm the public, and I don't have a clue what to tell them. Are we dealing with a killer who's targeting schoolgirls?'

'Rainey was also at the birthday party when Ava Sawyer went missing.'

'Do you think this is to do with Ava's party, then?'

'It seems increasingly likely. At the moment, we're examining every angle. There must be other factors that link these girls.'

'You sure you should be looking elsewhere? It seems quite a coincidence Audrey Briggs and Rainey Kilburn attended that party and now both are dead.'

'I completely agree with you but we really ought to explore other possibilities too. I've been in a similar situation where we've focused on only one suspect and one direction and overlooked the bigger picture.'

Aileen took a moment before she responded. 'You're in charge of the investigation, Natalie; however, if I were you, I wouldn't ignore the strong possibility these deaths are connected to that event.'

'I shan't. We'll be going back over what happened that day and looking for connections. I just have an inkling we ought to keep an open mind and ensure we're not overlooking a different reason these girls have been targeted. I'd hate for another child, who wasn't at that party, to be taken because we missed some vital clue.'

There was a brief pause as Aileen digested her words. Her musical voice was cautious. 'I understand. And if this is unrelated to the birthday party, I don't want the public panicking, but by the same token, they must be vigilant and ensure their children are not outside alone and vulnerable.'

Natalie understood the subtext of her words. Like her, Aileen was fearful they had a child serial killer in their midst.

Rainey's body was positioned at the base of a tree, some distance from the path known as Monks Walk. Over a white school blouse and skirt she wore a yellow dress, identical to the one found on Audrey.

'Similar ligature,' pointed out Ben Hargreaves, his long fingers hovering over the red mark around her neck.

'Was she strangled with the same object as Audrey?' Natalie asked.

'Initial examination would suggest so. I'll have to confirm it.'

Natalie noted the lipstick on the girl's lips. It was the same colour as Audrey had been wearing. Mike and his team were searching the area, inching their way across the grass and along the path. She joined him. His forehead was lined and his eyes looked heavy with tiredness.

'They're connected, aren't they?' he asked.

'Looks that way: the dress, lipstick, strangulation, both attended the same school and both were at the party at Uptown Craft Centre.'

'I had trouble looking at her,' he said. 'She reminded me too much of Thea.'

Rosy-cheeked Thea, with thick, black, wavy hair like her mother's and freckles sprinkled across a slightly turned-up nose. Natalie understood his dismay. She wanted to reach out and touch his arm to comfort him, but she daren't in case her actions were misinterpreted. Instead she looked away at the open-handed sculpture, an artist's representation of peace, and waited for him to speak again.

'We found her school bag.'

'Where?'

'It was propped against the foot of a bench. There are some schoolbooks inside with her name in them and a glazed clay object. Looks like a cat.' His words grew thick and he cleared his throat with a small cough.

'It wasn't abandoned, then, or thrown down?'

'Definitely propped upright.'

'Maybe Rainey stopped at the bench and placed it there.'

'We checked for fingerprints. Only found Rainey's on it.'

'Then it's unlikely the killer took it from her and rested it there. I wonder why he left it behind,' Natalie mused more to herself than Mike.

'Can't answer that. Maybe he forgot about it or didn't know it was there or got startled and ran off, leaving it behind.'

'You're right. Could be any of those.'

'We'll examine the dress once Ben's finished.'

'I'm done,' said Ben, turning up beside them. 'I'm prepared to go out on a limb and say death was through asphyxiation caused by strangulation. Body has cooled to outside temperature, suggesting she died sometime yesterday afternoon or early evening. Rigor and lividity also suggest death took place about that time. There's some substance under her fingernails. It's difficult to identify without a microscope, but I've taken swabs and will email you the results as soon as I have them. There's bruising along her neckline, but I'll look at that more closely in the laboratory.'

'Any signs of struggle?'

'There's some discolouration on her left wrist and upper arm. Might have been caused by somebody restraining her. I'd like to examine it more thoroughly. Again, I'll send you my full report as soon as possible.'

'If you could. This has to take priority.'

Ben and Mike moved back in the direction of the tree. Natalie returned to the entrance to Monks Walk, where she found Lucy waiting for her.

'I dropped Murray at Uptown Primary School. Ian rang us on our way here and asked me to run this past you. He uncovered something when he was going through the list of girls in the same ballet class as Audrey and thought you'd want to know immediately.'

'What is it?'

'Rainey used to attend Little Stars Dance Academy,' said Lucy. 'She was in that class but dropped out at the beginning of this year.'

'Really? Then I think we need to talk to the owners again.'

Carlton Kennedy was alone at the school, in jeans and a mauve shirt, sleeves rolled up to the elbow. He ushered them in and looked at them quizzically.

'We don't open until later. You were lucky to catch me here.'

'I won't beat around the bush. We've come to ask about another of your pupils, Rainey Kilburn.'

'But she isn't one of our pupils. What I mean is she hasn't attended a class this year. She gave up ballet. She wasn't really cut out for it.'

'But she used to attend the same classes as Ava and Audrey.'

'Has something happened to her?'

'I'm afraid we can't discuss that.'

His eyes widened. 'Something has happened, hasn't it?'

'Can you confirm your whereabouts yesterday afternoon?'

'I was here. Teaching. From three o'clock until seven.'

'And Bruce?'

'He was here too.'

'You saw him?'

Carlton hesitated. 'Not until I finished the classes, but of course he was here. There was no one else to man reception. Why are you asking me these questions? Is Rainey dead?'

'I'm afraid I'm not at liberty to divulge any information but I would like to ascertain your husband's whereabouts yesterday afternoon. Where can we find him?'

'I don't know. He'd already gone out by the time I got up. He didn't say where he was headed.'

'If he returns or rings you, would you please ask him to call me?'

'What's he supposed to have done?'

'If you see him, ask him to call me, please.'

Lucy screwed up her face. 'You reckon Bruce could be involved?'

'My gut says no but my head says we have to delve deeper. All three victims attended the dance academy. Bruce knew a bit about Ava and encouraged her to go to the party at the craft centre, then turned up at the same place, the very day she disappeared. Although he said he'd left by the time the party began, we have no proof that was the case or any idea of where he really went after his meeting with Mark Randle. At the time Audrey went missing, he was apparently painting stage scenery. Although Carlton claimed to have seen him in between classes, he might have gone out and returned later. The dance studio is within walking distance of both Queen's Park and Monks Walk. The problem I have is why? Why would he kill the girls? It doesn't make sense.'

'Unless he's psychotic and hates little girls.'

'True. We need to establish his whereabouts yesterday. I'll phone him on my way to the station. I'm calling a meeting for two p.m. Can you and Murray get back from the school by then?'

'I'm sure we can.'

Natalie nodded. 'Right. See you later.'

She jumped into her Audi and watched Lucy pull away in the squad car. Lucy and Murray would both check out Rainey's movements for yesterday afternoon, which meant she could concentrate on tracking down Bruce. She tried his mobile but it rang out so she put a call into the station and asked Ian to track down Bruce's vehicle using ANPR and safety cameras in and around Uptown.

CHAPTER TWENTY-ONE

Bruce Kennedy turned up within fifteen minutes of Natalie arriving at the police station. With Murray and Lucy out of the office, she took Ian to the interview with her, determined to get to the bottom of Bruce's whereabouts. She was shocked at the studio owner's appearance. His eyes were bloodshot and his hair dishevelled.

'I got your message,' he said. 'Thought it would be better if I came to the station rather than talk to you over the phone. What's this all about?'

Natalie waited until he was sat down. 'We need to establish where you were yesterday afternoon.'

He rubbed a hand over his beard and sighed. 'I was at the dance academy.'

'All afternoon?'

'I went out for a while at about four.'

'Where did you go?'

'For a walk. Not too far. I had to clear my head.' He let out a heavy sigh.

'Can you be a little more specific, please?'

'Carlton's no fool, and following your recent visit, he worked out I was keeping something back about the day Ava went missing. He kept needling me, asking me to tell him the truth, goading me, until I had no choice but to confess. I told him about being Mark's sponsor and of course it all came out after that: the addiction, my recovery and so on. I don't wish to go into the finer details but suffice to say, we had an almighty row before he took the first afternoon class. As soon as it began, I had to go outside to get some air.'

'Where did you go?'

He shrugged. 'I did a circuit around Uptown. Took the path from the academy towards the clock tower and looped back via Jasmine Avenue and St Chad's Road.'

Natalie looked at Ian, who knew the area better than her. He spoke up. 'That's about a half an hour walk which takes you past Monks Walk.'

'I don't know where you mean.'

'It's a cut-through, a garden behind the old library.'

'Library? Oh, yes! The arched entrance. Yes. I walked past it.'

Ian deferred to Natalie once more.

'What time would this have been?'

'I genuinely don't know. Maybe four thirty, four forty-five. I was too upset to be aware of what time it was. I'd just told my husband I was an addict; something I'd hidden from him all this time, and I was terrified he'd leave me over it.'

Natalie put her hands together as if in prayer and rested them in front of her lips, all the while studying Bruce's face. Could he be telling the truth?

'I'd like you to give us a DNA sample,' she said, eventually.

Bruce's mouth opened. 'Why?'

'You were in the vicinity of Monks Walk at around the same time a young girl was murdered there.'

'No! A girl was murdered there? Yesterday? Oh no! I had nothing to do with her death. Believe me. Take the sample. It'll prove it wasn't me. I didn't use Monks Walk.'

'You could easily have diverted from your route,' Natalie offered, staring hard at Bruce.

'But I didn't.'

'Can you prove otherwise?' Natalie asked.

'What are you suggesting? I went out for a walk because I was upset about a row with my husband, got it into my head to kill a girl and went in search of one? That's crazy!'

Natalie spoke smoothly. 'No, we're not suggesting that at all. We're merely trying to establish your movements yesterday afternoon. You might have seen somebody turning into or coming out of Monks Walk.'

'I don't recall seeing anybody.'

Natalie allowed a moment of silence before she next spoke. 'The young girl who was murdered yesterday. She was a pupil at the dance academy. You know her. Rainey Kilburn.'

Bruce's eyes widened. 'Oh my God! That's why you wanted to speak to me. Please believe me. I would *never* harm a child. I went out for a walk. I've never set foot on Monks Walk in all the time I've worked in Uptown. It's not a pathway I'm familiar with. I was deep in thought about how to handle Carlton and worried sick about what had been said. I wasn't paying attention to anything or anybody. That's it. I swear. Wait! I bumped into Effie Downing. She can vouch for me.'

'Effie Downing?'

'She runs evening yoga classes at our centre. She's Harriet Downing's mother.'

'Harriet Downing's mother saw you walking past Monks Walk?'

He shook his head to clear his thoughts. 'Yes. We drew level by the old library and exchanged a few words. She must have seen me walking along the road past Monks Walk. I remember now. The library clock struck once, so it'd have been four thirty. Harriet had been sent home from school because she was very upset by Audrey's death. Effie's mother was looking after her until Effie could get home from work. She was eager to get off, so we parted and I headed straight back to the academy. I was back at reception before the pupils began to arrive for the next class. The first came in at quarter to five.'

'We'll talk to Mrs Downing to confirm that. I'd still like to take a sample to eliminate you from our enquiries.'

He nodded his head in agreement.

Outside she asked Ian if it were possible for Bruce to have made the round trip in the time he stated.

'It's all viable. There are CCTV cameras on the library so we can confirm he was there at the time he said he was,' he said.

'Get onto it. First, take the DNA sample and then release him.'

Natalie took a quick stroll outside to collect her thoughts. When she returned, Ian was in the office looking at CCTV footage. He gave her a smile as she entered. 'I swung by the tech boys. Mark Randle's alibi checks out. They found him on footage going into Queen's Park and back out again two minutes later. Also, they confirmed Justine Woodman, his ex-girlfriend, entered the park ahead of him with a man, and emerged ten minutes later with the same man and a teenage boy.'

She rolled her eyes. 'Another suspect eliminated. Soon we'll be left with none.' She'd barely sat down when her phone rang. It was David.

'Josh's headmaster wants to see us as soon as possible. Josh is being suspended.'

'What? Why?'

'He says he'll tell us when we get there.'

'Christ!' She took a moment to process the news. 'David, you know I can't just drop everything. You got any idea what this is about?'

'None.'

'It must be some mistake. Josh is no troublemaker. Look, I can possibly manage to see the head later today, but I have a meeting in an hour. I'd never get there and back in time.'

'Natalie,' David began, 'Josh is in trouble. This is important.'

'I know. I know it is. But there's been another murder; another girl has been found.' She waited, hoping he'd understand. He did.

'Okay. I'll sort it.'

'Thanks, David. If I get the chance to come home for half an hour and see Josh, I'll do that.'

Natalie threw down her mobile. She couldn't think straight. What the hell had Josh been up to?

Ian looked up. 'Do you believe what Bruce said?'

'I think so. You found him yet?'

'Not yet, but even if I do, it would still be possible for him to reach Monks Walk, kill Rainey and reappear on St Chad's Road before four thirty.'

'Only if he isn't telling us the truth and went directly to Monks Walk, rather than take the route via the clock tower.'

Natalie slumped into her chair and drummed her fingers against the desk. 'But why? He'd have had to stumble upon Rainey. It would have had to have been a chance killing. And then there's the dress. Did he have it with him when he went out or did he go back later and put it on her body?'

Ian shrugged. 'Took a chance going back, if that were the case.'

'We got no other surveillance cameras in the area to confirm his movements?'

'There's only the one by the library.'

'What about the academy itself? They must have some security cameras. Maybe we could get hold of their footage and see if Bruce left the premises carrying a dress or a bag containing the dress. No. If he dressed her, he'd surely have left behind DNA or some forensic evidence, even if he was wearing gloves, and he willingly gave us a sample. He wouldn't do that unless he was certain of his innocence, would he? This is hopeless! Have we got a number for the Downings?'

'Must have. We had all the numbers from Ava Sawyer's file,' said Ian, turning his full attention to the CCTV footage.

Natalie rummaged through the folder containing all the information on Ava Sawyer until she found what she was looking for. She punched out the number and waited while it rang. Effie Downing answered. Natalie introduced herself and explained she was following up some information.

'Could you confirm you saw Bruce Kennedy yesterday afternoon?'

'I did. I was walking home from the health food shop where I work. I ran into him near the library and had a few words with him.'

'How did he seem?'

'Downhearted. That's why I stopped. He's normally cheerful and says hello. I didn't have much time to talk. I had to get home.'

'I understand Harriet was sent home from school.'

'That's right. This whole business with Audrey Briggs really upset her. I'll probably keep her off again tomorrow.'

'Your mother fetched her?'

'That's correct. There were only two of us at the store yesterday, Kylie and myself. Kylie is only just eighteen. I couldn't leave her alone. I rang my mum, who collected Harriet and stayed at home with her until I could get back.'

'Can I ask one more thing? When you spotted Bruce, was he headed out of Monks Walk?'

There was a slight hesitation in her voice. 'No. I don't think so. He was walking along on the same pavement as me. That's why I noticed him. There wasn't anyone else about at the time and he had his head down, looking sorry for himself.'

It appeared Bruce had been telling the truth.

'And you didn't spot anybody coming out of Monks Walk at that time?'

'Has something happened there?'

'We're investigating a crime that took place there. I'd appreciate your help. Did you see anyone other than Bruce in the area?'

'Can't say I did. I was parked up the road from Monks Walk. Apart from Bruce, I didn't run into anyone else.'

'What time did you get home?'

'Quarter to five, I think.'

'And you were at the health food store all day?'

'Yes, I took my lunch break there. I didn't leave the place until just after four.'

'You shut at four?'

'No, it's late-night opening on Thursdays. The store manager came in to take over from us at four. I left then.'

'Do you work there every day?'

'Apart from Saturdays. I do nine to five with the exception of Thursdays, when I finish at four, and Saturdays, which I don't work.'

There was little more to be said on the subject and Natalie ended the call. Effie Downing certainly couldn't be put in the frame. She'd been at work when both Audrey and Rainey had been killed. Natalie turned to face Ian, who was still staring at the CCTV footage captured by the library camera.

'Effie Downing confirmed seeing Bruce. I don't think she has anything to do with the killings but I wonder if her own daughter might not be in danger.'

'You mean because it was her birthday?'

'Exactly. If the killer is after children who attended that party, he'd almost certainly go after the birthday girl, wouldn't he?'

'There's a strong possibility of that happening. Oh my God!' Ian squinted hard at the computer screen. 'Look who I've just found on this footage.'

He held down a button, talking all the while. 'I came across Bruce Kennedy as we suspected, standing outside the library at bang on four thirty. I rewound the tape to double-check he didn't appear on it earlier, and I spotted this person heading towards Monks Walk at four fifteen.'

He paused the recording and Natalie peered closely at the figure caught mid-arm swing as he marched briskly. It was Carl Sawyer, Ava's father.

CHAPTER TWENTY-TWO

FRIDAY, 28 APRIL – AFTERNOON

Loud voices echoed down the corridor as Lucy and Murray waited outside the head teacher's office at Uptown Primary School. The last of the pupils burst through the exit, leaving the door to crash shut behind them.

The office door opened and Patrick Horn, the head teacher, showed them in. A dark-haired woman was already there. She introduced herself as Jennifer Collinswood, Rainey's form teacher.

'I'll fetch another chair,' Patrick offered.

'It's fine. I'll stand,' Murray replied.

Patrick looked young to be a head teacher, a sporty-looking individual with lanky limbs and a fresh face. 'Absolutely dreadful news. We were just discussing how we should best approach this. The children were already upset about Audrey Briggs and now Rainey. We're at a loss as to how to handle it. I expect the parents will be thinking about keeping their children at home until you've captured whoever is behind this. Do you think the school is being targeted?'

'I expect we'll be issuing a statement later, sir, and somebody will be in touch with you regarding how best to deal with the news.'

'Good. Good,' he said, half to himself. 'We don't want everyone in a blind panic, do we?'

Lucy shook her head. 'We're trying to establish some facts to help us with our investigation. When did you last see Rainey?'

Jennifer cleared her throat. 'I had to leave immediately after lessons ended for a dentist appointment. I spotted Rainey as I drove out of the staff car park. She was waiting near the staff gate. I stopped to ask if she was getting a lift home. She said she was waiting for her brother to walk home with him and his friends. Main school was coming to an end – they finish ten minutes after us – and I had to get off, so I left her there. I wish now I'd stayed long enough to make sure she met up with her brother, Tyler.'

'Did she usually go home with her brother?'

'She and Harriet Downing usually walked home together. They were best friends, but Harriet kept bursting into tears all day because of what happened to Audrey. I took her over to the school secretary during first break and her grandmother came to collect her.' She swallowed hard and looked Lucy in the eye.

'I feel really bad about this. Miss Goffrey and I spoke at length to all the classes about the dangers of wandering off on their own, or talking to strangers. I don't know what happened, if somebody pulled up and offered to give her a lift after I spoke to her, or if she took it into her head to go home alone, but I am convinced of one thing: she wouldn't have gone with a stranger. Not after the talk.'

Patrick spoke up. 'It was really most unfortunate. Tyler, who's in year ten, got up to some mischief yesterday afternoon during a science lesson and was kept behind after school to help tidy up the lab as punishment. He didn't leave until ten past four. I suspect Rainey got tired of waiting for him and went home alone.'

Lucy wasn't going to draw any conclusions. Natalie had taught her it was best to be in possession of all the facts before making any assumptions. Rainey might have got into a car or walked home with someone else.

'Were Rainey and Audrey good friends?' Murray asked.

Jennifer shook her head. 'Rainey was Harriet's best friend. Thick as thieves. Audrey got on with just about everyone but didn't have a close friend. Not that I knew about. I don't know how they'll cope with this latest news. Poor little souls. It's going to traumatise them.'

Lucy had no answers. It was true.

'I'm sure the authorities will send in appropriately qualified teams to help you deal with this,' she offered.

'But you never really get over something like this, do you?' said Jennifer. 'I think I might blame myself forever.'

'It wasn't your fault. It was a series of unfortunate incidents. And we don't know what actually happened. We have yet to piece everything together.'

Jennifer bit back tears. Patrick took over. 'I spoke to some members of the staff as soon as you rang me earlier, including the caretaker and secretary. None of them saw Rainey after school. Most of them were either working in their classrooms, or in the staffroom, and didn't leave until well after four.'

Murray had already spoken to all the teachers while waiting for Lucy and had established the same.

'Where do the parents pick up? Are they allowed to wait outside the front gate?' Murray asked.

Patrick shook his head. 'We don't encourage pick-ups or drop-offs from the front of the school. All parents collect from the sports centre car park next to the school. We have a gate that leads to it that's only unlocked before and after school – from eight thirty to ten past nine in the morning, and again from three twenty until four twenty.'

'It's unlikely anyone would have picked up from the front gate, then?'

'Only staff members are allowed to use that particular entrance. As you know, it is coded or entry is admissible by intercom. We don't want anyone getting onto school property who shouldn't be here.'

'Rainey would have had to have used the back entrance to get out of the school.'

'Unless she slipped out after a member of staff opened the front gate, yes.'

'Have you noticed any people hanging about or acting suspiciously?'

'We've had no reports of anyone.'

'Would it be possible for you to open the gate to the sports centre now for us?'

'I can arrange that. The pupils should be having lunch in the dining hall for the next half hour but please ensure you shut it behind you.'

Murray stood at the edge of the car park in front of the walled sports complex.

'It'd be impossible for anyone to see out of that,' he stated, staring up at the windowless building.

'If she came this way, there must have been one or two parents still lingering in the car park who'd have seen her. We could appeal for witnesses.'

'Then why didn't somebody come forward yesterday when the missing person's team was trying to find her? You know what I think? I reckon she took a slightly different route. I think she either went out the front way, after Jennifer left, or she got a lift,' said Murray.

'Or she took a shortcut,' said Lucy, staring at trampled grass to the side of the sports complex. 'Where does that lead to?'

Murray pulled out his phone and drew up the map. 'You might be on to something. It appears to skirt past some fields, and from this point,' he said, pointing at the map, 'it feeds into St Chad's Street.'

'Isn't Monks Walk off St Chad's?' Lucy asked.

'It is. Want to check it out? I'll fetch the car and meet you there.'

'Okay. Give me a head start.'

Lucy walked at a steady pace, shadowing the hedgerow to her right. The route skirted around one field and over a wooden stile leading to another larger field and the edge of a series of allotments, bordered by lower hedges. She stuck to the allotments, which could be accessed by the main road to the far side of the plots. Halfway down, the hedging stopped, to be replaced by a post and rail fence for several metres. She peered over the allotments, a scattering of various-sized vegetable patches, pots, painted sheds and plastic sheeting. There was nobody about to speak to so she continued on her way. From here, she made out the church tower and knew she was nearing the town centre and then spotted another stile ahead. She hastened to it and clambered over it, her pulse quickening. Now she was almost on Monks Walk itself. She scoured the tall hedges until she found what she hoped for: an access point where the shrubbery had died back enough to allow a person to squeeze through. This was the area known as Monks Walk, and ahead of her were forensic officers bent over examining the terrain. She called out to them.

'Hey! Is it okay to come through this way?'

Mike Sullivan looked across, spotted her and waved her in. 'Yeah. Come through. We've checked there.'

'Did you find anything snagged on the shrubbery?' she asked.

'Picked up some fibres, which we've sent to the lab for analysis.'

'It's possible Rainey came this way from school,' said Lucy, lifting her arms high, turning sideways and sliding through the opening. 'If her killer was following her, he'd have to be slim to get through that gap.'

'He might have already been here. He could have been lying in wait,' Mike suggested, his lips stretched into an apologetic grimace.

'True. Still worth running the theory past Natalie,' Lucy replied, tucking her blouse back into her trouser waistband. 'We're meeting soon.'

'Tell her I've requested top priority on all the evidence we've lifted from here. We'll get everything back to you post-haste.'

'Thanks, Mike. Catch you later.'

Lucy kept on the path until it passed through an archway and joined St Chad's Road, where Murray was waiting.

'Didn't take you long,' he said.

'Twenty minutes from school to Monks Walk, which would have got her there at about four fifteen or so unless she ran all the way. I think she took this route. There's a load of allotments back there. We ought to find out who rents them and see if anyone was on-site yesterday afternoon.'

He glanced at his phone. 'Good idea. We're cutting it fine now. Best get back for the briefing.'

As Murray navigated the traffic, Lucy chewed over what she'd discovered in the car.

'Murray, do you think the murderer could have been waiting at Monks Walk and poor Rainey was an unlucky victim, in the wrong spot at the wrong time?'

'I think it was a deliberate act. Somebody followed her from school. First Ava, then Audrey and now Rainey. I reckon it's to do with the birthday party.'

'But Ava disappeared in 2015. Why wait until now to attack the children who attended the party? It just doesn't make sense.'

'It makes sense to me. Ava's body was unearthed on Tuesday. It's opened a wound for somebody.'

'Then the most logical conclusion is that someone who was close to Ava is attacking the children who attended the party.'

'They're certainly targeting the girls. They've yet to attack a boy.'

'The people closest to Ava were her folks. Reckon one of Ava's parents is behind this?'

Murray wasn't going to be drawn. 'Beatrice Sawyer is in Sheffield under the watchful eye of her mother. She isn't in the area.'

'Could be Carl.'

'Without proof, we shouldn't make accusations. These are wild guesses.'

'I'm talking to you like a friend not a copper. Just shooting the breeze,' she said in a bad American accent.

'Facts first,' he replied with a grin. 'We have to remain open-minded.'

'Which was what I was being when I suggested she was an unfortunate victim in the wrong place at the wrong time. This might not be anything to do with the birthday party in 2015.'

'You really are buying into the Natalie Ward school of checking every possibility, aren't you?' he joked.

'I think we should consider all likelihoods, yes.'

'But you can't ignore the yellow dresses, the lipstick or the fact they were all at the birthday party together.'

Lucy shook her head. 'I get what you're saying. What about if Rainey walked home with somebody she knew, who turned on her?'

He threw her a look. 'Another child?'

'Oh, I don't know. I'm trying to consider every event.'

'Fair enough. We'll run these theories past Natalie. See what she thinks.'

Lucy wondered if Carl or Beatrice Sawyer could possibly be behind the murders then suddenly her thoughts turned to Rainey's mother, Paula Kilburn. She couldn't conjure up the pain the woman would be feeling. To lose a child must be one of the most heartbreaking situations in the world. Lucy wanted to understand, but try as she might, she couldn't quite summon such depth of feeling. She had no real comprehension or experience of motherly love. Her own mother had abandoned her as a baby, and until she'd met Bethany, she'd never really known true compassion or care. Bethany wanted a child so badly. She'd make a wonderful mother. Lucy desperately hoped she'd be able to step up to the mark when it happened.

CHAPTER TWENTY-THREE

THEN

The boy sits towards the back of the bus where he can overhear Sherry and Gail talking excitedly about Sherry's birthday party which is later that same day. It sounds wonderful. There are going to be outdoor games, dancing, a barbecue and a proper magician. He sits back in his seat, invisible to the girls whose excited voices float over him.

The bus pulls up at Sherry's stop and he observes her and Gail as they stand on the pavement then scurry off in separate directions, Sherry's school bag bouncing on her shoulder and hair shimmering in the afternoon sunlight as she flies up the road towards her house.

Sherry is eleven today and has invited almost all of the class to her party but he hasn't been asked. He can't understand why not. He hasn't frightened her recently and she hasn't seen him hiding behind the wall watching her play tag with the other girls. The bus slows again and wheezes to a halt. He waits until it has completely stopped before squeezing out of the narrow seat and waddling down the aisle. The doors open with a long 'phew' as if it's all too much of an effort to keep opening and closing, and he clambers down the steps.

'Thank you. Bye,' he says to the bus driver. He always thanks the driver, who drops him right outside his front door.

In his bedroom, he rests on his bed and stares at the ceiling. He would love to go to the party. He's never seen a magician and he'd like to play some of the games they've got lined up: Postman's Knock, Twister and outdoor skittles. Then, he has a brilliant idea. He can go. If he turns up with a gift for Sherry, she'll have to let him in and maybe she'll finally get to like him. He has just the present for her. He bounds off the bed and shuffles under it to pull out the box he keeps his doll in. He brushes down her dress and tidies her hair. What could be a better present than a doll that looks like her? He'll visit her house on his bike. He won't tell his mum in case she insists on accompanying him. She'll be pleased he wants to use his bike. She keeps telling him he should go outside more.

Two hours later and he's ready. His mum doesn't suspect a thing even though he's wearing his favourite T-shirt and best corduroy trousers with the elastic waist he got for Christmas. She's so busy in the garden with Dad, she only has time to register he's on his bike as he's halfway down the path.

'Whoa. Where are you off to?' she shouts, leaping up from the bed of pansies where she's been gardening and waving a trowel at him.

'Just for a ride,' he says, hoping she doesn't notice the plastic bag containing the doll hanging from his handlebar. He blocks it with his body. 'I won't go far. Only to the park.'

She looks doubtful. His father speaks to her and she shakes her head then shouts, 'Promise you won't ride in the road. You'll stick to the pavements.'

'Promise,' he yells and pedals off before anyone can call him back.

Sherry lives close to the village green on a cul-de-sac, which is a French word for a road that's a dead end so you can only come out the way you go in. His teacher told the class that when they were all asked about where they lived. He lives in a terraced cottage, which doesn't sound anywhere near as nice as a cul-de-sac, but that's where he's always lived.

It takes six minutes of hard pedalling to reach Sherry's road, St Catherine's Close, and he's out of breath and a bit sweaty from the exertion. He soon forgets his discomfort as he sees Gail disappearing into Sherry's house. She's carrying a wrapped present. He's on time.

He dismounts his bike and wheels it up to number 12 and lets it rest on the grass outside. There's a glass porch in front of the main door and he has to ring the doorbell on it. He plasters on his best smile and holds the plastic bag containing Sherry in front of him. He spots movement behind the frosted glass of the main door and his heart thuds against his ribs. The door opens and Sherry stares at him with the biggest eyes he's ever seen. She's in a bright yellow dress with yellow ribbons in her hair and her lips are red with lipstick like the colour his mother sometimes wears. She's wearing white ankle socks and patent leather black shoes and he's so pleased. She looks as pretty as a daffodil or one of his mother's yellow pansies, and just like the gift he's brought.

'What are you doing here?' she gasps.

'Happy birthday,' he stutters.

A gentle voice comes from behind Sherry and a woman appears. 'Who is it, Sherry?'

'A boy,' she replies. 'I didn't ask him to come. He's the boy from my class.'

He waits, his hand outstretched. Sherry retreats behind her mother, who has the same colour hair as her daughter but hers is coiled in a huge bun. She's in a blue shift dress with flowers on it. Her eyes aren't the same shade of blue as Sherry's. They're deeper, like a clear sky on a perfect summer's day.

'Why are you here?' she asks, her voice not unfriendly.

'I brought Sherry a present. I'd like to come to the party.'

She gives him a gentle smile and crouches so she is face to face with him.

'That's really nice of you,' she says, 'but there aren't any boys at the party. It's only for girls. I'm sorry but you can't join in.'

She actually looks sad and he doesn't know how to reply. He hears whispers behind the door and knows Sherry and her friends are listening to the conversation. He has to get away and quickly.

'Oh, okay,' is all he can say. His mission has failed but he can still win Sherry round. 'Will you give her this please? It's a special present from me. I hope she likes it.'

He shoves the doll at Sherry's mother.

She regards the plastic bag with narrowed eyes and shakes her head. 'I don't think so. Do your parents know you're here?'

His cheeks burn. He can't respond.

'I thought not. It'd be best if you went home and please don't come here again. If you do, I might have to say something to your parents.' The sad look has turned stern. He nods a response and still clutching the bag containing the doll, races off back to his bike. He picks it up, jumps on it and pedals away as fast as he can.

CHAPTER TWENTY-FOUR

FRIDAY, 28 APRIL – AFTERNOON

The office was uncomfortably warm and Natalie conducted the briefing with her sleeves rolled up past her elbows. Thanks to Lucy and Murray, they had a picture of the route Rainey had taken from school and a rough idea of when she was attacked. They also knew Bruce Kennedy was unlikely to have been behind the assault. Although his path had taken him past the entrance to Monks Walk, he had not had time to locate Rainey, kill her and dress her in the yellow dress before meeting Effie Downing beside the library.

Of more immediate concern was Carl Sawyer, Ava's father, spotted in the same vicinity at around the time Rainey would have appeared in Monks Walk.

'He has a motive,' said Murray. 'His daughter disappeared during a birthday party. He might harbour a grudge against those children who attended the party.'

'It's certainly possible but why wait until now to attack them?' Ian asked. It was the same question Lucy had asked in the car.

'His daughter's body's just been unearthed. I'd say that's reason enough. It's brought it all back to him. His daughter was found on Tuesday. Since then two girls have been murdered. It's logical to think it could be him,' Murray suggested.

'It certainly looks like this is all related to Harriet's birthday,' said Natalie with a slight shake of her head, 'and yet I'm still not a hundred per cent convinced.'

'Even with the whole yellow dress thing going on?' Murray sounded indignant. 'It screams retaliation to me.'

'I agree,' said Ian. 'It seems too staged. Besides, the dresses Audrey and Rainey were wearing weren't like the one Ava wore.'

'Oh, come on!' Murray was incredulous.

'That's why I'm slightly dubious. A tiny part of me wonders if maybe somebody wants us to believe it's to do with the birthday, but it isn't.' Natalie folded her arms. She wasn't going to exclude any other possibilities. She wasn't going to mess up by only exploring one avenue. 'First things first. Interview Carl. There might be an innocent explanation as to why he was there. We also can't ignore the fact all three girls attended the dance academy. We might have run into a wall with Bruce Kennedy but there could be somebody watching the place and choosing victims who attend or attended the classes. We also can't ignore the fact all the victims were in the same class at school. Check out their form teacher, Jennifer Collinswood, and anyone she is living with.'

Ian looked like he wanted to speak again but caught the look Murray threw him and remained quiet.

'Get a list of all of the people who rent allotments and see if anyone was at their plot yesterday afternoon.'

Murray nodded at the request. He'd already tracked down somebody at the council who might be able to help.

'I don't like the fact we've drawn so many blanks with Audrey Briggs, either. I'm going to request a dramatic reconstruction of events as well as an appeal for witnesses. Somebody must have seen her. I refuse to accept she left her house and vanished in a park where other people were walking dogs, riding bikes, playing or just wandering about, even if she was found in a less populated area. We've got lots going on and I'm grateful to you for giving your all. I understand this isn't an easy investigation and I needn't tell you that I'm concerned we're dealing with a child serial killer. Let's get this clear: I haven't discounted the idea that the perp is hunting down girls who attended Harriet's birthday. It would be foolhardy to do so. However, I'm concerned the assailant will act again. At this stage, we need to notify the parents of the remaining girls who attended that party in 2015 and ensure those children don't go off alone. I believe they're in no danger if they stay with adults or other children. Finally, the yellow dresses. Any news from that website?'

Lucy shook her head. 'I'll send another email to the Etsy vendor.'

'Etsy?' Ian's brows furrowed.

'Online shops where people sell home-made stuff,' Lucy explained.

Natalie ended the meeting, and as everyone went about their business, she took Murray to one side.

'I have to go out for an hour. Can you keep on top of everything here and ring me if you need me?'

'Sure.'

'Thanks. Appreciate it.'

'Have you spoken to him about it?'

'I tried but he ended up yelling at me and saying I didn't understand. Of course I fucking understand.' David's face was dark with anger. 'I was more pissed off with the headmaster's attitude than anything. You'd think Josh had filmed the bloody sex scenes himself rather than watched them.'

'Where's Leigh?'

'She went home with Kelly. She'll be dropped off about six. I don't think she's got any idea of this.'

'Good. We need to let him know it was wrong but for the right reasons.'

'What reasons? He's growing up and he's curious. He watched some porn. It's not the end of the world, is it? It's only natural he's curious about it. I was at his age.'

'Oh, come on. It's not like it was in your day, looking at pictures of naked women in copies of *Playboy* or whatever you kept hidden under your bed. These sites contain seriously degrading images of both women and men.'

'He was trying to learn more about sex.'

'But this isn't the way to do it. You know what's on those sites: sexually explicit scenes, degrading stuff like fantasy rape scenes, fetishes, molestations. And there's the advertising that flashes up from time to time. It's not healthy for a young mind to watch that crap. I want him to end up in a wholesome relationship not re-enacting sexually explicit scenes he's watched online.'

'He's not stupid. He won't think that's how people behave.'

'That's exactly the point I'm making. He's young. He *will* think that's how ordinary people behave. It'll have a bearing on how he perceives sex. He needs to be made aware of the difference.'

'How do *you* suggest we deal with it, then?'

'We don't lose our rags for one thing. Keep it calm. He knows he's done wrong but maybe he doesn't really understand why, or why we're concerned. You should talk to him again.'

'No.'

'No?'

'It's all very well you racing home and telling me how to look after our children but that's not how I want to play it. You're rarely here, Natalie. I am. I'm the one who has to sort them out in the mornings and listen to them bickering in the car and make sure they eat the right food, or drag them away from their iPads and social media and tell them to get on with their homework. Have you forgotten what that's like? They're teenagers. They don't like being bossed about and I'm the one who's been tasked with that ever since I lost my job and you got promoted in yours. I'm permanently playing the role of bad cop around here. You waltz in, ruffle Josh's hair, watch movies with Leigh and can do no wrong in their eyes.'

Natalie put her head in her hands. 'We've talked about this. I'll make more time once this investigation is over.'

'You always say you will and you do for a while, then another case comes along and you're out all hours. I don't want to have a heart to heart with Josh about the wrongs of downloading and looking at pornography.'

'Why? You of all people ought to be able to talk to him frankly about sex. You're close to him.'

'Exactly. You try and tell a teenager you want to talk to him about porn and see what reaction *you* get. I don't want to fall out with him over this. I want him to be able to come to me and not think I'm some sort of prude.'

Natalie was astounded. 'David, it isn't about being prudish. There's evidence to suggest that porn has serious effects on teenagers' psychological health. It promotes unrealistic attitudes to what constitutes consent, and unwholesome views about sex and relationships. All I'm suggesting is that you chat to him about it. Maybe he has some questions about sex he'd like to ask you. You know how low his self-esteem is at the moment. This won't help it.'

David pursed his lips and released a hiss of air. 'You sound like a bloody counsellor.'

'I've seen what can happen thanks to exposure to pornography. I've come across rape victims and abused children and other sights I wish I'd never seen. I believe pornographic sites foster an unhealthy attitude, that's all. I'm only being a parent – hopefully a good parent. There is no ideal way to deal with this but I think treat Josh as an adult and we'll be doing the best job we can as parents.'

David sighed wearily. 'Okay. I get it.'

'Did he show you the pictures?'

'The head teacher confiscated the phone, and when he passed it to me, I didn't really look closely at them. Josh was sat there, head down. I didn't want him to have to suffer the indignity of me scrolling through them.'

'Did he tell you how he came by them?'

'A friend of a friend got them off a site on his dad's computer and messaged them to Josh and a few others. They've all been suspended. The school has a no tolerance policy on the matter.'

'I'll have a quick word with him and get off. You'll be fine. It won't push you apart. If anything, it'll prove you're a good listener and the sort of dad he should go to when he's in trouble.' She took his hand. He didn't pull away.

'You reckon?'

'Yeah. I reckon.'

Josh was hunched over the kitchen table, staring at a chemistry textbook.

'Hey!'

He grunted a response.

'Look, we're not angry with you,' she said.

'You're not?' Josh looked up in surprise.

'No. However, it doesn't mean it's okay.'

Josh wrapped his arms around his body, his mouth turned down.

'We're not going to preach to you but we'd like to have a chat about it.'

'I don't want to talk about it.'

'How about you and Dad go for a burger, and if you feel like talking to him, you can?'

David spoke up. 'Come on. Leigh's out and there's no decent food in the house. What have you got to lose?'

'I suppose,' Josh said, scraping back his chair. 'I'm going to get changed first.'

'Sure,' said David.

Natalie looked him in the eye. 'You okay about this, then?'

'Looks like I'll have to be, doesn't it?'

'I'm not making you do this. I just think it's the best way.'

'If he clams up, I'm not going to force the issue.'

'Fair enough.'

'And for the record, I don't like being manipulated into these awkward situations.'

'I know. I promise I'll talk to Leigh about it. Make sure she has all the facts. How about that?'

He nodded a response. 'You going back to the office?'

'Got to talk to the parents of the latest victim and then I'll go back.'

'I'll stay up. Let you know how it went.'

'Thanks. I'll try not to be too late.'

Natalie waited until they'd driven away before leaving the house. David had touched a nerve. She wasn't fulfilling her role as a good parent at all. It was true that ever since she'd accepted the promotion, her family had had to get on without her. Was Josh beginning to rebel because of the situation? Part of her couldn't shake the feeling she was at fault. Finding a work–life balance was horrendous. Mike hadn't managed. She hoped she could. She had too much to lose if she couldn't.

CHAPTER TWENTY-FIVE

FRIDAY, 28 APRIL – LATE AFTERNOON

The Kilburn family lived on the enormous Hounton Park estate in one of the first houses to have been built during the 1980s. Since then, the development had grown to such proportions it had become a suburb of Uptown with its own community centre, shopping precinct and various pubs.

Donald Kilburn came to the door using a pair of walking sticks. He was large-framed and towered over Natalie.

'Come in,' he said in a gentle voice that seemed at odds with his appearance.

His wife, Paula, was puffy-faced through crying. She stood in the middle of the kitchen, clutching a tea towel. Tanya Granger was sitting on a stool.

'Put that down, pet,' Donald said. 'The detective wants to talk to us.'

Paula ignored him. 'I have to dry up these cups first,' she insisted. 'I'm making Tanya a cup of tea, aren't I?'

Tanya shook her head. 'I can sort out the tea. Why don't you sit down? I'll bring you yours. You take one sugar, don't you?'

Paula nodded and pulled out a box of teabags, dropping them in front of the kettle.

'She's been like this all morning,' Donald whispered to Natalie. 'Can't get her head around what's happened.'

He shuffled onto a stool. 'Do you want a drink?' he asked Natalie.

'No, thank you. I won't stay long. You've been through enough.'

Tanya busied herself with the kettle. Paula edged towards Natalie, tea towel still in her hands.

'We have and it's not over yet,' he replied.

'I really am most sorry for your loss,' said Natalie.

'Aye.' Donald's eyes misted for a minute, and he wiped them with the sleeve of his sweatshirt.

'Are you feeling up to a couple of questions?'

His head moved up and down imperceptibly.

'I understand Rainey used to take ballet classes at the dance school in Uptown.'

'She did. Gave them up though. Two left feet.' Donald sniffed back a smile. 'She tried, mind. Bless her heart. Her friends were doing ballet and she wanted to do what they did. In the end, she preferred swimming. She was like a little fish in water. Much better choice of activity for her.'

'She didn't go back to the dance academy once she gave up lessons?'

'No.' Paula's voice was even quieter than her husband's. 'She loved swimming though.'

'Where did she go swimming?'

Paula waited while Tanya placed a cup of tea in front of her and continued, 'Leisure centre next to the school. She went Saturdays along with a couple of others in her class.'

'Who would that have been?'

'Audrey Briggs and Harriet Downing. Everything Harriet did, Rainey did too,' said Paula, then she stopped suddenly. Tears poured down her face.

Tanya put an arm around her shoulders. 'It's okay. Let it out.'

The woman cried silently into Tanya's shoulder.

Donald's face crumpled. 'It's so hard to take in,' he said.

'I understand. It's a traumatic time for you. I really am most sorry.'

He swallowed hard. 'I was at physiotherapy yesterday afternoon. I go three times a week. I had an accident at work last year. Slipped on a wet platform on an oil rig. Busted both hips. It's been a long journey to get back on my feet. Paula was at work. I keep thinking, if only one of us had been around to meet her from school, this wouldn't have happened. If Paula hadn't had to take on extra shifts, she'd have been here and we'd have known Rainey was missing sooner. We'd have maybe saved her.'

'You mustn't think like that. Neither of you are responsible for what happened.'

'And Tyler won't come out of his room. He thinks it's his fault. If he hadn't been pratting about in lessons, he'd have walked home with her. I don't know what to say to him. Part of me is angry with him.' Donald looked at her with imploring eyes.

'It's natural to hunt for reasons why this happened and to point the finger of blame at yourself or others, but the fact is a series of events occurred that were out of your control. You must talk to the liaison officer and let her help you. You'll need that support.'

'What I really need is for this to be a horrid nightmare, and for my daughter to return home,' said Donald. 'But that isn't going to happen.'

Natalie allowed him a minute to compose his features once more then asked, 'Was Rainey good friends with Audrey Briggs?'

'It's no coincidence, is it? First Audrey, now Rainey.'

'We're examining several leads and possibilities at the moment.'

'I see. Okay. Rainey was in the same class as Audrey and they'd known each other since they started school together. She got on with her, I think. Audrey's name would crop up from time to time and she came back here on a play date or for tea once or twice, I believe. Paula can confirm that. Of course, they took dance classes together and played netball and swam; the usual things girls of the same age do.'

'Where did they play netball?'

'At the leisure centre. There were after-school clubs.'

'Was Rainey friends with Ava Sawyer?'

'Not to my knowledge. I work as a derrickman, so I was often away on various rigs, and didn't do school runs or get involved with my daughter's activities at that time. That was Paula's area of expertise. She'd do the ferrying about for both Rainey and Tyler. I don't know if they were friends but I do remember Ava disappeared at Harriet's sixth birthday. It was big news at the time, and of course Paula was horrified at what had happened that day. I heard on the radio the other day, Ava's body had been discovered.'

'That's right.'

'Three missing girls. Three dead girls,' he said slowly and let the words hang in the air before sighing heavily and speaking again. 'I don't know what else I can tell you. It's all too raw for me to be of much use to you.'

Tanya caught Natalie's eye and nodded. Paula's sobs had lessened. 'Paula, can you talk to Natalie?' she asked.

Paula's face was red. Tanya passed her a tissue and she wiped her running nose.

'I'm sorry,' she said, gulping back final tears.

'I quite understand. Take your time. What can you tell me about Rainey and Ava? Was Rainey friends with her?'

Paula gave a quick shake of her head. 'She stayed away from Ava. Found her too volatile. That wasn't the word she used. She just said Ava was too up and down. Ava and Harriet Downing used to be inseparable until just before the birthday party. Something happened between them and they fell out. Rainey became Harriet's closest friend around that time and they remained best friends from that day.' She swallowed hard and fresh tears sprang to her eyes. Tanya handed her the cup of tea, which she sipped.

'And would you say Rainey was also good friends with Audrey Briggs?'

'She was good friends with all the girls in her class.'

The doorbell rang and Tanya stood up to answer it. Another liaison officer had arrived. Natalie decided it was time to leave them all, and thanking them, she departed. Her thoughts were no longer on the birthday party. Audrey and Rainey had both attended swimming classes and netball club. She had another avenue to pursue.

The office was a hive of activity on her return, with each member of her team fully occupied.

'Carl turned up a few minutes ago. Murray's in the interview room with him,' said Lucy.

'Good. I'll sit in.'

'Before you go, I got a reply from the American lady who made the yellow dresses.'

She swivelled her laptop around. The yellow dress on the screen looked very like the ones Rainey and Audrey had been wearing. 'She makes them to order in a variety of colours and had an order from the UK for five identical dresses.'

'Five?'

'I'm afraid so. There's more bad news. They were delivered to a Mrs Smith at a collection point in Uptown, and the dresses were paid for with an Etsy gift card so we don't know who ordered them. I got an email address for the supposed customer – mrs-smith12345@hotmail.co.uk – but the tech boys say the account's been deleted and was set up with a false name and address.'

'Oh, for fuck's sake! The bastard's one step ahead of us. Okay, there has to be a way to find out who collected them. Where's the collection point?'

'Warehouse the other side of Uptown.'

'Head over there and ask around. Maybe they don't have loads of parcels from the States and they'll remember who came in for it.

Ask the tech team if they know how to identify a purchaser of an Etsy gift card and track down the recipient. The perp's not getting away with this.'

Ian looked up. 'I've made some progress too. I checked out Jennifer Collinswood, Audrey and Rainey's form teacher. She still lives at home with her parents and doesn't have a boyfriend. She has an exemplary work record and does volunteer work for a disabled children's charity at weekends. I've also located Elsa Townsend. She isn't in Spain as we thought. She's been back in the UK for the last three weeks.'

Natalie's eyebrows lifted. 'How did you find her?'

Ian grinned. 'Got the techies to track down the IP address for her email and then called in a favour from a mate who used to be a copper but who now lives on the Costa del Sol. The address was an Internet café in Puerto Banús, so he went in and asked about her, showed her photo to the café owners, who are British, and found out she returned to the UK. Checked with immigration and she came into Manchester on Thursday, 6 April.'

'Well done. Any idea where she might be?'

'The tech boys are searching for any information that might give us a clue.'

'Good. Good.' Natalie turned towards the door. Even though this revelation had spiked her curiosity, Carl Sawyer still had some explaining to do. 'Oh, Ian. Can you find out who runs the after-school netball club and the times for the swimming lessons on Saturdays at the Uptown leisure centre for me?'

'Will do. Dealing with a list of allotment owners for the moment.'

'Do that first and then chase up the leisure centre.'

She strode into the corridor. Suddenly, there was a lot of information to process. She hoped they could do so speedily because at the front of her mind was the chilling knowledge that whoever was behind this had purchased five dresses, and to date, only two had turned up. The dresses were significant and important to the killer. If only she could understand their relevance, she might be able to put a halt to this before any more children died. Was this because of Ava Sawyer, the girl in the original yellow dress? Maybe Ava's father could help her answer that question.

CHAPTER TWENTY-SIX

THEN

It's Monday morning and he's been waiting with bated breath for Sherry to join the school bus, face pressed against the window to get a first glimpse of her before she boards. The doll is hidden in his satchel and he will give it to her on the bus in spite of what her mother said. The night before, he dreamt that instead of heading directly for the back seat where she usually hangs out with her friends, she stopped at his seat and sat down next to him. He handed her the doll and she loved it. She gave him a kiss and wanted to be his friend. He'd woken with his heart thudding at such a possibility.

Back on the school bus, he cranes his neck to get his face closer to the cool glass and peers out. It's a beautiful, bright morning with hedges full of white hawthorn blossom and clumps of daffodils pushing up from grassy verges. The bus draws into Acton village and takes the route, as always, around the pond towards the wooden bus shelter. Now he can make out the group of children waiting, identical in their school uniform. There are only six who regularly get on at this stop: four kids in the year above him, then Gail Shore and Sherry Hunt. There are sometimes one or two parents who like to make sure their kids are on board but today there's a small group of parents who stare solemnly at the bus and watch as everyone troops on board. Sherry isn't among them. His heart sinks. He's waited impatiently all weekend to hand

Sherry her gift and she isn't here. Worse still, Gail has joined the older kids and their heads are lowered and he has no idea what they're saying. He slumps in his seat, deflated. Is Sherry ill?

It suddenly hits him. The children up front are talking about him going to Sherry's house. They're saying things behind his back again. He's going to get into trouble and be sent in front of the headmaster for going to her house. If his mother is brought into school again, he'll be in major trouble.

The bus picks up at the next two stops, and lost in his own misery, he barely registers the fact all the children are sitting towards the front of the bus, leaving him alone at the rear. Ostracised. He knows what it means. He looked it up in his parents' big black dictionary they keep in the sitting room. It means to be excluded, rejected from a group.

He reaches school and hides in the toilets until school begins. His palms are soaking wet. The bell sounds for the start of lessons and he has to join his class in the line-up outside the form room, in silence. Gail glances at him as he shuffles to the back of the line and then away again. She hisses something to another girl and they both give him a look that chills him. He is in trouble.

They troop into class. He stands behind his desk as he must every morning, wondering why Sherry hasn't come into school. Is she that frightened of him, she doesn't dare come to class? Her desk looks lonely without her.

The form teacher looks really serious, her mouth pulled down at the corners. 'Good morning, children.'

'Good morning, Mrs Tideswell,' they chorus.

'You may sit down.'

The sound of scraping chairs fills the room. He stares at the large times table charts on the wall rather than look at Mrs Tideswell. He knows she is going to say something about him going to the birthday party. The class settles and she stands.

'I'm afraid I have to start with some terrible news,' she says. He can't hear for the drumming in his ears. She's going to tell them all

about him having a doll and how he tried to give it to Sherry for her birthday. They'll call him names and laugh at him.

'It's about Sherry. Some of you might already have heard rumours but it's been confirmed. I'm sorry to say, Sherry and her family were involved in a car accident on Sunday evening and have tragically all lost their lives.'

He sees Mrs Tideswell's lips move but he can no longer hear her words. Sherry, pretty Sherry in her yellow party dress, is dead. She'll never know about the present and he'll never have her as a friend.

The class turn their heads as one towards his desk and it takes a while for him to register he is sobbing uncontrollably.

He knows his mum is concerned about him but there's nothing he can do to stop her worrying. She keeps looking over at him from her ironing board. She's put on some cartoons for him but he can't concentrate on them. He's been morose since she came to fetch him from school. Mrs Tideswell told her he was in shock. All he knows is Sherry has gone – forever.

His mother is heading upstairs with the basket of ironing to put it in the airing cupboard.

'I'm going outside to play,' he says.

She halts on the third step and half-turns towards him. 'Good idea. Don't leave the garden though.'

'I won't. I don't want to.'

As soon as she's out of sight, he reaches into his satchel that's leaning against the wall by the front door and pulls out the plastic bag. He can't bear to look inside. He scurries to the back door, changes into his outdoor shoes and slips out into the garden.

The garden is awash with colour. His parents take pride in it and spend much of their free time working the flower beds. There's a special shed at the bottom of the garden containing all the gardening equipment. He sometimes helps out but he has to be supervised in case he pulls out a flower instead of a weed.

He visits the shed then approaches the freshly dug patch his parents were clearing that weekend. They're going to plant a variety of daffodil bulbs here in September. He's seen the bulbs, in paper bags in the shed, bulbs of all sizes that look dried up and dead at the moment but will bloom into a vibrant display of yellows and creams next year. This is the right spot.

He makes quite a deep hole. He doesn't want his parents to find what he's going to bury there. It doesn't take long to scrape back the freshly dug earth, its damp warmth permeating his nostrils as he digs. When the hole is large enough, he peeps inside the bag, checks the doll's dress is neat. His heart lurches once more at the sight of her pretty face.

'Bye-bye, Sherry. I'll miss you.'

He wraps the bag around her and places her gently in the hole before covering it back up, and then, wiping the dirt from his hands, he heads back towards the house.

CHAPTER TWENTY-SEVEN

Carl Sawyer filled the seat in the interview room. The tops of his biceps bulged from his T-shirt sleeves and his wide hands rested on the stretched fabric of his jeans. His face was blank.

'Good afternoon, Carl,' said Natalie.

'Why am I here?'

'You're of interest to us.'

'Oh, I am, am I? And why would that be?'

'Where were you yesterday afternoon at around four o'clock?'

'Out and about.'

'What's that supposed to mean?'

He lifted his shoulders and his mouth turned downwards. 'What I said. Out and about.'

'Would that have been in Uptown?'

He refused to answer.

'Let's cut to it. You were spotted on CCTV in Uptown yesterday headed along St Chad's Road in the direction of Monks Walk.'

'And?'

'Why were you there?'

'I'd met up with somebody and was going back to my car.'

'And who was this "somebody"?'

'Why's it important?'

'Because you happened to be in the vicinity at about the time a young girl was attacked and killed.'

His face remained impassive but his eyes darted left and right as the reality of what was being said dawned on him.

'So, I'll ask you again, who were you meeting?'

Carl shifted uncomfortably in his seat. 'She didn't want anyone to know she was in Uptown.'

'Who didn't?'

'Elsa Townsend.'

'The woman who owned Uptown Craft Centre and Farm with her husband Barney?'

'Yeah.'

'Why were you meeting up?'

'She contacted me on Thursday morning. She'd heard Ava's body had been found. She wanted to talk to me.'

'What did she want to talk to you about?'

'About how sorry she was and how guilty she felt. She was anxious I'd think she had something to do with it, given Ava was found at the centre.'

'Where is Elsa now?'

'I don't know. I met her at the Dove and Horses. There weren't many customers. We had a drink. She cried a lot and said she was really sorry about Ava, that she'd read about her body being recovered from the site, and how she needed to reassure me she knew nothing about it.'

'How did that make you feel?'

'I didn't feel anything. The stupid cow was in charge that day and no matter what she says, she was accountable for what happened. She should have kept an eye on my daughter. She may not have killed Ava but she sure as hell was responsible for what happened to her. I told her as much. Left her in tears.'

'You were pretty angry, then?'

He glowered at Natalie. 'You could say that.'

'Where did you go after your meeting?'

'Back to my van. It was in the multi-storey car park on St Chad's Road.'

'What time did you leave town?'

'I have no idea. I sat in the van for a while. I was worked up. I suppose it was about four thirty. I went straight home.'

'Do you have a car park ticket that will verify this?'

'No, I don't. There'll be some recording though, won't there? There's a camera at the barrier that reads the number plate.'

Natalie looked at Murray, who left the room to confirm the statement.

'Carl, where were you on Wednesday afternoon?'

'Home.'

'You weren't at work?' With no one to confirm his whereabouts, he had no alibi for the afternoon Audrey was killed.

'I took a few days off.'

'You stayed at home all day?'

'Yeah. I stayed inside with a few tins of beer. It's been a shit week, what with Ava being found. I drank a bit. Beatrice rang me. We talked about what we're going to do for Ava. We've got to organise a funeral for her, only Beatrice can't face it. I went to the funeral parlour to try and sort it out on my own but I couldn't. You get a book, you know? A book to go through like a fucking shopping catalogue, full of things you might want for your kid's funeral: white horses to pull a white hearse, fingerprint keepsakes, coffins decorated with your child's favourite fascinations, and it's like being stabbed in the heart. Even though I suspected she might be dead, all the time she's been missing, there's always been a possibility she was out there, somewhere. Soon, all I'll have to remind me of her will be a headstone and whatever pottery ornaments we choose to leave beside it. She was a life. She was my life. It hurts so much. She's gone. Forever.' He stopped and bit on his lower lip to stop it from trembling.

His pain was palpable. Natalie couldn't ignore it.

'You will get through this and you'll remember happier moments and times you spent with Ava, those occasions that filled you with joy and made you laugh, and your memories will keep you connected to her. She'll never be gone completely.'

He wiped the back of his hand over his eyes. 'It doesn't feel like I'll ever be able to get to that point.'

'You will. It's early days. You need time.'

He didn't reply. Natalie still wasn't sure if he had enough anger in him to harm other children who'd been at the party. She wanted to probe further but if it came back that he'd left the car park at around four thirty as he claimed, it was unlikely he'd have murdered Rainey.

'When you went back to your van, did you see anybody else walking along the pavement?'

'Nah. It was quiet. Didn't see a soul.'

'On Wednesday, is there anyone who can vouch for you?'

'I kept the door locked and had the telly on all afternoon. I didn't speak to anyone. Apart from Beatrice.'

'Did Beatrice ring you on your mobile?' asked Natalie, thinking it would be easy to check to see what time she had called.

'Nah, she rang the fixed line cos I'd switched off my mobile by then.'

'Any idea what time that was?'

'I was a bit sozzled by then. Couldn't tell you. Sometime during the afternoon. She'll know exactly when. Why?'

'Audrey Briggs was murdered on Wednesday afternoon.'

He lifted his face. 'You think I killed her?'

'I think we need to eliminate you from our enquiries. There's a difference.'

'I didn't. I was far too drunk to drive. I didn't leave the house at all.'

'You wouldn't object to giving us a DNA sample?'

'No. Take it. I've nothing to hide.'

'Thank you.' She left the room to arrange for Ian to take the sample. In the office Murray was pouring over a screen.

'I've found him,' said Murray. 'He left the car park at four twenty-seven. Look. He's alone in the van.'

The photo showed a serious-faced Carl at the wheel of his van.

'I also rang the pub, the Dove and Horses. The manager said there were two customers in at about three thirty p.m. The man who matched Carl's description banged his glass down and stormed out after about fifteen minutes. The woman, who was wearing sunglasses, followed him a minute or two later. Both left behind unfinished drinks. Manager said he thought they were rowing but they kept their voices down so he couldn't hear what about. The Dove and Horses to the car park is about thirty minutes on foot, which accounts for how he was picked up on the library camera at four fifteen. He's unlikely to have murdered Rainey.'

'Ian, will you take a DNA sample, please, and then let him go home?'

'Another dead end,' said Murray, folding his arms.

'But another lead. What was Elsa really doing back in town?'

'You suspect it wasn't because she wanted to tell Carl she was sorry about Ava?' Murray asked.

'Strange, isn't it? She had many opportunities to speak to Carl in the past but came back to the UK a couple of weeks ago, just before Ava's body was unearthed, and then happened to be in town the day Rainey was killed. Can you see if the tech team has worked out her whereabouts yet? I'd very much like to talk to Elsa; and Ian, ask Beatrice Sawyer what time she phoned Carl on Wednesday.'

Lucy looked up and spoke. 'Natalie, I've rung the warehouse that distributes parcels. They're shut at the moment and open again at eight tomorrow. I'll head down there first thing.'

'Thanks.'

'The swimming lessons are at nine tomorrow,' said Ian as he edged out of the door. 'I've left the details of the netball club on your desk.'

Natalie read through them. She'd be able to talk to the organiser the following morning. She'd start her day at the leisure centre. 'Lucy, why don't you get off too? It's late and I don't think we can do much more this evening.'

She dropped down at her desk, thinking back over her conversation with Carl. He hadn't come across as a man who'd want to harm children. Did she trust her instincts enough to believe this? Her phone buzzed. It was Mike.

'Hey. Got some news for you. I'm with Naomi and we've identified the substance under Rainey's nails. It's a mixture of clay, presumably from the clay cat in her school bag, but there are fibres which we believe to be leather and a hair we think might have come from an animal – a dog.'

'I wonder how the fibres got under her nails.'

'Here's a couple of theories for you. They're under her right hand and she is right-handed, so maybe she was strangled by something leather – a belt or equivalent – and tried to tug it away from her throat, or, she picked them up earlier in the day at school, from a bag or from pulling at a belt.'

'And the dog hair?'

'Got caught up with the clay. She patted a dog. She picked them up from the bushes she squeezed through to reach Monks Walk. Can't think of anything else.'

'Fair enough. Good suggestions.'

'We've run tests on the fibres we lifted from the bushes we think she came through, and they're a match for her school skirt and socks. There were also other man-made fibres, black cotton, not from any of her clothing.'

'From her attacker's clothes?'

'Maybe, or might have been there for a while. I'm sure other kids would have tried to use that as a cut-through in the past. School uniform is black trousers and white shirt.'

'Okay. Cheers, Mike.'

Murray reappeared with a sheet of A4 in his hand. 'Could have something here. Elsa was in contact with Barney.'

'Her ex-husband. He said she'd been in touch for his birthday a couple of weeks ago and they hadn't been in touch for a while.'

'He lied. She sent him another email, asking him to meet her when she was in the UK.'

'When did she send it?'

'Thursday, 20 April. Just over a week ago.'

'He must have known she was in the UK when he spoke to us. Bastard. Right, you up for speaking to him now?'

'You bet.'

As she left the office, she sent a text to David, explaining she'd be out much later than she intended. She hoped he'd had a chance to sort things out with Josh. As much as she wanted to go home and be a mother to her son, she couldn't leave this. Children's lives were at risk, and whether she liked it or not, her family had to take a back seat.

CHAPTER TWENTY-EIGHT

FRIDAY, 28 APRIL – EVENING

Barney Townsend opened the door a mere crack and peered out at Natalie and Murray. He was in a dressing gown, cord wrapped tightly around his lean frame.

'What is it?' he asked.

'We'd like a few words,' said Natalie.

'Can't it wait until morning? I was in bed.'

'It's a little early to be in bed, isn't it?'

'Not for me. I'm an early riser.'

'I'm afraid it can't wait. It's regarding your ex-wife Elsa. You lied to us, Mr Townsend, and that's something we can't ignore.'

He visibly deflated and opened the door.

'I prefer to say that I withheld information. Information I believed to have no bearing on your investigation.' He shut the door quietly behind them.

'That's not for you to decide. You could have impeded our investigation and that's something I don't take lightly.'

He didn't move from the door. 'What do you want to know?'

'Why you didn't tell us that Elsa was back in the UK?'

'I didn't think it was important.'

Natalie clenched her fists tightly and spoke deliberately. 'Children are dead. In my book that's more than reason enough for you to tell us everything you know about Elsa.'

He shifted from one slippered foot to the other. 'I didn't think—' he began. He was stopped immediately by Natalie lifting her hand up.

'We want to talk to Elsa and we suspect you know her whereabouts.'

'She had nothing to do with Ava's disappearance.'

'Have I not made myself clear, Mr Townsend? We shall decide what is and isn't relevant in this case. Not you.' Natalie drew herself up to her full height and looked him in the eye. 'Where is she?'

'Here,' came a voice from the staircase.

Natalie's head whipped in the direction of the woman speaking. Elsa Townsend stood at the top of the stairs. She descended slowly, clinging to the banister. Barney ran a hand through his thick hair.

'It's not what it looks like…' he began.

Natalie shot him a steely look.

'Can we sit down to discuss this?' Elsa asked. 'I'm not too good on my feet for a long spell. I've been quite ill recently and don't have much energy at the moment.'

Barney led the way to the sitting room. Elsa took the chair nearest the window that faced a two-seater settee and an old rocking chair.

'I'm sorry. It's totally my fault Barney didn't divulge my whereabouts. I made him promise. I was terrified you'd think I was to blame for Ava's death, what with her body being found on the craft centre premises. I needed time to digest it all. I'd not been back in the UK five minutes when I heard about that. I ought to have come forward immediately and cleared it up but you'd been to talk to Barney and he told me Audrey, who'd been at the centre that day, had also been killed, and I didn't know what to do. Here I was in the UK and a second child dead, and me with no proof of my whereabouts at the time. I thought it would be better if you all believed I was still in Spain.'

'Why did you return in the first place?'

Elsa shuffled her bottom further back into the chair. 'I kept getting headaches that got worse and worse. I had them for a few years, even before I went to Spain, but the last few months, they've been impossible to live with. I went to a specialist in Spain and discovered I've got a tumour on my brain. When you're facing something like that, your priorities change. I became homesick. I wanted to sort things out between me and Barney before I have surgery. Put my affairs in order, if you like.' She gave him a half-smile. 'I was staying in a motel but I had a blinder of a headache yesterday and he let me use the spare room.'

'You met up with Carl Sawyer yesterday?'

'I did. I tried to talk to him soon after Ava went missing. I visited him and his wife several times to tell them how sorry I was, but they wouldn't speak to me. They thought I was responsible and I suppose to a certain degree I was. I let that little girl out of my sight and she disappeared. I met up with Carl because I wanted to try one last time. I wanted him and his wife to know that there hasn't been a single day I haven't wished I could turn back the clock and relive that one day. When I heard Ava had been found, it seemed even more important to speak to them both. I didn't know they'd split up. I tried their house but Beatrice's mother refused to let me speak to her. With Barney's help, I located Carl and met him in town.' She looked away for a second and shook her head sadly. 'It made no difference. He still hates me and blames me.'

'What did you do after Carl left you at the Dove and Horses?'

'Walked to the top of the road and waited for Barney to pick me up. I can't drive at the moment.'

'Barney was in town with you?'

'I was,' he replied.

'What did you do while Elsa was talking to Carl?'

'Hung around the shops, waiting for her to ring me. It was only for about an hour.'

'Where did you park?'

'In one of the bays near the pub. You get up to two hours' free parking there.'

'I'd like to know your exact movements for that time, please.' Natalie looked directly at him.

A deep furrow appeared between his eyes. 'I went to the newsagent's and browsed through some magazines. I bought a gardening magazine then sat on the bench near Greggs and had a takeaway coffee and read my magazine until Elsa rang me.'

'Have you got your till receipt for the magazine?'

'I threw it away. It might be in the kitchen bin.'

'Would you check for me, please?'

'What's this all about?' he asked, rising as he spoke.

'It's about the murder of another girl.'

'You don't think I'm a suspect, do you?'

'Could you just locate the receipt please, sir?'

Elsa continued speaking. 'I didn't kill Ava. I have absolutely no idea who might have done such a thing. I didn't kill Audrey. I remember her. She was a sweet little thing with a snub nose and gap-teeth. She was the one who first noticed Ava wasn't with the group.'

'What about Rainey Kilburn? Do you remember a girl called Rainey?'

'I do. She went off on the ponies with Harriet. She kept squealing loudly.' She winced at the memory. 'I remember her vividly. I remember them all. I won't ever forget them. I see twenty children in my dreams most nights. I see their faces and hear their voices and I count all twenty of them, then I wake up and remember there were only nineteen. Is Rainey dead too?'

'She was killed yesterday afternoon.'

Elsa's eyes grew large and she spoke in a whisper. 'So that's why you want to know where we both were.' She was interrupted by Barney.

'I think this is it,' he said, handing a crumpled piece of paper to Murray, who opened it and read out the time of the sale.

'Three fifty.'

Natalie would have to check how far away the newsagent was from Monks Walk, but she was fairly certain Barney couldn't have got there and back in time to have murdered Rainey and then picked up Elsa. Their phone records would confirm when Elsa made the call to be collected, and safety cameras would have registered his car in that area as they left. It was looking like both had strong alibis.

'Are you staying here for long?' she asked Elsa.

'For the foreseeable,' said Barney. Elsa gave him a grateful look.

'We might need to talk to you again,' said Natalie.

'We'll be here,' said Elsa.

'Can't be them, then,' said Murray as they drove away.

'It's not looking that way. I don't know where to turn next,' said Natalie. 'We really need a lucky break. I hope tomorrow gives us one and that it comes in time. I really don't like the idea of the killer buying five yellow dresses.'

'I'll go back and confirm Barney couldn't have reached Monks Walk and strangled Rainey,' said Murray.

'I was going to do that. You get off.'

'Yolande's out with her mates tonight. I'm fine to do it.'

'Cheers. I could do with getting home. Got a few family issues.' She bit her tongue. She must be overwrought. It wasn't like her to discuss personal matters with a colleague. Fortunately, Murray didn't push her on the matter.

'We haven't overlooked anything, have we?' he asked.

'I don't think so.'

'You worry though, don't you?'

'About missing something important? Every time.'

He kept his eyes on the road and indicated to pull out past an SUV. She spoke more to herself than him. 'I think we're handling it properly but what we really need is some evidence to send us in the right direction.'

As Murray accelerated past the SUV, she looked out of her window, her eyes gazing on the faces of those inside. In the passenger seat was a girl, about the same age as Rainey and Audrey. Natalie pressed her lips tightly together and prayed the breakthrough would come soon.

CHAPTER TWENTY-NINE

SATURDAY, 29 APRIL – MORNING

Natalie was awake before first light, head throbbing and mouth dry. It had been a long night. David had been up when she'd finally got through the door after eleven and had poured her a glass of red wine. Having not eaten dinner, the alcohol had taken hold quickly, and she'd made the mistake of pouring a second glass after David had stomped off to bed. Now she was paying the price.

She listened to the rhythm of his light breathing, envious he was dead to the world. He didn't have trouble sleeping after an argument whereas she'd been awake half the night, chewing over all the finer points of their disagreement and the cold words spoken in anger that had stolen into her mind and heart.

David hadn't been willing to discuss his conversation with Josh…

'I have a right to know what was said and how you left it.'

'If you're so big on rights all of a sudden, then maybe you ought to be around more often for the kids.'

'Fuck off, David. Fuck right off! If it hadn't been for your gambling, I would be able to stay at home and know what my children were up to and to talk to them more often instead of agonising over what they're

going through and being powerless to assist because I'm involved in an investigation, miles away.'

'Trust you to throw that back at me again. You'll never let it go, will you?'

'I'm sorry. I was out of line. I've had a really bad day.'

'Well, boohoo! I've had a fucking shitty day myself.'

She winced at the memory of what had followed. She'd been as forthright as David and given as good as she'd received, her anger fuelled by his whinging attitude and the effects of a difficult investigation. They'd begun amicably enough and she'd listened to David's gripes about having had to speak to Josh, but he'd already consumed several beers and the wine had turned his mood sour. It had quickly become apparent they were not going to talk about Josh like grown-ups or parents. They were going to bicker and head back down the path they'd trodden too frequently of late. She'd been relieved when David had stood up abruptly and gone to bed.

Now she wanted to shake him awake and say she was sorry she'd been less than sympathetic, and at the same time, she wanted to impress how much pressure she was under. The case was getting to her. Big time. Olivia's face drifted to the front of her thoughts. 'I know what you're saying,' she whispered. 'I have to find this killer.' She couldn't bear any new nightmares about young girls and endure more regret and further guilt at failing them.

She stared at the ceiling, mulling over her plans for the day and waiting for David to come to. She searched for information on Etsy gift cards on her phone and worried about the three remaining yellow dresses. Who were they intended for? Was the killer after three other girls who attended the birthday party, and if so, could one of the dresses be for Harriet Downing, whose party it was? The thought mobilised her into action. She'd go back over DI Howard Franks' files from the original MisPer case in July 2015, and check how many girls in total were at the party and then try to work out which ones might be targeted next. David stirred and threw himself onto his left side, his back to her. There was nothing to be gained from waiting to make peace with him. He could be out for another couple of hours. She had more pressing matters to attend to.

The Ava Sawyer files revealed eight girls, including Ava, Audrey and Rainey, had attended Harriet's birthday party in 2015. Natalie looked up addresses for all of them, noting one had moved to Scotland and another was now in Derbyshire. That left four in the area, including Harriet herself. She wrote down their names on a sheet of A4: Avril Jones, Victoria Kelly and Harper Webb. Then she tried to establish what connected them. All three were in the same class as Audrey and Rainey. None of them attended dance classes at the academy. All lived in and around Uptown but not on the same estate as Audrey and Harriet.

After a while, the thumping in her head became too much to ignore and she headed to the drinks machine on the ground floor to buy a bottle of water so she could take some headache pills. Mike was in front of the machine, feeding it coins.

'You're in early,' she said.

'Been here all night with Naomi and Darshan,' he said, scratching at the growth on his chin. 'Might go back for a shower in a minute. I'm out of fags. Needed some chocolate to tide me over.' He lifted the large, wrapped bar up for her to see.

'Nutritious breakfast,' she joked.

'Come on, then. What are you going to have?' he asked, nodding at the machine.

'Bottle of water and two aspirin.'

'Even more nutritious.'

'My own fault. No food last night and too much wine. I ought to know better.'

'Age does not necessarily bring wisdom,' he said as he unwrapped the foil and jammed half the bar into his mouth.

'All night and no breakthrough?'

Mike chewed a while before answering. 'I have nothing conclusive to offer you. There's no DNA traces anywhere on the material. Killer probably wore gloves.'

'There must have been something. What about from the person who made it or packaged it?'

He shook his head. 'DNA is not always transferred through touch. Some people shed more skin cells than others. Maybe the person who made the dresses was one who shed very few cells. The dresses were machine-stitched, and if the person was a good seamstress, they'd whip the material through a sewing machine so quickly they'd hardly make contact with it. Also, hand-washing gets rid of skin cells so fewer cells are deposited. If I were sewing dresses like those, I'd keep my hands very clean so as not to spoil the fabric. All of which means we came up with diddly squat – no DNA.'

'You have nothing whatsoever?'

'We're still working on it and we've eliminated a load of evidence we brought back from both scenes. It's a question of being patient, Natalie. You know how hard we all slog, and we're working as hard, fast and accurately as we possibly can.'

'Yeah. I know. I'm getting edgy about this. I have a dreadful feeling the killer is going to try and strike again and I don't have anything on him. I ought to have something by now and I haven't. It doesn't seem right.'

'This is the real world, Natalie. Sometimes, we can't make it right. We can only do our best.'

'What if our best isn't good enough?'

'It's too early for philosophical discussions. I'm going to get showered and have a rest. I suggest you take those aspirin and ease up on yourself.' He stretched his neck left and right and popped the remainder of his chocolate into his mouth.

'Good advice but I don't think I can. I have to find this per-petrator.'

'You know you're taking this investigation too personally, don't you? This is more about you than you're willing to admit. Want to know what I reckon?'

'No. I don't,' she said, stuffing a pound coin into the slot and waiting for the bottle of water to drop into the drawer.

'You can't make up for other people's mistakes,' he said, kindly.

'I'm not—' she began then caught the look in his eye. He knew her well.

She was comforted by his presence and comprehension. David hadn't understood in the same way Mike had. Mike knew she'd never forgive the people who'd screwed up on the Olivia Chester investigation, or herself for her own part in it.

'Yeah. Okay. I know. Bugger off for your shower and spare me the pep talk.' She lifted the water bottle from the drawer and twisted the cap from it.

'You're welcome,' he said and winked.

She smiled a response and waved him away.

The aspirin had done their job, and having cleared her head and visited a local coffee house for a coffee and pastry, Natalie was more able to focus on the day ahead. Murray was getting out of his car when she got back to the station, and instead of heading upstairs, they drove directly to the Uptown leisure centre.

They were only five minutes down the road when Ian phoned her.

'Beatrice Sawyer rang her husband Carl at four thirty on Wednesday. They were on the phone for half an hour, discussing funeral arrangements. Her mother spoke briefly to him too. He has two witnesses who can confirm his whereabouts.'

'Thanks, Ian.' Turning her head slightly in Murray's direction, she said, 'Carl's got an alibi for the time Audrey was killed.'

A lift of eyebrows was his response. She stared out of the windscreen. They'd left Samford and were driving past fields of bright yellow rapeseed. *Yellow like the party dresses.* She pressed her lips tightly together and quietly fumed. She was rapidly running out of suspects.

A woman in her early twenties, with wavy dark hair swept back in a headband and dressed in a pale-blue tracksuit, was manning the desk. Her name badge read Helena Dickinson and she was responsible for the netball club that took place at the centre. The echoing shouts coming from an instructor and the heavy beat of music indicated some activity was already taking place in the room behind reception. She scanned the list of names of all the girls who attended Harriet's party, including Harriet, and stabbed at one. 'I don't recognise this name,' she said, pointing at Avril Jones.

'But you know the others,' Natalie urged.

'Sure. They're regulars, although Harper's been dropping off attendance recently.'

'Have you known them long?'

'The club's been going a year. They've all been coming since it started. We run different sessions for different age groups. I've been in charge of this particular group so I know them well enough. Harriet usually plays centre and Audrey was a terrific goal shooter. Rarely missed the net. Rainey was goal attack. We cancelled the last session in light of what happened to Audrey. And now Rainey too. It's dreadful. I think we'll hold off a while before we start it up again.'

'Do you get regular spectators?'

'No. We don't play competition matches, only mixed friendly seven-a-sides. It's a fun session. I teach them some skills – how to shoot, pass the ball, that sort of thing – and a mini-game. The parents usually wait at the in-house coffee shop. There's no viewing area. When we host matches in the large court, then parents come to support.'

'How long have you worked here?'

'Since July last year. I worked in Cornwall before that – surf instructor!' She smiled.

'That's quite a move. Cornwall to Samford,' said Murray.

'Boyfriend was here. We met in Cornwall in 2015 when he was visiting the area,' she said. 'Stayed in touch online and he visited me as often as he could, but the travelling was crazy. Apart from the fact we were both knackered after a journey, it cost a fortune to visit each other. I miss the sea but we get away to Wales now and then. Still keep up my surfing.'

'Does your boyfriend work here too?' Natalie asked.

'No. He's at the Sudbury Wildlife Centre.'

'Guy Noble?'

'Yeah, that's him.'

'He used to work at Uptown Craft Centre and Farm.'

'Yeah. I met him just after one of the children had gone missing during a birthday party. He left the place soon afterwards. He didn't like working there any more. He told me you found her body. Poor little soul.'

'Does Guy come and visit you here?'

'Sure. He comes over from time to time to hang out if I'm on reception or not too busy.'

Natalie digested this new information and thanked Helena before heading towards the swimming pool housed in another section of the leisure centre, reached by a separate entrance. She'd found another connection. Not only did several of the girls who attended Harriet's party play netball, Guy would probably have known them too. Was he as squeaky clean as he appeared to be? She dragged herself back to the present. She'd come here to try and work out if there were any other possible links between the girls. Avril hadn't played netball. She still needed to talk to the swimming coach to confirm if she attended swimming lessons. The three remaining dresses were intended for three victims. She had to work out who before it was too late.

*

Lucy waited at the reception point at the warehouse on the edge of Uptown. It was far larger than she'd expected, and through the glass panel in the shut door she could see rows of racking, stacked with parcels and packages of all sizes, and a bright-orange forklift truck buzzing up and down the aisle. The young bloke on duty had told her he'd only be a minute but she'd waited fifteen full minutes already, all the while listening to tinny, piped music. It would drive her insane to work there. She drummed her fingers against the counter. Through the door she could see the youth now talking to an older man who'd stopped the truck. There was a great deal of arm-waving and head-shaking going on. She wished they'd get a move on and tell her what she needed to know.

The whole investigation was getting to her. On one hand, she and Bethany had decided it was the right time to bring a child into the world, and on the other, she was dealing with a person who took children out of it. The prospect of becoming a parent was troubling her, and the old feelings of self-doubt she harboured had started to consume her. What if she was a shit mother? She had no idea of what constituted a good one. Hers had abandoned her and she'd never really gelled with any of the women who'd attempted to foster her. Bethany said that was because she was prickly and defensive because she was hurting inside. She hadn't allowed any other maternal figure to get close. Bethany was sure a baby would transform her. Lucy wasn't totally convinced.

Bethany, however, would make a great mum. She drew solace from that fact and that they'd have outside support. Yolande and Murray had been incredible. Yolande, her only true friend from her youth, also rejected by her parents and fostered out, had become a lifelong friend to both her and Bethany. They'd been through many tough situations together and helped each other on lots of occasions. Yolande was one in a million with the biggest heart. If she loved a person, she loved them completely. Who else would allow their husband to be a sperm donor for her friends?

The spotty-faced youth returned, a sullen look on his face, trailed by a thickset bloke wearing overalls and an air of superiority.

'Sorry. We can't help you,' said the bloke. 'We don't keep a tab on every package. Customer comes here with a collection number. We match it to the one on the parcel, swipe the barcode to prove it's been collected, then hand it over.'

'You don't have any names or records of who picked it up, then?'

'No.'

'So, anyone could have collected it?'

'Not without the number.'

Lucy had already ascertained the woman in the USA had arranged the delivery of the parcel and a confirmation email had been sent to the bogus address. This verified it. The killer had been able to get the parcel almost undetected. All he needed was the identifying number.

'You wouldn't happen to recall handing over a package from the USA?' She looked at the youth, who shook his head.

The guy in the overalls spoke again. 'We handle hundreds of packages from all over the world. Never notice where they come from. It's all about technology these days. We deal with numbers and work with computers. I'm very sorry but we don't stand a hope in hell of finding out when the parcel came in or who collected it.' He lifted his square shoulders in apology.

'Do you have any CCTV cameras?'

'There are CCTV cameras in the warehouse itself and in the back area where shipments get unloaded, but not on reception where customers enter to pick up packages.'

Lucy waited until she'd got back to the car before swearing loudly and thumping the steering wheel in frustration. She was so close and yet couldn't establish the identity of the person who'd picked up the yellow dresses. Her hopes now lay with the tech team, who were working on the Etsy gift card used to buy them. She threw the car into reverse gear. They had to nail this bastard. He or she wasn't as clever as they made out. They'd slip up soon and Lucy would be ready for them when they did.

*

As soon as Natalie entered the swimming pool area, the pungent aroma of chlorine wafted over her, a sharp reminder of trips to the local pool with Josh and Leigh when they were so little the brightly coloured armbands seemed to swamp their tiny arms and elbows. She inhaled the friendly smell and the warmth. A few families were already in the water, and as she walked across to the man in red T-shirt and shorts, standing at the far side of the pool, she spotted a face she recognised. Howard Franks, the ex-detective who'd worked the Ava Sawyer case, was standing in the shallow end, his arms supporting a young girl about six years old, in a bright yellow swimming costume and goggles, who was kicking legs back in a convincing, frog-like manner. He shook his face to clear it of droplets that had splashed onto him and acknowledged Natalie and Murray, who paused to say hello.

'Hi. Didn't expect to see you,' Natalie said.

'Every Saturday without fail. Kerry's with her grandma but Sage and I have some time together – don't we, baby?' She beamed a happy smile back at him. 'She's doing really well. Made heaps of progress these last few weeks. Might go for a full length together today. What brings you here?'

'The investigation.'

'Hang on a minute, chick,' he said to his daughter. 'Practise those leg kicks, holding onto the side. Daddy will just be here, okay?'

The girl splashed across to the side nearest Natalie and did as asked. Howard hauled himself from the water onto the side of the pool then stood up; he reached for a towel on the seat in front of him and wrapped it around his waist self-consciously.

'I heard about Rainey,' he said quietly.

'That's one of the reasons we're here. Checking movements. You know how it is.'

'Unfortunately, I do,' he replied. The door clattered open and a couple of lads came through, heading straight for the steps into the pool. An elderly man carrying towels followed them. Howard lifted a hand in greeting.

'Ned Coleman,' Murray said. Natalie recognised the name. He was the man who lived opposite Queen's Park.

'You know him?' she asked Howard.

'Oh yes. Known Ned a while. Lovely fellow. Met him during the investigation into Ava's disappearance. That's his grandson, Freddie, in the water. He's in the same year as Audrey and Rainey and was also at the birthday party. Ned was one of those who helped search for Ava. Came every day. He was terribly upset about it because Freddie was one of the reasons Elsa Townsend lost sight of Ava. He and his friend were playing up and distracted her. Ned felt they were in some way responsible. He brings Freddie to swimming club every week and waits for him here. His daughter's divorced and works Saturday mornings, so he looks after the boy. Lost his wife to cancer early 2015. He understood what I was going through when my own wife was taken ill. Talked to me when I was at my lowest. Got a lot of time for him.'

'He lives opposite the park where Audrey was found.'

'He didn't see anything?'

Murray shook his head.

'That's a pity. He was a big help on our investigation. Has a very good memory.'

'He was at the centre the day Ava went missing?'

'He came to collect Freddie from the party. Freddie's mother dropped the boy off and Ned came to collect. He remembered a lot of faces in the shop and helped us locate a few customers who'd been at the craft centre at the time. Of course, nothing came of it but he was able to describe them in detail and that gave us the edge.'

'He was watching television and didn't hear or see anything when Audrey went missing,' said Murray.

'That's a shame.'

'Daddy!' came the voice from the pool.

'Coming. Better go. We don't have too long before the club begins and we have to get out of the water.' He dropped the towel back onto the seat and slipped back into the water.

The lifeguard had moved and was talking to Ned. Natalie and Murray approached the pair. Ned nodded a greeting to them and then shuffled away to the seating area, where he set out his grandson's towel, a newspaper and a flask.

'Do you take the swimming club?' Natalie asked the young man.

'Yes, I'm a lifeguard and swimming instructor.'

'I have a couple of questions about the club,' Natalie said. 'Do any of these children attend?'

She handed him the list of names that Helena had already perused. The young man stopped halfway down the list and wrinkled his nose apologetically. 'They've all been to the club in the past, but to be honest, I'm not very good with names and faces. I just bark instructions to the children. I only remember the ones I see more regularly. I know Harriet Downing, for example, although I haven't seen her for quite some time. Some weeks they come along, others they don't. Audrey was one of the more regular attendees.'

'What about Rainey? When did you last see her?'

'I can't remember if she was here or not last week. It's quite difficult to see who's who in the pool, and we don't keep an attendance register. It's a free class and if the children want to participate, they can. Maybe Ned can help you on that. He might have noticed. Would you excuse me? I have to clear the pool before we can start the club.'

He lifted a whistle and blew it loudly. Natalie searched the water for Howard, who was at the deep end of the pool. He swam easy strokes, maintaining a watchful eye on his daughter's progress as she battled to reach the edge of the pool and the steps to get out.

Freddie and his friend pulled themselves onto the side of the pool and waited obediently, joined now by other children. The place was filling up with parents and children and a hubbub of noise. Family swimming was at an end and the club was about to begin.

Ned was unscrewing the top of the flask as Natalie and Murray approached.

'Mr Coleman, do you mind if we ask a few questions?'

He put a hand to his ear. A group of six children had arrived and their excited voices bounced around the walls.

'Do you know Rainey Kilburn?' she asked more loudly.

'Of course, I do. She's in my grandson's class. That's my grandson. Freddie.' He pointed out the boy on the poolside.

'When did you last see her?'

His thick eyebrows almost met each other as he pondered the question. 'She was here last week. She usually comes with her friend Harriet, but Harriet hasn't been to swimming club for a while. Freddie says she's given it up. I saw her then. Has something happened to her?'

'I'm afraid Rainey died Thursday afternoon.'

A look of concern crossed his features. He looked around at the children near the lifeguard. 'Oh, goodness gracious. This is dreadful news. That's two children dead in the same week.'

'Do you happen to know if any of these girls came to swimming club?'

She handed him the same list she'd shown the lifeguard and Helena. 'I've seen them all here at one time or another. They're all in the same class as Freddie at school too.' He lowered his voice, looked around to make sure nobody was listening and leant in closer. 'Is this to do with what happened to Audrey?'

'It is. We were wondering if you'd seen anybody acting suspiciously here, possibly watching the girls or hanging about outside.'

He rubbed at his chin. 'I'd have noticed if anyone else was about. Sometimes the parents wait for a while but it gets boring watching the kids splash about and they go off for a coffee. I see the same faces come and go most weeks and I haven't spotted anyone new or behaving suspiciously.'

At that moment, he looked up and a warm smile filled his face. 'Yes, lad?'

Freddie was rushing towards them, a flash of white flesh.

'I haven't got my nose protector,' he said. He hopped from one foot to the next, arms dangling, droplets of water pooling around his bare feet.

Ned rummaged in the bag next to him and withdrew the silicone swimming training protector. 'Here you go.'

'Thanks, Grandpa.'

'Freddie, can I ask you a quick question about Rainey?' Natalie crouched to meet the boy's eyes. 'Did she come to swimming club last week?'

'Yes.'

'Did you notice any grown-ups talking to her at the swimming pool or outside?'

He shuffled again and cast an eye towards his friends by the poolside. They were getting into the water. 'No. Only Guy. They laughed about something. I remember that. It was when we were leaving. I walked past them and she laughed at him and punched his arm.'

'Guy was here?'

'By the wall. I said hello to him. He's nice. He works with birds at the wildlife centre. He let me stroke an owl when we went.' A friend called for him, voice echoing in the pool. 'I have to go.'

Natalie nodded and he bounded lightly back to the pool. She turned her attention back to Ned, who was watching his grandson fit his nose clip and jump into the water with the others.

'Did you see Guy?'

'Yes. He chatted to Terry the lifeguard for a while.'

'Have you seen him here before?'

'I don't think I have, no.'

'And you come here most Saturdays?'

Ned's cheeks lifted. 'Every week. I look after Freddie on Saturday mornings. Only time I get with him and he's growing up so fast. We come here first and then go for a burger or roll afterwards, without fail. He loves swimming.' He paused for a second and his face changed again; the enthusiastic spark that had been there when he spoke about the boy disappeared as he stared at his flask. 'Wicked thing to have happened to those girls.'

'If you can think of anything that might help us, would you get in touch with the sergeant?'

'Naturally. If anything strikes me as important, I'll do that.' His attention was drawn to Howard, now wearing a shirt over his towel and walking towards the changing rooms.

Natalie's phone buzzed. She thanked and left Ned, speaking as she walked off. It was Ian.

'We've had an anonymous tip-off. Somebody thinks they spotted Rainey on Thursday afternoon, near that dance school in Uptown, around three thirty or three forty. They claim there was a small black car around that area too, and Rainey might have got into it. No make or model. Caller wouldn't leave a name and said they couldn't be sure it was her, as they were on a bus at the time going past that spot, but they wanted to help us.'

'Yet they wouldn't leave a name so we could talk to them in person, which would actually be even more helpful. Okay, best follow it up.'

A pulse beat steadily in Natalie's neck. Had Rainey been picked up from school? This went against what they'd believed so far. She might not have walked at all. The dance school had once again been brought to their attention.

The lifeguard blew his whistle again and shouted for the children to pay attention.

They left Ned to his newspaper and tea and hastened away.

CHAPTER THIRTY

FRIDAY, 24 JULY 2015

AVA SAWYER

Ava watches Freddie and Thomas fighting over some plastic dinosaur, their faces red with anger, and fumes inside. It's a stupid party. She didn't want to come. Her mum had insisted.

'You'll be the only one in the class not to go,' she had said.

That would have suited Ava just fine. She doesn't care for any of her classmates, not since Harriet Downing decided to be mean and told everyone that Ava wet the bed. Horrible Harriet who unwrapped the carefully chosen birthday present – a jewellery-making set – and barely glanced at it before sliding it on the table next to the other gifts. Ava had spent all her saved pocket money on the gift, and Harriet had looked down her pointy nose at it and mumbled thanks she didn't mean.

Audrey Briggs is starting to annoy her. She tries too hard to be friends with everyone, and the last few minutes she's been grinning her idiotic, gap-toothed smile at Harriet every time Harriet squeals. It's too much for Ava. Audrey's her friend not Harriet's. Rainey Kilburn, who's taken over the role as Harriet's best friend, whispers something in Harriet's ear, and both girls look across at Ava and begin giggling. Ava can't stand the smug expressions any more. She told Harriet about her bed-wetting in strictest confidence and now everyone knows about it. She's going to make her pay for it.

The woman in charge of the party, Elsa, is still dealing with the boys. No other adults are about. Guy, the nice man who looks like a human bear, has gone off. Ava knows what to do. She'll ruin Harriet's party. She's going to disappear, and everyone will have to spend time searching for her instead of playing games. Elsa will soon realise Ava's gone. And if she doesn't, Audrey will say something, and then Elsa will have to stop all the fun and games and send people out to look for her. Ava gives a wry grin at the prospect. Ava is good at hiding.

'I'm going to the toilet,' she tells Audrey.

Audrey gives her a dumb, open-mouthed look. 'You have to tell that woman first.'

'I'm big enough to go to the toilet on my own, and besides, I know where it is,' says Ava. She ducks out of the back door and into a corridor. She doesn't head for the toilets, signed to her left, but heads to the right. She's been to the centre before with her parents and she remembers there are sheds and stables out here.

No one sees her as she races along. If anyone stops her, she'll burst into tears and say she's lost. She soon reaches the stables and heads for the furthest one. The door is shut but she can open it with the latch. It's empty inside and quiet. It smells of warm straw and earth. Light filters through the slight gaps in the wood, and as her eyes adjust to the gloom, she spots a pile of blankets at the far side. She moves towards them and squeezes in behind them, pulling the top blanket over her head. They'll not find her in here for a long time. By the time they do, Harriet's party will be over.

Ava is pleased with her plan. Harriet should never have told everyone her secret. She thinks about what she'll say when she's found. Maybe she'll just cry and say Harriet was so horrible to her she ran away.

A sound makes her stiffen. There were no animals in the stable when she came in. She strains to listen. It's the door latch. It clicks as it opens. The door creaks open and then shuts again. She waits. There's nothing. Then suddenly a voice calls softly.

'Hello, little girl.'

She doesn't reply. The voice is scary.

'I know you're in here. I saw you come in. You look very pretty in that yellow party dress.'

She doesn't dare move. There's something about the voice that frightens her.

'Where are you hiding?'

She keeps stock-still. This isn't what she expected to happen.

'You shouldn't hide in dark places like this. Nasty things might happen to you.'

She suddenly wishes she wasn't alone in here with this person. Mummy warned her about strangers.

'Do you want me to look for you?'

She presses her lips together to stop from crying out.

'I'm going to find you.'

It falls silent in the stable. Ava's knees begin to tremble. She's made a big mistake. She could jump up and race for the door and get away from this person with the silky-soft, frightening voice. She counts to ten and then throws off the blanket, jumps up and runs straight into a solid shape. An arm grabs the top of hers and holds it tight; too tight. She whimpers.

'I'm not going to hurt you,' says her captor. 'Aren't you pretty? Far too pretty to be hiding all alone in a barn.'

He strokes her hair, scaring her further. She struggles to free her arm. It's released but two heavy hands are placed either side of her face.

'I'm not going to hurt you. I just want to be your friend.'

'I don't want… to be… your friend,' she gasps and kicks out.

'Don't say that.' The heavy hands slide around her neck and suddenly she can't breathe. She sees flashes of stars like the jewels in the jewellery-making set and imagines she can hear the laughter of children playing party games. She remembers her mother in the car, blowing her a kiss she pretended to ignore, and then she sees no more.

CHAPTER THIRTY-ONE

SATURDAY, 29 APRIL – AFTERNOON

'Guy Noble. What do we know about him?' Natalie spoke on the hands-free set so both she and Murray could listen in.

'Nothing more than we had when we were looking earlier,' said Ian. 'No convictions. He shares some rented accommodation with Helena Dickinson, who works at the leisure centre.'

'We spoke to her. She runs the netball club,' Natalie said. 'Go on.'

'Guy's parents live locally at Shelley's Drive. There's a brother, Sam, who currently lives in Brisbane. Guy graduated from Samford College with a degree in horticulture. Worked for Uptown Craft Centre until 2015. Nothing else. Not so much as a parking ticket.'

'What does he drive?'

'Nissan pickup truck in silver.'

'So that wasn't the vehicle our witness claims to have seen outside the dance school, then. What about his girlfriend? Does she have a car?'

'Nothing registered in her name.'

'Okay. We're going to interview him now. How's Lucy getting on?'

'No-go at the warehouse.'

Natalie rolled her eyes. She'd really been pinning her hopes on somebody at the warehouse remembering who'd collected the parcel containing the yellow dresses.

'She's talking to the techies again. I'll ring if we find out anything.'

'Thanks. Should be back once we've spoken to Guy.'

Traffic was heavy as they drove through the town centre, the streets busy with families and groups of youngsters shopping. She thought about her own children at home and wondered what David was doing with them today. She was going to ring and ask, then changed her mind. Home and work didn't mix.

Guy answered the doorbell immediately in bare feet, dressed in tracksuit bottoms and a T-shirt, an almost empty bowl of cereal in his large hand.

'Sorry. Just got up. Had a late night.' He ambled into the kitchen and deposited the bowl by the sink. 'Tea?' he asked affably.

'It's not really a social call. We'd like to know why you were at the swimming pool last Saturday.'

Guy wiped his hands. 'To invite Terry to the pub.'

'Why didn't you ring or text him?'

'I was at the centre, waiting about for Helena to finish a class, and dropped in to see him.'

'Even though he was running the swimming club?'

'It's only a splash-about session, not training for the Olympics!' he scoffed. 'I was only there a few minutes.'

'What did you say to Rainey Kilburn?'

'Rainey? Why?'

'Answer the question, please.'

'I can't remember.'

'Try.'

'Some random aside about her brother. I'd seen him outside, skateboarding with his mates. He was showing off as usual and came a cropper. Landed right on his arse. I told her he was skateboarding like a girl.'

'You know her and Tyler well enough to make such a comment?'

'They live in the same street I used to live in. I've known them pretty much all their lives. They'd often be hanging about or playing football. I'd always say hi to them and even join in the odd game. Nice kids. My parents sold up a few years ago and we all moved to the house at Shelley's Drive. I moved out when Helena came up here.'

'When was the last time you saw Rainey?'

'Where are you going with this?'

'I'm afraid Rainey was killed on Thursday afternoon.'

His jaw dropped. He spluttered a response. 'No. How?'

'I can't tell you that, but I am keen to know when exactly you last saw her.'

'Last Saturday. At the pool. I haven't seen her since. Oh crap. Her folks are going to be so cut up.' He shook his head in disbelief.

'Where were you Thursday afternoon?'

'Work. I was cleaning out cages until about four. I left after that. Came home. Got showered, had a bite to eat, watched some telly and went out with Terry.'

'Were you anywhere near the dance academy or Monks Walk on Thursday?'

His head moved from side to side several times. 'I came straight home from work.'

'In your truck?'

'Yes.'

'Okay, I think that'll be everything for the moment,' said Natalie.

'Was Rainey murdered? Audrey was. Was Rainey?'

Natalie didn't answer but instead thanked him for his time and strode back outside where she lifted her head to the sky and gritted her teeth. 'We can't prove he was anywhere near Rainey on Thursday afternoon,' she said. 'If he drove back from work when he said he did, he couldn't have gone to either the school or Monks Walk. Shit!'

'We can run checks on ANPR and see if his number plate was picked up, which'll confirm his story and route,' said Murray.

'Do it but I think he's telling the truth. I don't think it's him.' She released a lengthy groan before getting back into the car. 'Who is it? And who the fuck are they going after next?'

'A small black car outside the dance school at about three thirty or three forty. Any chance you picked up such a vehicle on ANPR or CCTV?' Natalie paced the office floor, aware time was racing by and they were no closer to uncovering the murderer.

'No, guv.' Ian was looking as downbeat as Natalie felt.

Natalie ceased her pacing. 'I wonder if our possible witness really did see Rainey or just thought they did. We have the forensic evidence that puts Rainey at Monks Walk. There were fibres in the shrubbery where she entered. I think they were mistaken.'

'What if she didn't come into Monks Walk via the bushes but was trying to get out?' Ian suggested. 'How about if someone dropped her off at the dance school, or even the entrance to Monks Walk, and she tried to flee from them?'

Murray spoke up. 'No. We'd have spotted her on the library CCTV. That makes no sense either.'

'No, it might make sense,' Ian reasoned. 'Especially if she got picked up by the dance school and dropped off near Monks Walk and avoided the camera.'

'Nah. That'd mean two people were involved: one who collected her from school and let her out at the dance school, and another who picked her up there and set her down a little way along the road,' said Lucy.

Ian rested the back of his head against the top of his chair, staring at the strip lights above him. 'Yeah. You're right. The witness is mistaken. Rainey wasn't there and didn't get into a car. We'd have some way of tracking her if she'd been anywhere on St Chad's Road.'

Natalie spoke. 'I have to agree. It makes far more sense if Rainey walked home using the shortcut that Lucy discovered, and ended up coming into the back of Monks Walk via the gap in the bushes. The witness was mistaken.'

'It wastes time when we have to check out these false leads,' said Ian.

'We still have to follow them up. Just in case,' Natalie replied.

Exhaustion was setting in. It was visible on the strained faces in front of her. 'I'm calling a break. Go grab a sandwich, pint, a walk, whatever you want. We'll meet up again in an hour. We need some time out.' She scraped back her chair and stood up.

Murray stretched and yawned. 'You staying in?' he asked as he flung his jacket over one shoulder.

'No. I'll nip out in a minute.' Natalie waited until the office was empty and then dialled David. It went to answerphone. She texted Leigh, asking what she was up to, and sent another message to Josh. There was no instant reply from either of them. She shoved the mobile in her bag and headed off outside.

The green near Samford Police Headquarters was mostly used as a cut-through to a housing estate but on the more pleasant days was a spot frequented by employees of the many businesses scattered on the enormous business park surrounding it. One of the companies, a construction firm, had dug out a decent-sized reservoir and erected a sculpture in the middle of it, along with a walkway around it. Natalie chose to follow the circular path and give her mind a chance to digest the facts. The problem was she didn't have enough information to act upon. Ava's body had been uncovered and Audrey and Rainey were now both dead, strangled like Ava, and all of them wearing yellow dresses. Without a doubt the cases were connected but who was behind them?

Her phone vibrated in her pocket and she lifted it to her ear, waiting to hear the excited jabbering of her daughter, the most likely of the three to call her, but it wasn't Leigh. The voice was urgent and fearful. It was Howard Franks.

'Natalie. Sage has disappeared. She went to her friend Louise's house about an hour ago and hasn't come home.'

CHAPTER THIRTY-TWO

Howard's face said it all. It was contorted as if in great pain, the corners of his mouth pulled downwards. There was an edginess to his movements that had not been apparent during other meetings, a nervous tightening and untightening of his hands, and his eyes darted crazily from left to right as if to suddenly alight upon his daughter.

His house, a simple semi-detached, was the last at the end of a row of similar properties on Lavender Rise and bordered a lane that led away from Uptown. A bright red phone box opposite his home and a signpost stating the village of Garrington was seven miles from this spot were the last indicators of civilisation as the main tarmac road ebbed away into lesser B-road, flanked by tall hedgerows that created an impression of an ever-narrowing route that came to a full stop in the distance.

Natalie stood by the sitting room window that overlooked the road. It was a comfortable, homely room furnished in good taste and cluttered with knick-knacks and china ornaments only a woman could have purchased. She studied the photograph Howard now held out to her. It was of him, his wife and their two daughters, each mini copies of their mother with high brows, sparkling green eyes and soft, light-brown hair that tumbled in curls. The youngest, Kerry, was only about two in the picture. Howard had the widest smile Natalie had ever seen. One hand was placed on his wife's shoulder in an easy gesture that was not merely posing for the camera.

'She's wearing that necklace,' he said. The necklace was a silver locket bearing a delicate pattern and Sage's name engraved across it. 'It contains a photo of her mother. She only puts it on at weekends. She's in a pink, check shirt dress, a blue denim jacket and white, laceless trainers. This is a more recent photo of her.' He pulled out his phone and scrolled to a picture of her smiling softly. His face crumpled again. 'Oh God. The number of times I've been in your position, trying to locate a missing person, and now, the horror is mine.'

Natalie put a hand on his arm. 'Howard, we're on this. The team are already canvassing the street and we've officers searching the route she took with Louise. We've got people interviewing Louise and her family and all of Sage's friends. You did the right thing contacting us immediately. We haven't lost much time. Try not to stress too much. I know they sound like empty words but they're not. The more focused you are, the better the chance we have of locating her. Can you run through what happened again for me, please?'

'Louise Harbourn lives on the road behind this one, in Larkspur Close. She came by half an hour after we returned from swimming with her new puppy, Benji. She asked if Sage could go back to her house to play with the dog. I agreed and told Sage not to be too long because we had to go and pick up Kerry from my mother's. I watched them set off, then my mother rang me, so I went back inside to talk to her. Kerry, my youngest, wanted to stay with her grandma for an extra couple of hours so she could watch a Disney film. I checked my watch. It was two thirty on the dot. I said it was fine and I'd pick Kerry up at five to give them plenty of time.'

He raked his fingers through his hair and then rubbed his scalp before continuing. 'I put the dishwasher on and went upstairs to sort out the girls' rooms. They're supposed to keep them tidy but they only do half a job. I was about twenty minutes in Sage's room, picking up clothes and toys, and when I looked at my watch I was surprised to find it was already gone three.'

He drew a lengthy breath. 'I became a little agitated. It wasn't like Sage to lose track of time. She knew we had to collect Kerry and had no idea her sister was staying for longer than planned, so she ought to have returned. I went around to fetch her. Louise told me Sage had left twenty minutes earlier to come home. It's two minutes away. That's all. Two minutes. There's a grassy path that passes to the left side of our house next to the brook, and from there you can reach Larkspur Close. I returned, thinking maybe she'd come back the longer route along the road, but she wasn't here, and then… then I knew something terrible had happened and I rang you.'

Natalie kept a steady gaze on him. He was about to fall apart and she needed him to keep clear-headed. His recollections were vital. 'Did you hear any traffic pass by when you were inside?'

'After I finished talking to my mother, I turned on the radio,' he said. 'It was quite loud.'

'You didn't glimpse anything or anyone from the window?'

'No.'

'This is going to sound awful but Sage wouldn't have deliberately run off, would she?'

A pitiful sound escaped his lips. 'No. We are sound. She and I are best buddies. More so since her mum passed away.'

'She hasn't been upset recently?'

'No. You saw her at the pool. She's quite cheerful at the moment.'

'Have you been threatened by anyone either recently or in the past? Has anyone ever suggested they'd harm you or your family?'

He shook his head and a solitary tear rolled down his face.

'We're going to do everything, and I mean *everything*, to get her back, okay?'

His Adam's apple bobbed up and down several times before he could speak again. 'Do you think it's because of Ava Sawyer? I was the investigating officer and I didn't find her. Audrey and Rainey, who were at the birthday, have died and now Sage has been taken.'

'We can't leap to conclusions, Howard. You know that, although we'll obviously be mindful of it. We'll explore every angle and set up taps on your phone in case anyone tries to contact you and demand a ransom. I'm going to leave you with the liaison officer and will come back as soon as I can.'

It was hard to tear away from the man who was clearly in shock and despair.

'I want to help search for her.'

'You can't. You must stay here in case this is a kidnapping. Or in case she returns.'

Her words had the desired effect and he sat down. 'Okay.'

The street outside was busy with officers and vehicles. The dog unit van had manoeuvred into a space in front of her car and was parked on the grassy verge opposite the houses. Howard had already pulled out some of Sage's clothes for the hounds to pick up a scent. The neighbourhood was awash with activity. Lucy was talking to the next-door neighbour. She came away from the door and, catching sight of Natalie, shook her head. Natalie refused to accept the person who'd taken Sage had not been seen. He wasn't the invisible man and the police had arrived on the scene very quickly. Ian was already examining ANPR points in the area. If the kidnapper's vehicle was on any of them, they'd find him.

Murray approached her. 'Not looking hopeful.'

'It's a quiet road. It'd be most unusual if one of the residents didn't spot something, and if nobody saw any unusual activity, then I'm guessing whoever took Sage didn't drive down Lavender Rise and then follow the lane,' she said, turning to check the route. The main road curved to the right and disappeared from view. She looked towards the lane. 'They might have come from the direction of Garrington, turned around and headed back that way.'

'And made a three-point turn in the road?'

Natalie chewed on a thumbnail. 'No. You're right. That's quite risky and might have drawn attention to their vehicle. They're more likely to have driven into Larkspur Close, which runs parallel with this road, and parked up there, then taken the cut-through by the brook and waited around Howard's house. It's unlikely this was a spur-of-the-moment act. The perpetrator wasn't just "passing by", saw Sage and decided to snatch her. They planned this. Either they parked in the close or hid a vehicle somewhere, up an empty driveway, maybe?'

'What about the cut-through? Could they have hidden along there?'

Natalie and Murray walked to the trodden-down pathway. It was a narrow grass strip, large enough for one person to walk along, that ran alongside a small stream. Natalie strode ahead. To her left were tall fence panels painted dark green that enclosed Howard's garden and prevented anyone from peering in. To the right of the path and down a slight slope, the crystal-clear water babbled over smooth pebbles. They continued past Howard's garden. Where his fence panels ended, new, brown ones began. The house behind his was equally shielded from view. A few more paces and the path opened into the turning circle at the bottom of a cul-de-sac, with houses to the left and right. Louise's house was on the bend to the right. Natalie observed the two officers walking up pathways, gathering information from residents.

'It's possible to park up here,' she said. 'Look at the number of cars strewn about. I bet the kidnapper could have left their vehicle anywhere along this road and driven away undetected. What I don't get is how they knew Sage had gone out.'

'They might have been hanging around here,' said Murray.

'No. Too risky. And if they'd been lurking on that path between Lavender Rise and this road, they'd have been at risk of being spotted.'

She turned around and began pacing back to Howard's house, checking left and right. There was nowhere for anyone to hide. When they reached the main road once more, she faced Murray and, cocking her head to one side, asked, 'How could the perp know Sage was outside and alone? Were they watching the house?' Natalie turned a full circle slowly. 'What about that phone box?'

'What about it? It's one of those old-fashioned ones. I'm surprised there are still boxes like that around,' Murray said.

'They were put out of commission a few years ago and the phones removed.' She tapped her chin thoughtfully. 'When you get used to seeing something every day, it blends into its surroundings. What if somebody was actually standing inside the cubicle, casing Howard's house? Howard might not have noticed anyone, especially if the person inside didn't move. The abductor might have waited there before, hoping for such an opportunity. They might even have dragged Sage into the box for a while until he could escape with her, maybe after Howard went running off in search of her. Where's Mike?'

'He's not here.'

'Anyone from Forensics?'

'On their way.'

'When they arrive, ask them to check out that phone box and also get background checks on all these neighbours and those in Larkspur Close. Someone knew Sage went off with Louise, and that person could only have known if they'd seen her go.'

She returned to the house and called out, 'Howard. Does anyone use this old phone box?'

He appeared immediately. 'No. It's empty. The locals wanted the structure left. Something to do with bygone British. There's a campaign to have a defibrillator installed inside it so it'll be more useful. I know what you're thinking. I opened the door and looked inside just in case Sage was hiding there or worse. Nothing there.'

'I'm thinking the person who took your daughter might have been spying on you. I'm going to get Forensics to examine it.'

'Thank you. The thought hadn't crossed my mind. I was so concerned about Sage. Who'd be watching me?'

'I don't know but it's a possibility we can't ignore.'

The dog handlers were approaching the house and she made way for them.

'Speak to you later,' she added as she hastened away. Time was of the essence.

CHAPTER THIRTY-THREE

Superintendent Aileen Melody stood at the back of her office, arms folded, head resting against the wall. Natalie stood opposite her. Following the news about Sage, Aileen had come into work and wanted an immediate update. Natalie had left her team, who were frantically collecting information two floors below, to get Aileen up to speed.

'This has to be connected to the disappearance of Ava Sawyer. What about her family? Have you spoken to all of her relatives?'

Natalie had done little else since she'd returned to the office. She and Ian had contacted everyone related to the girl, while Murray had run checks on every household member in Larkspur Close and Lavender Rise.

'Beatrice has been staying with her mother in Sheffield since Thursday. She's not left the house other than to go to town accompanied by her mother. Beatrice's father remarried several years ago and lives on the Isle of Wight. He hasn't been back to the mainland in the past year. Carl Sawyer has an alibi for the days the girls were killed and also for today. He was at a football match with a friend until an hour ago. He doesn't have any close family connections. His older brother, Pete, works on an oil platform in the Hebrides and hasn't visited Carl in months. Carl's parents are both deceased and he isn't close to his only other living relatives – two uncles who live in the south of the country. That doesn't really leave us with many relatives who might be out for revenge.'

Aileen gave her a disapproving look at odds with her gentle Irish lilt. 'I know you're in charge but I can't fathom out who else could be responsible. The killer went after two girls who attended Harriet's party and has now taken Howard's daughter. It's no coincidence. Howard was in charge of the investigation. I'm presuming the perpetrator snatched Sage because he couldn't get his hands on any of the remaining girls who attended the party in 2015. Whichever way we look at it, it comes back to that event in 2015.'

'I know it appears that way but I can't shake off the feeling there's something else we've missed or haven't yet established. I'm following up every lead and every piece of information. You have to trust me on this.'

Aileen pushed herself away from the wall with a sigh. 'I don't need to remind you this is a high-profile case, and if you aren't able to deliver results very soon, I'll have to find somebody else to handle it. Have it your way for now but we need results and we must find Sage Franks – alive.'

'I know. I want that more than anything. We've got search parties, dogs and a helicopter out. The missing persons team is handling that side of it. We're doing what we can to identify and track down the perpetrator.'

Aileen pressed her elegant fingers against her forehead. 'And you have no clear idea of who it might be? No suspects? Nothing?'

'It's not proving easy.' Natalie bit back what she really wanted to say, that she needed to end this pointless conversation and return to the action downstairs. Aileen knew witnesses and suspects couldn't be conjured up from thin air and it took time to establish alibis. If she'd come in on her day off, it was because she was under pressure from her superiors to resolve the case. Nothing put fear into the general public more than a child killer on the loose. Aileen must have picked up on her tone and dismissed her with a sigh.

'Look, I'm keeping you from the investigation. You'd better get back to your team.'

Natalie hastened back to her own office. Ian was on the phone and Murray at his laptop. Lucy beckoned her over.

'Etsy gift card. It had a sixteen-digit code on it. The techies have come up with a name. Grace Coots. She lives in Moreton, about ten miles out of Uptown.'

'You got hold of her?'

'Her husband answered the phone. Grace was at the hair-dresser's. Due back in the next half an hour.'

'What do we know about her?'

'Works as a childminder at the Humpty Dumpty nursery for babies and infants under school age.'

'Okay. We'll head over there now.'

Grace Coots was dragging out some shopping bags from the rear of an aged Mercedes estate car when Lucy and Natalie pulled up outside her house. An enthusiastic red setter bounded over to greet them, tail wagging, and then raced off into the house.

The woman looked up at them. 'You the police? My husband said you'd rung while I was out.'

They produced identification and asked if they could conduct the conversation inside.

'Sure. What's it all about?' asked Grace, marching towards the house. The dog reappeared and rushed about, getting under her feet. 'Out of the way, Rufus. Tony! Will you take the dog? The police are here.'

A deep voice called for the animal, and Grace beckoned them into the kitchen where she deposited her bags then shut the door.

'How can I help?'

'It's regarding an Etsy gift card you used.'

Her face screwed up in confusion. 'Etsy card?'

'We understand you purchased some goods online using a gift card.'

Her head turned to one side and the other then her eyebrows rose. 'I did receive a gift card but that was ages ago. I lost it soon after I got it.'

Lucy gave a tight smile. 'I'm afraid we'd need more information than that. A gift card owned by you was used to purchase some clothes from America.'

'You've lost me. I really don't understand what you're getting at. I used the card once to buy some stationery, just after I got it. I put it back in my purse with my credit card, and when I went to use it next, it had gone. It probably dropped out when I was shopping. I could easily have pulled it out with my credit card, I suppose, and it must have been picked up by somebody who used it. What's the big deal?' Her voice began to tail away as she spotted the serious look on Lucy's face. She opened the door and shouted, 'Tony. Here a sec.'

She hung by the door until her husband arrived, a large man in a rugby top and jeans that were fastened tightly under his swollen stomach.

'You remember that gift card I got a couple of Christmases ago?'

'What gift card?'

'The one my stepfather gave me. You must remember it. You said at the time it was a weird present to give me. I had to explain what Etsy was.'

'Oh yeah. I remember now. You lost it soon afterwards. We turned the house upside down looking for it.'

'Thank you.' She turned back to Lucy, a look of triumph on her face. 'See. I lost it.'

'As much as we'd like to believe you both, the card is relevant to a murder enquiry.'

'Christ!' Grace's eyes opened wide. 'I don't know what happened to it. Really, I don't!'

'Mr Coots, do you have any idea?'

His mouth had fallen open, making him appear gormless. 'No idea.'

'Because of the serious nature of our investigation, we'll have to interview you both more formally at the station.'

'I haven't got the bloody card. It slipped out of my purse.' Grace's voice rose a couple of octaves. 'Tell them, Tony.'

'Calm down, Mrs Coots. I'm sure we can work out what happened. You say you received the card as a Christmas present?'

'From my stepfather. He was stumped what to buy me and happened to remember I'd told him and my mum I was thinking of setting up my own Etsy online business at the time, so he got me a gift card to buy craft supplies. It was for two hundred quid and I only used ten pounds of it. I was pissed off I lost it at the time. Two hundred quid's a huge amount of money. I looked all over the house for it and even went into a couple of shops and the big supermarket in Uptown where I'd been, on the off chance it had been handed in, but of course, it hadn't.'

'And could we take your stepfather's details please?'

'Why? I don't see him at all these days. He gave it to me the first Christmas after my mum died and we've drifted apart since then. I bet he doesn't even remember giving it to me. He's quite elderly.'

'Just give us the details, please,' said Lucy, pencil in her hand.

'Ned Coleman.'

Natalie cocked her head to one side. 'Ned Coleman's your stepfather?'

'He was married to my mum for ten years. She died early 2015.'

'Do you have any brothers or sisters?'

'Yeah. Roselyn. She lives in Uptown.'

'What's her surname?'

'Momford. She kept her married name although she's divorced.'

'And you have a nephew?' Natalie asked.

'Freddie. That's Roselyn's boy. Why?'

'Just ensuring we have the correct facts,' Lucy explained, making notes as she spoke.

'Would you mind if we examined your computer, if you have one, and any smartphone you own?'

'I would mind. Are you saying I'm a liar?' Colour rushed to Grace's cheeks.

'We are not. What we'd like to prove is your innocence and confirm you have not been involved in a serious crime.'

'Put like that it's a good idea to let them look, love,' said Mr Coots. 'It's not like we've got anything to hide, is it?'

Grace glowered at Natalie a moment then her shoulders fell forward. 'No, I suppose not. Go ahead. Tony, will you get it?'

Her husband disappeared with the dog trotting behind him.

'Have you used any Etsy sites recently?'

'I did a few months ago. I bought some paper and decorations to make some birthday cards and a couple of patterns for Easter rabbits.'

'You ever bought anything else?'

'Only craft materials.'

'Not clothes?'

'No. I only buy clothes from the high street. I don't trust the sizing online. I once got a jumper and it was way too tight for me. Had to send it back and it was a nuisance having to queue to post it back and then wait for a refund.'

'You ever see any dresses like this?'

Natalie handed over a picture of the yellow dresses.

'Can't say I have, but we don't have any children ourselves, so I wouldn't be looking for anything like this.'

Tony reappeared with an iPad and a mobile. 'That's all we have. I've got a pay-as-you-go phone but it's one of the old ones. No Internet.' He held it up to show Natalie.

'That's fine, thanks. We'll return these as quickly as possible.'

*

Natalie stared out of the car window. It had been one of the brightest days so far this year but not one she had enjoyed. There was still no sign of Sage. Her stomach was twisted into tight knots.

'I don't know what to make of this investigation,' she said. 'There are clues but they don't make sense to me.'

'Run them past me. See if it helps.'

Natalie turned towards Lucy. 'Okay, Ned gave one of his stepchildren, Grace, an Etsy card for Christmas in 2015. Grace lost the card and a killer found it. Freddie's Ned's step-grandson and Freddie was at Harriet's birthday when Ava disappeared.' She paused as she reflected on her own words.

'Go on. That sounds like it's leading somewhere.'

'Ava was wearing a yellow dress. The killer bought five identical yellow dresses with the Etsy card. That's as far as I can get. It's like I have the pieces of a puzzle but none of them slot exactly into their right places.'

'How about if Grace and Tony lied. What if Grace didn't lose the card and instead bought the dresses?' Lucy offered.

'But why? It makes no sense for her to.'

'That's true. She had no reason to kill Audrey or Rainey. I see what you mean. It's a conundrum and, meanwhile, we're no closer to our killer. I keep thinking we're making progress and then we're thrown off scent again. And all the while I keep thinking of Howard and Sage.'

'I know how you feel. I'm really concerned about Sage now.'

'What if the killer's taken her?' Lucy asked.

Natalie had been considering that very possibility, yet if the same person who'd killed Audrey and Rainey had also abducted Sage, they'd changed their modus operandi. She thought carefully before she spoke. 'Audrey and Rainey weren't kidnapped. They were surprised, killed and their bodies left behind at two different locations. We haven't found Sage's body near her house where she might have been ambushed. The teams haven't found any sign of her. So, unless the killer has changed their MO we might be dealing with two different people.'

'I hear what you're saying but is that what you really believe? Do you think we're dealing with two different perps?'

'No. My gut tells me we're looking for one individual and that person has plans for Sage. We must find her before they can be carried out. We'll talk to Ned then get the iPad back to the lab. The sooner we get to work on it, the sooner we can eliminate Grace and Tony from this investigation.'

'But then what?'

Natalie turned her head to face her young colleague. 'Honestly? I haven't a clue. Keep bashing away at all the people we've suspected. We can't trust anything any of them say. Every alibi has to be watertight.'

'If it is to do with Ava, who else could we look for? We've tried everyone who knew her.'

'Look harder. That's all we can do.'

'Can I be honest?' Lucy asked.

'Sure.'

'I've never been on a case that has filled me with such horror. I'm frightened this bastard is going to keep taking children from under our noses and get away with it. I'm scared for all those little girls who were at the party and even more scared this is not to do with the birthday and the killer has only just begun.'

Natalie had had the same thoughts. They'd burrowed into her mind and were causing her the same anxieties. 'We're not far off, Lucy. We've been methodical. They won't get away with it.'

'I wish I had your positivity,' said Lucy. 'I'm dreading the thought of failure.'

'We won't fail,' said Natalie. 'We can't afford to.' She lifted her head higher and hoped with every fibre of her being she was right.

CHAPTER THIRTY-FOUR

SATURDAY, 29 APRIL – EVENING

'Hello again,' said Ned, opening his door wider. 'We spoke at the swimming pool. DI Ward, isn't it?'

'That's correct, sir. And this is Sergeant Lucy Carmichael.'

'Come in, ladies.'

His checked slippers swished against the carpet as he shuffled forwards and opened the door to a sitting room. 'Come in,' he repeated.

The room was small but comfortable with two chairs in front of a television, each electronically operated to allow the occupant to lie back if necessary. An old black dog was curled up in a basket at the foot of one of the chairs. It opened its eyes at the presence of intruders but didn't stir. Ned pulled up a dining room chair from under a round table covered by a floral tablecloth and sat on it.

'It's about a gift card you gave your stepdaughter Grace.'

'I haven't seen Grace for about eighteen months or so. Not much at all since her mother passed away.'

'You saw her Christmas 2015.'

His face took on a faraway look. 'That was my first Christmas without Lorna. So hard. I missed her terribly. Still do.'

'You spent Christmas with Grace.'

'Did I?' His brow furrowed. 'No. Only Christmas lunch. She had me, Roselyn and the lad over. We opened some presents under their tree. I didn't get a tree for here. It didn't seem right. Lorna loved Christmas. I was always the stick in the mud, you see? She'd decorate the whole house and have everyone over on Christmas evening for eggnog and to sing carols. I'm not much of a Christmas person. Sorry, where was I? I went over for lunch and came back mid-afternoon.'

'You gave Grace an Etsy gift card.'

His brows lowered further. 'That's right. I didn't know what to buy her. Lorna usually dealt with all that sort of thing. She was great at knowing exactly what people would like. I remember wondering what on earth to get them all and then I recalled a conversation we'd had one afternoon when Grace told us about a great website where she could buy all sorts of craft goods. I asked Roselyn about it. I'm hopeless with this modern technology, and she helped me buy the gift card. I bought Grace's husband, Tony, a card to use on Amazon. It seemed the easiest option. Although in hindsight, they probably didn't appreciate the gifts because they haven't invited me back again for Christmas lunch.' The disappointed look on his face touched Natalie. He was a lonely gentleman. The room harboured memories of bygone times, stuffed full with books and memorabilia undoubtedly collected during his time with Lorna: glass ornaments and assorted pottery vases; pictures in a variety of frames, mostly of Freddie, from a baby to more recent times; a couple of larger photographs of Ned and a striking redhead in her fifties.

'And you didn't hear any more about the Etsy card after you gave it to Grace?'

'She thanked me of course but I have no idea what she bought with it. As I said, I've not seen much of her since that Christmas. I understand why. She and Roselyn didn't really know me very well. In Grace's eyes, I was some sort of usurper who'd replaced her own father in her mother's affections and she wasn't very keen about that. She voiced her opinion on a few occasions. I hoped she'd take to me in time, but she didn't really. She was a grown-up with her own husband when Lorna and I tied the knot. It's not as if she was a youngster who'd grown up with me as a stepfather, so it came as no surprise she didn't want to include me in her own life. Roselyn was more accepting. She'd been through a divorce and knows what it's like to live alone. She lets me see Freddie even though he isn't my flesh and blood. She understands that to me, he is. I don't have any other family. Lorna was my one and only love.'

'Did you purchase an Etsy card for Roselyn?'

'No. She isn't into buying goods from online shops any more than I am. I got her a large bottle of perfume. She wears the same perfume as Lorna used to wear – Chanel No. 5. Has that helped you at all?' He shook himself free of the memories and looked at Natalie.

'You've been most helpful.' Natalie smiled at the man, who stood up and replaced the chair under the table that was probably no longer used for eating meals. His dog shifted in his basket and dozed back off to sleep.

'If you want to ask me anything else, you'd be very welcome,' he said. 'I don't get too many visitors.'

'I felt sorry for him,' said Lucy. 'He looked so… lost.'

'I got that impression too.'

'I suppose we could ask Roselyn about the card but it seems we're barking up the wrong tree. Ned gave it to Grace, who lost it. All it means is somebody who lives in or around Uptown might have found it and used it.'

'Possibly but why wait until now to use it? The card was lost sometime late 2015, early 2016. The person who found it hung onto it until a few months ago. When were the dresses ordered?'

'January this year.'

'They had the card a year before using it. Doesn't that strike you as peculiar?'

'Sort of.'

'Let's get the iPad back to the lab and run checks on the family. There might be some skeletons in their closets. I also want to find out if we've anything on Sage. It's been almost six hours since she went off with her friend Louise.'

Natalie threw the office door wide open and marched inside.

'Please tell me you've found out something useful. We've got nothing on the sodding Etsy card other than it was lost and probably found in Uptown.'

Ian raised a forefinger to indicate he was onto something. With his mobile tucked under his chin and head tilted to hold it in place, he was talking as he typed.

Murray spoke up. 'Two things: using ANPR cameras, the tech team confirmed Guy's whereabouts the day of Rainey's disappearance. His alibi checks out and he was nowhere near Monks Walk. And second, Mike turned up after you left. A pink cardigan matching the one Audrey was wearing was found in a litter bin a couple of streets away from the park. There were two one-pound coins in one of the pockets. It's in the lab being checked for DNA. Mike's dusting the phone box for prints. There were quite a few, left by people over time; however, he believes somebody was in there recently. There are signs of disturbed dust, especially to the rear of the box, and indicators somebody was leaning against the glass. He's trying to lift any prints that might be on those panes and any footprints.'

'Our child snatcher could well have been watching Howard's house as we suspected.'

'Mike and I tested out that theory. He waited in the box while I stood outside on Howard's path. Dressed in dark clothing and making little movement he could easily have remained undetected in the phone box.'

'What about the dog unit? They find a scent?'

'They did and as expected they followed it along the grass to Louise's house, but lost it soon after, which seems to indicate she disappeared around that area.'

Ian ended his call. 'A neighbour thinks they saw a dark-blue Toyota Yaris parked outside number 12 Larkspur Close. They didn't think anything of it and assumed it was somebody visiting there because he's seen it parked up on a few occasions, but it's come to light that the occupants of number 12 are away for the weekend.'

'No chance they got a registration for it, did they?'

'Nah. At least he recognised the make and model. It's a start. What's really of interest is that number 12 is the first house on the right as you come out of that path linking to Lavender Rise.' He tapped his pencil against his front teeth and rocked on his seat. 'Thinking what I'm thinking?'

'The assailant was in their car, watched Sage go to Louise's house and then followed her down the path when she came out?' Murray said.

'What if they parked their car, took the grassed path and staked out Howard's house from the phone box? They watched Sage leave with Louise, and when the girls took the path to Louise's house they followed them and waited in their car for Sage to come back out,' said Natalie, who then shook her head. 'Too messy. They'd risk being spotted. How about instead of waiting in the car where they stood a chance of a neighbour seeing them, they lurked on the path, waiting for Sage to emerge? They must have known she'd take that route back home and might have even heard Howard telling her they were going to collect Kerry, so they knew they wouldn't have long to wait. Yes, that's plausible,' she said, rubbing her hands together in thought. 'Search all the cameras in the area for a dark-blue Yaris. Any of our earlier suspects own one?'

Ian spun back round on his seat and started typing again. Murray moved across to the fixed computer to examine footage.

Lucy returned with a scowl on her face. 'They're overwhelmed with work. I had to plead to get them to check the iPad.'

'They doing it?'

'Yes. I'm good at pleading,' she said straight-faced. 'What's going on here?'

'A dark-blue Yaris was parked outside number 12 Larkspur Close,' said Ian, eyes trained on the screen. 'It might belong to whoever snatched Sage.'

'Good. A lead at last.' Lucy plonked down on her seat and began reading through a file. Natalie looked across. It was going to be a long night. She ought to ring David.

'Anyone want anything in particular to eat?' she asked. 'I'm going to ring an order through to the Chinese takeaway on Salt Street. I'll just get a mixture if that's okay with everyone.' She received appreciative noises and nods and slipped outside to order the food and speak to David, but her first call was to neither.

'Hi. Everything okay?'

'Complete fucking chaos,' said Mike. 'Teams out here, there and everywhere at the moment. However, we're pretty certain the assailant was hanging out in the phone box near Howard's house. We uncovered similar sole patterns that indicate they'd been there several times. Your theory appears to be spot on. They were spying on Howard and his daughters.'

'Okay. That's something,' she said, slowly. 'They must have come from the phone box and met her on the path then bundled her into their car. Shit, they could have driven her anywhere.'

'They might be local to Uptown.'

'I'm going around in sodding circles here. I feel they're near and yet I have no idea where they're hiding!' She stomped around the car park as she spoke.

Mike picked up on her tone. 'You okay?'

'It's so fucking difficult. A little girl's been snatched and I know in my gut the killer's got her. I'm scared. I'm scared for her and

I'm terrified we won't find her in time. I don't think I could take it if we're too late.'

There was a pause before Mike answered. 'Natalie, let it go. If you get wound up, you'll make rash decisions. You know what went wrong with the Olivia Chester case. You're in control here. You've got the best people you could have on this investigation, and whatever happens, you will have made the right decisions. That's all you can do. Like me, you work with what you've been given. Don't turn your attention to what might happen. It hasn't yet.'

His words had the desired effect. Once again, he'd known how to handle her and what to say. The burning in her stomach subsided for a moment.

'Thanks, Mike. I needed to hear that.'

'Any time. That's what friends are for.'

She resisted the urge to say more and hung up. She had to let David know she wouldn't be home. She decided to text him instead to avoid an argument and then rang for a takeaway. They'd all work better if they had some food. They had leads. They knew about the car and that the kidnapper had been watching Howard's place. It was certainly looking increasingly like this was connected to the disappearance of Ava Sawyer so she'd go back to the beginning. She told herself they *would* find Sage, and she marched back inside more determined than ever to locate the child.

CHAPTER THIRTY-FIVE

SATURDAY, 29 APRIL – AFTERNOON

SAGE FRANKS

He's watched this house on many an occasion. The little girl who lives here looks very like Sherry's friend, Gail Shore. From the first time he set eyes on her, he was reminded of delicate Gail with huge green eyes and ringlets of light-brown hair, who looked as thin as a twig and who'd laughed so cruelly at his attempts to befriend Sherry and her. Sage isn't like Gail. She is friendly and sweet and charming. He doesn't want her ever to change. She's perfect as she is.

The phone box is the perfect place to observe the house and its inhabitants. Howard doesn't draw his curtains until late in the day so sometimes he sees the girls playing or watching television in the front room. He likes to observe the trio going out together, dad holding onto both girls' hands, Sage looking up with adoration on her shining face. Howard is her world for now. Her love for him shines like a halo around an angel. The sight of her face creates a pocket of warmth in his chest swiftly followed by the familiar heaviness of sorrow. He's never experienced such affection. Howard is fortunate. However, times changed and children grew up and had families of their own, and

Howard would lose that complete and utter dependence and breadth of affection. He'll be doing Howard a huge favour. This way, he'll always remember Sage like this. There'll be no arguments, fallouts or suffering. Howard will always have his perfect little girl.

He knows Howard's routine. Saturdays he drops off the little one, Kerry, at his mother's house then takes Sage swimming. They go to town for a drink and a treat – a cake or sandwich – and then do the weekly shopping together. They return around 2 p.m. and then leave to collect Kerry again. Those moments when it's just Sage and her father are the best. It's magical to watch them.

He shifts slightly in the phone box. Dressed in black, he is invisible in his hidey-hole. He can stand still for hours if he has to. Practice makes perfect. He had plenty of practice standing in the corner of the school classroom.

Another girl, tugging a gambolling puppy that stumbles cheerfully into the car tyre, has appeared from the cut-through. He's seen her before. She lives close to where he left the car. He's been parking there every Saturday. Most people are off work and the close is filled with cars. One extra won't be noticed. In his experience, people aren't very observant, and he uses that knowledge to his advantage.

The girl rings the doorbell, pulling at the puppy, who is trying to eat a flower. She lifts him up. Sage comes to the door with her father. Her face lights up when she sees the dog. There's a conversation and Howard nods. He can hear Howard telling Sage not to be long. Howard walks part way down the path with the girls. His heart is thudding against his chest wall. If Howard comes any further and looks up, he'll have the phone box in sight. He'll be spotted for sure. He isn't sure what he'll say if that happens. He holds his breath and waits. The girls skip on ahead but Howard turns slowly and fumbles for a mobile in his trouser pocket and answers it. The distraction was meant to be. Howard ambles back towards his house and disappears from view.

From his position he watches the girls race towards the cut-through, squealing with excitement as the puppy chases alongside.

This is his chance. He follows them and stops at the car, extracting the large shopping bag on wheels he keeps in the boot. This is it. The moment he's been hoping for. It's perfect. He hastens back down the path and stops a third of the way down. Here he is completely out of sight. There are no windows overlooking this area. He can hear no other noise than the tinkling of the water running alongside. He takes a moment to enjoy the solitude and to prepare. This time he's ready. He played it wrong before. He tried to befriend the girls when he ought to have taken them by surprise.

He feels the cloth in his pocket. He's doused it with chloroform. The bag is unzipped and open. Sage is small for her age, and so slight she'll easily fit into the bag. He hums a rhyme; a distant memory of a lonely childhood.

It's not long before he sees her. He assumes the position and cranes his neck then looks in surprise as she approaches.

'Hi,' she says.

'Shh! Look. Baby ducklings. There are five of them. So sweet.'

She moves next to him and looks where he's pointing. Her face screws up. 'Where—'

He acts immediately. He clamps one hand containing the cloth over her face and holds her body tightly to his so she can't escape. She struggles but is no match. Within seconds she is limp and he bundles her into the shopping bag and wheels it to his car. He opens the boot and places the bag in. It weighs very little. There's no sound from the bag. He's managed it. Now he must get away before Howard comes looking for her.

He pulls away in his car slowly as to not draw attention to himself. He's the master at that. No one usually notices him. He ought to feel sorry for Howard, who will be anxious and upset, but he doesn't. He's given Howard the greatest gift imaginable – everlasting love.

CHAPTER THIRTY-SIX

SATURDAY, 29 APRIL – NIGHT

'Fuck all,' said Ian, lifting his hand from the mouse and falling backwards against the back of his chair. 'No sign of a dark-blue Yaris on any of the footage.' He rubbed his eyes and yawned.

'Then they must have taken a route where there are no safety cameras, no ANPR and no CCTV,' said Natalie. Her hair stuck up from running her hands through it repeatedly and her mascara was smudged, but she didn't care. She threw up the map of the area on the overhead projector. Lavender Rise and Larkspur Close were circled in red and the camera points all marked in green. 'To avoid the cameras altogether the perpetrator would have had to have taken these roads,' she said, drawing red lines down several streets. We need to work out the possible routes they might have taken and see if they lead us to a specific area in Uptown.'

The empty boxes that had contained the Chinese food were now stacked in a neat pile outside in the corridor. Ian stood up and stretched. 'I'm going for some air and a fag,' he said.

'You want to go home?' Natalie asked.

He shook his head. 'No chance.'

She knew how he felt. There was a sense of urgency and determination in the office. Mike had been right when he told her she had the right team for the job. It struck her she felt an affinity with these people that she'd not experienced in her last position. They may have their ups and downs but they worked so well together. Her musings were interrupted by Lucy, who entered holding the iPad and smartphone taken from Grace and Tony Coots. 'They're clean. Nothing to link them to the purchase of those dresses.'

Her face said far more than her words. It was clearly infuriating her that she could make no headway with the Etsy card. She settled back down to her laptop and, ignoring everyone, puzzled over some information she had on her screen.

Natalie was trying to work out the route the dark-blue Yaris might have taken. It was the only clue they had to Sage's where-abouts. She hadn't rung Howard. With no fresh information for him, there was no point in adding to his misery. He was at home with Tanya and another liaison officer who would alert the team should a ransom demand be made or, if by some miracle, Sage reappeared.

Naomi tapped lightly on the open door and entered. She brought with her the smell of lilies of the valley. Her eyes were bright and she showed no sign of fatigue as she stepped up to Natalie's desk, slid across a manila folder and waited for a reaction.

Natalie opened the file and read its contents. Naomi had identi-fied fibres found on Audrey's cardigan and matched them to those found under Rainey's fingernails.

'It's not just ordinary leather,' said Naomi. 'It's known as bridle leather, which refers to the way it's treated at a tannery. This particular type is harder wearing because both the flesh and the grain sides are treated with beeswax, fats and tallow, all of which is labour intensive and expensive. I suspect your killer used the same or similar piece of leather to strangle both girls.'

'The killer strangled them with a pricey belt,' Natalie said.

'A belt, strap, bridle or a dog lead,' said Naomi.

'It certainly gives us some food for thought,' said Natalie. 'Thanks for working so quickly on this.'

'I wasn't going home until I'd identified the fibres. I just hope it helps you find the little girl who's been taken.'

'Me too, Naomi. Me too.'

Naomi glided out, leaving Natalie poring over the findings. She wondered how easy it would be to buy bridle-leather goods and began a quick search for them.

'Natalie, we think we have an idea where the kidnapper was driving,' said Murray. The map was now a mess of colours from where he and Ian had been testing out routes. 'We took out all the roads where there are cameras and that left only two possible directions they might have taken before hitting a security camera. This all hinges on the fact he actually drove into Uptown and didn't stop and park up anywhere along the route.'

He threw up a new transparency with the roads removed. The two possible directions the kidnapper might have taken were obvious. Dodging CCTV cameras, the kidnapper could only have driven towards Uptown Primary School and beyond to St Chad's Road, or to Queen's Park. Natalie blinked at this new information, her eyes gritty with tiredness.

'Has he taken her to the park?' Her brain was working too slowly.

'We could head there,' Murray said.

'I can't shake off the feeling the killer has snatched Sage. We can't ignore the fact Howard was working the Ava Sawyer case and the other victims were at the birthday party when she disappeared. I know it's only assumption on my part, but I think we should consider it a real possibility.'

'Okay, we'll run with that. It makes sense and we don't have anything else to go on.'

Natalie continued to voice her thoughts. 'If I'm on the right track and he has taken her, then why would he go back to the same crime scene unless he's sending out a message? I don't think he retraces his steps. He's killed in two different places and kidnapped three girls from three different spots. I could be completely wrong.'

She pulled a face then made the decision. 'Go on, Murray. Take a unit and go to the park. I'm not sure he'll have taken her there but we can't ignore that possibility.'

Ian spun around to face her. 'I think I have something relevant. I was going through the list of allotment owners to see if anyone noticed Rainey walking past on Thursday afternoon, and I've received an email from the allotment committee with new information. Two plots, previously owned by gentlemen on my list, were allocated to new owners this month. One of them now belongs to Ned Coleman. If he'd been on the allotment, he might have spotted Rainey the day she died.'

'He'd have told us if he'd seen Rainey. He knows we're investigating the disappearances,' Natalie said.

Murray gave a slight shrug. 'It's still worth asking him about it. Just in case.'

She glanced at her watch. It was almost twelve. He'd probably be asleep. The thought of Sage trapped by a killer spurred her on to make the phone call. Ned answered on the tenth ring.

'Mr Coleman, it's DI Ward. I'm sorry to disturb you so late at night, but we need your assistance.'

'Go ahead. I wasn't asleep. I was reading. I don't sleep much these days.'

'You have taken on a plot at the allotments, haven't you?'

'That's correct. I've had an application in for quite some time but there haven't been any spaces. Two came up recently. I got one.'

'Were you tending it Thursday afternoon?'

'I went over first thing after lunch to set up some cloches and I was there about an hour. Why?'

'You didn't happen to notice Rainey Kilburn walking past while you were there?'

'I'm afraid not. I was working on my patch and then I left and caught the bus home. I like to get back for afternoon tea and my quiz shows. I enjoy those.'

'You don't drive any more?'

'I sold my car soon after Lorna passed away. I don't stray far from Uptown so it didn't seem worth hanging onto it. They're expensive to run, what with maintenance, MOTs, tax, insurance and, of course, the fuel. It's easier to get about using my bus pass.'

'What about transporting your gardening tools and plants and so on?'

'I usually get everything I need delivered to the plot. I have a shed there to store the essentials and there's invariably someone willing to help out a fellow gardener.'

'Was there anyone else on the allotments on Thursday afternoon?'

'A couple of chaps were leaving for lunch when I arrived but no one else turned up while I was working.'

'Thank you. Sorry again for ringing so late.'

'It's not a problem. Always happy to oblige.'

Natalie gnawed at a hangnail. Ned didn't own a car. He hadn't been on his allotment when Rainey had gone by. She almost felt sorry she'd disturbed the old gent so late at night.

'Natalie?' Lucy's voice was filled with a sudden eagerness. 'Ned's stepdaughter, Roselyn, owns a blue Yaris.'

'You're kidding.'

'Bought it in 2011. It's registered to her.'

'Grab your coat. We're going to pay her a visit.'

After several failed attempts to find Roselyn, Natalie decided to return to the station. She rang Ned once more and asked if he had any idea where his stepdaughter might be. The man sounded wearier this time but was polite with his response.

'I think Freddie is staying with his father tonight, so I expect she went out with friends. She's probably stayed over with them or hasn't got home yet. Most likely the former. I'm afraid I can't help you with who they are or where they live. I'm not privy to her personal life.'

Natalie apologised again for disturbing him. There was little more they could do and they needed some rest. The missing persons team was out searching for Sage, and until it was daylight, her own team couldn't get going again.

It was after 1 a.m. when she and Lucy got back to the office, and she dismissed everyone with instructions to be in by eight the following morning.

Before she turned out the lights, she took one last look at Sage's photograph, which they'd attached to the wall of victims. She had to find her alive yet she was powerless for the moment. She'd be up first thing and talk to Roselyn. For now, she had to hope Mike and the missing persons team were having more luck than her.

'Stay alive, Sage. We're going to find you.'

CHAPTER THIRTY-SEVEN

SUNDAY, 30 APRIL – MORNING

Natalie hammered on the front door. Eventually a figure, visible through the glass door, made its way down the stairs, wrapping a dressing gown tightly around herself.

Roselyn opened the door a mere crack, revealing an eye, a nose and section of ghost-white face.

'Roselyn Momford?' Natalie asked, holding up identification. 'Could we come in for a minute to ask some questions?'

'You have any idea what time it is?' the woman hissed. 'Can't this wait?'

'I'm afraid not. You own a dark-blue Yaris, don't you?'

'Yes.' The response was hesitant.

'Where were you yesterday afternoon?'

'I was at a friend's house. She lives near the big supermarket in Uptown.'

'Was that all afternoon?'

'Most of it. I was here to start with, with my son. My ex turned up at about three thirty, came in and had a cup of tea before taking Freddie home with him. He has Freddie every other Saturday. They left at about four. I had a bath, got changed and went across to her place. We went out for drinks, met up with friends and ended up at Hot Pink nightclub in Samford. Got home about three.'

'Did you leave your car outside her house?'

'I didn't use my car.' Roselyn's fingers tightened around the door, knuckles white against the dark frame. 'Hang on. I have to release the chain.'

The door shut with a quiet click followed by the sound of a chain dragging back along a slider before it opened again. Natalie and Lucy crossed the threshold. Roselyn tugged the edges of the dressing gown, which was a couple of sizes too small for her.

'It's only a fifteen-minute walk to her house from here. I didn't drive it. I was going to, but Ned asked if he could borrow the car to take some stuff to the allotment, and given he's been good enough to take Freddie swimming every Saturday while I'm at work, I couldn't refuse him. He doesn't own a car, you see?'

'Has Ned borrowed your car before?'

'Only since he's been buying compost and plants for this new plot. He can't carry heavy bags and gardening tools on the bus, can he? Besides, the garden centre isn't on a direct bus route. It's outside Kingstone, ten miles away. I offered to ferry him about but he said he's such a ditherer, it takes him ages to decide what to buy and he thought I'd get bored waiting about for him. He does take forever, even to choose something simple like seeds. I've been with him in the past. He loves garden centres.'

'Can you remember the days he borrowed it?'

'I suppose I could work them out. It was always when I was at home. I need it for work and to run Freddie about the rest of the time.'

'And he told you he was going to the garden centre yesterday afternoon?'

'That's right. What's happened?'

'We're trying to identify the driver of a car spotted at a crime scene yesterday afternoon and we suspect it was your vehicle.'

'Where?'

'Larkspur Close.'

'I don't know where that is.'

'It's a road linking to Lavender Rise that leads to Garrington.'

'Oh, I know where you mean. I doubt he'd be there. He doesn't know many people and I'm pretty certain he's never mentioned anyone living there to me. He's somewhat of a recluse. Loves gardening and has his old dog for company.'

'He's your stepfather, isn't he?'

'Met Mum after Dad died. I was surprised when they got married. He's quiet and shy and Mum was gregarious and full of life. He loves Freddie so much though. You can't think Ned was involved in any crime,' she scoffed. 'He's a kind old man. He's not likely to have robbed anyone.'

'It wasn't a robbery.'

Roselyn's mouth opened and she cocked her head. 'Well, he definitely won't have been involved in anything criminal. It can't have been my car that was spotted there.'

'Does the car have a navigation system in it?'

'It does.'

'I'd like to ask somebody from the technical team to run a programme to check where it's travelled in the last forty-eight hours.'

'You're serious, aren't you?'

'I know you think it's unlikely Ned was involved, but we have to be totally satisfied that he wasn't. We're investigating a serious crime and we need hard evidence your car was nowhere near the scene.'

She lifted her arms palms upwards and threw her head back. 'Whatever. It'll only prove my car wasn't where you think, so go ahead. The car isn't here, though. It's still at Ned's. He wanted to transport some stuff to keep in his shed on the plot, and I don't need it until Monday, so I told him to hang onto it until later today.'

'Then I'll arrange for somebody to check it at his house.'

'You want me to ring him?'

'That won't be necessary. I'll sort it out. Do you remember helping Ned buy an Etsy card for your sister?'

'I remember it. It was the first Christmas after Mum died. He spent far too much money on Grace. Told him not to buy one for two hundred pounds. He was adamant. I think he hoped by spending loads of money on her and Tony, they'd let him into their lives. Stupid bitch went and lost it. I was well pissed off with her. Took me ages to sort it out for Ned. He's rubbish with the Internet.'

'Did he buy you an Etsy card too?'

She snorted. 'No.'

'Have you bought another gift card since then?'

'No, why would I? I wouldn't waste my money on Grace. She's a tight-fisted leech.'

'You don't get along?'

'Never did. Used to fight like cat and dog. Not everyone gets on with their family members. Glad Freddie's an only child. At least he won't fall out with any brothers or sisters.'

Natalie thought about her own sister, Frances. It was true. Not all sisters were close.

'You want to ask anything else?'

'That'll be all for now,' Natalie replied and opened the front door. 'Thank you for helping us with our enquiries.'

Natalie tried ringing Ned as they got back into the car. It rang out.

'No answer.'

'Might be out.'

'It's eight o'clock. The shops don't open until ten. Where could he have gone?'

'Could be walking his dog.'

Natalie bounced her knee up and down. 'I reckon Ned could be involved.'

'Really?' Lucy's eyebrows lifted.

'He didn't mention borrowing Roselyn's car when I spoke to him last night. He told me he got gardening equipment and goods delivered to the allotment, yet he asked to borrow the car to visit a garden centre.'

'He could still be telling the truth. He probably buys some things at the centre and orders other stuff. He can't keep asking Roselyn to lend him her car. He wouldn't want to take liberties.'

'It's a feeling I can't shake off,' said Natalie. 'You've been to his house.'

'And?'

'He has a garden. Why would he own an allotment plot as well as a decent-sized garden? I don't know why I didn't query it before.'

Lucy released a sigh. 'I hate to rain on your parade but plenty of people have both gardens and allotments. The soil could be wrong in his garden for growing certain vegetables: maybe too acidic or too much clay. Besides, he owns a dog. I imagine it'd dig up anything he planted. They can be quite destructive.'

Natalie sat in silence. The roads were quiet with only a few vehicles travelling on them. They overtook a small group of joggers clutching water bottles and running in a pack. It was Sunday morning and they still had no idea where Sage might be. Thoughts swirled in her mind. She spoke again. 'Ned's our only possible suspect at present. He has a plot close to the route Rainey took. He lives opposite the park where Audrey died. He saw nothing on either occasion. I'd accept that but there are other coincidences that mount up: he was at the garden centre when Ava went missing; he knows Howard and probably also knows where Howard lives; and now, a car that is the same make, model and colour as his stepdaughter's vehicle was spotted on Larkspur Close.' She counted each revelation off on her fingers, halting at her little finger and saying, 'And he gave an Etsy card to his other stepdaughter. A card that mysteriously disappeared.'

'True but he has no motive for killing the girls and there's nothing in his file to indicate he has mental issues or any past history that would suggest him to be capable of harming children.

He also spent a lot of time assisting Howard when he was hunting for Ava. He felt responsible for what happened. He loves Freddie, who technically isn't his real grandson. He likes kids. I can't see why he'd want to harm them.'

Natalie heard what was being said but a buzzing had begun in her ears, the sound of blood rushing. Olivia Chester could have been saved if the team had explored all possibilities and not been blinkered.

'I know this may seem crazy but let's go to the allotment, take a look around. If Ned did snatch Sage, he might have hidden her there or somewhere nearby. There are loads of sheds and outhouses on those plots. He could have hidden her in any of them.' Seeing the look of doubt creep across Lucy's face, she continued. 'I understand this goes against what we know about the killer's MO, and Ava, Audrey and Rainey were left in the locations where they were murdered. In theory, if the same killer is responsible, they ought to have found Sage on that cut-through from her house and murdered her there or nearby, not taken her away. Her disappearance might even be unconnected to the investigation, but I can't get away from the fact that Ned *could* be our perpetrator or involved in some way. Killers can change their routines, and I think we should explore all possibilities. We'll head to the allotment. In the meantime, I'll send one of the others to his house to check it out and see if the Yaris is there.'

The area containing the allotments was accessed by a small lane off the main road but the gate to the plots was padlocked. Natalie smacked her hand against it and cursed.

'We could get in the other way, the route Rainey took from her school, by the fields. It'd mean cutting across a field to join the path that runs beside the allotments and close to Ned's plot,' Lucy offered.

As they spoke, an old Volvo appeared, rattling up the lane, and pulled up beside them. A woman with steely grey hair, in a green Barbour jacket and jeans, emerged from the vehicle.

'Are you to do with the allotments?' Natalie asked, extracting her ID card and holding it up for the woman to see.

She put on a pair of glasses that were dangling around her neck on a thin chain. 'Barbara Whitmore. I chair the allotment committee. What's going on?'

'Could you let us in, please?'

'Why?'

'We're investigating the disappearance of a child.'

'And you think they've wandered onto this site? Most unlikely. We keep the place locked up.'

'I expect you know all the allotment members?' Natalie asked, opting for a friendlier approach.

'I know most of them.'

'How about Ned Coleman?'

'I know Ned. Tremendously nice chap. He's been coming here for years. As long as I can remember.'

'I understood him to have only recently obtained an allotment.'

'That's correct. He took over Albert Grimshaw's plot. Albert was too old to manage it any more. Before that, Ned would drop by regularly to help out anyone who needed a hand: turn over some earth, plant seeds, anything really. Never took a penny for his efforts either. He's got green fingers and what an extensive knowledge. He ought to have been a professional gardener. Ned's been a fixture here for a very long time. Why are you asking about Ned?'

'It's just part of our investigation. Could you show us his plot?'

Her face screwed up. 'Have you spoken to him about it?'

'He's not answering his phone and it's imperative we check it out.'

'I don't see why.'

'Please take us to his allotment.' Natalie's voice took on a steelier edge that had the desired effect.

Barbara pulled out a large key ring from her coat pocket and fumbled a key into the sizeable padlock. It clicked open. Lucy pushed the gate wide.

'Be careful where you tread.' Barbara took the lead and skirted around several patches of weeded earth and areas covered by green and blue polythene, along narrow grass paths to the far end of the site. 'Here,' she said.

It was well-tended and had recently been turned. It was divided into six equal sections by thin green string. A slate plant marker was buried in the earth of the first section. Lucy bent to read what was written on it. 'Lily of the valley,' she said.

Barbara frowned. 'There's no sign of them. Must have been left there from last year although I don't remember Albert planting any lily of the valley there.'

Another vehicle had arrived and two men strolled onto the site.

'Two more of our merry band,' she said. 'Want to ask them about Ned? I think you'll find quite a few people here have time for Ned Coleman.'

'I'd like to look inside his shed first.' Natalie walked towards it.

Barbara's nose wrinkled. 'I don't think that's appropriate. You ought to ask him for permission first.'

Natalie knocked on the sides of the shed. There was no sound from inside. There was no padlock; the door was locked with a key.

'You really should check with Ned before prying into his personal space.' The words came out in a less aggressive tone.

'We're conducting an investigation into the abduction and murder of children. Given Mr Coleman is not about for us to ask him, I think it would be perfectly acceptable for us to look inside his shed.'

'My shed key fits his lock.' One of the men had walked up behind them. 'It's easy to forget to bring your key, and most of us have similar types of shed. I unlocked it a few times for Albert. He was always forgetting his key. I don't suppose Ned would mind.

He's got nothing to hide. Nice bloke. Helped me out when my back was playing up.'

Barbara scowled at the man, who ignored the look and instead pushed past to open the door. He stood aside, leaving Natalie to enter.

'Well, if there's nothing else, I'll leave you to it,' said Barbara huffily. She strode away, her wellington boots leaving imprints along the borders of Ned's plot.

'Bossy old cow,' said the man. 'What are you looking for?'

'Just checking it out,' said Lucy, blocking the man, who was craning his neck. 'If you wouldn't mind waiting there for a second?'

'Okay,' he replied.

Lucy walked in. Light filtered through a couple of warped boards and cast pale, golden rays onto neatly arranged tools that hung on the wall and shelves containing a wooden basket, secateurs and gardening gloves. Three huge bags of compost were stacked in a pile on the floor next to a pair of shears and a bucket. On the wall to the left of the building were rows of shelving with open wooden boxes, each containing seed packets, all displayed so the fronts were visible. Natalie read each out: 'Sherpa cucumber seeds, broad beans, sweet wonder peppers, blanched golden celery, pea seeds…'

'I thought you planted peas from a pod,' said Lucy. 'Sounds like he's really into gardening. There's nothing here. No sign of anyone, no rope, no evidence of a struggle. Nothing.'

Natalie had to agree. There was nothing to indicate Sage had been taken to the shed. She'd made a bad call. She glanced one last time at the seed packets. The man was so tidy. The vegetable seed packets had been arranged alphabetically. The flower seeds had been arranged according to colour. As her eyes scanned the Latin names, none of which she recognised, it struck her they were almost all yellow flowers: sunflowers, daffodils, blanket flower and tickseed.

'Lucy, he's got numerous packets of yellow flower seeds.'

'Yellow?'

Natalie raked through the packets and looked at the pictures of the blooms on the front. They were all yellow. She turned when she heard her name spoken.

'Natalie, look.' Lucy's voice was wary. She held the gardening gloves in one hand. Natalie immediately recognised the object that had been hidden from view under them. It was Sage's silver locket. Had the girl been here? Her mind flipped back to the six sectioned patches on Ned's plot. Each were wide and long enough to take the body of a child. Her pulse quickened as she considered the possibility of Sage's body being in one of them. 'I need to put in a call and get a warrant,' she said. The man was waiting nearby. 'Thank you, Mr…?'

'Mount. You done now? Want me to lock it up?'

'Leave it open, please. I don't suppose you have any idea where Ned might be?'

'He usually turns up round about now. We have a bit of a Sunday morning club thing going on here. A few of us who don't have families meet up for tea and cake. I'm surprised he isn't already here. He catches the eight o'clock bus.'

'I'd like you all to keep away from the allotment today.'

'Why?'

'We can't discuss an ongoing investigation but I'd appreciate it if you could contact your friends and tell them the allotments are out of bounds. Now, if you wouldn't mind packing up, we need to clear the area.' She strode towards Barbara Whitmore, who was watering some plants.

'I'm going to have to ask you to lock up the gate to the allotments, hand me the key and leave the premises.'

'But Sunday is one of our busiest days of the week.'

'Sorry. Not this Sunday.'

The woman put down her watering can. 'I'd like to protest about this.'

'If you'd like to put in an official complaint, please do, but I shall still have to ask for your cooperation. Could you please vacate the premises immediately and hand the key to my colleague?'

Natalie ignored the woman's huffs of irritation and hastened to the Audi. She rang the office and Murray answered. 'Natalie, glad you called. Ned's not at his house and there's no sign of the Yaris. Ian's still in position there in case he returns.'

'Put out a call on the car.'

'Done. Tech team are searching for it on safety cameras too.'

'Good. I need a warrant to search his house and another for the allotments. I don't like it, Murray. He's got packets and packets of seeds for yellow flowers – only yellow – and we've found Sage's locket in his shed. His patch has recently been turned over. There are six areas of equal size marked out on it. One has a marker for lily of the valley but there's no sign of any flowers or plants. I want to dig it up.'

'You don't think he's buried Sage there?'

'I hope to God he hasn't.'

'I'll sort it. Do you want to try Ned's house or stay there?'

'I'm leaving Lucy here. Will you come over and bring a team to search the plot? I'll head to the house and join Ian. Let me know as soon as you've got the warrants.'

'Natalie, I typed lily of the valley into a search engine. This website says the flowers represent sweetness and purity of heart.' Lucy lifted her mobile to show what she'd found. 'I think he might have buried her there.'

The gnawing, like hundreds of tiny teeth trying to eat through her stomach lining, began again. She fought the pain. This had to end now. If they found Sage in the allotment plot, she would never forgive herself.

She tore away from the allotment, praying she was wrong.

CHAPTER THIRTY-EIGHT

SUNDAY, 30 APRIL – MORNING

Ian was in his car, seat reclined, eating a chocolate bar when Natalie tapped on his window.

'Morning, guv,' he said. His eyes were bloodshot from lack of sleep. 'Fancy some breakfast?'

He held up two more bars of chocolate.

'Cheers. Okay if I join you?' She headed around to the passenger side and got in, took a bar from him and ripped off the wrapper. Maybe the chocolate would help ease the writhing in her stomach.

'Think it's him?' said Ian, eyes trained to the end of the street. There were no cars.

Natalie looked across at the entrance to the park. It'd only been three days since she'd been here staring at the sweet face of Audrey Briggs, and since then, another child had died and yet another was missing. 'Yes.'

'Who'd have thought it? My money was on Ava's father or mother. I figured they were seeking some sort of warped revenge. Goes to prove you can't trust anyone. They're a worry.'

'Who?'

'Kids today. My girlfriend's expecting our first. Due in six months' time.'

'I didn't know. Congratulations.'

'I try not to bring personal life to work. Thanks. Have to say I'm a bit worried about it though. This job doesn't help. I see loads of shit stuff and know my little one is going to be journeying through a dark world.'

'It's always been a dark world, Ian. We managed to navigate its pitfalls as did millions of others. Warn your children of them, try not to put too much pressure on them and listen to them when they need you to. That's all we can do as parents and hope they don't make too many mistakes.'

'You get on okay with your children?'

'I could do better.' She finished the chocolate, balled the wrapper and shoved it into her pocket to dispose of later. Her phone rang. Murray was to the point.

'Got them. I've sent an officer across with yours. On my way to the allotments.'

They waited a further ten minutes. Natalie chewed over every detail of the investigation, trying not to focus on the passing time, or on the possibility of Howard's daughter being buried at the allotments. Ian left her to her thoughts. Eventually, a police car came into view.

'Let's go.' She threw open the car door, collected the warrant and marched up to Ned's house. She knocked loudly and rang the bell then walked around to the back door. 'Mr Coleman, open up.'

There was nothing. Having proclaimed her intentions to enter using force, she nodded at Ian, who broke open the back door with the police-issue battering ram, sending it crashing against the jamb and splintering the wooden panels.

Natalie called out again. 'Mr Coleman, if you are at home, please answer me.' She was met with silence. She pulled on plastic gloves and spoke to Ian. 'You take downstairs. I'll take upstairs. We're looking for anything that links him to any of the girls.'

The house was tidy and clean, and the bathroom smelt of pine. She noticed the old-fashioned shaving brush hanging from its stand next to a recently used bar of soap, covered in a light foam.

There were two bedrooms upstairs. She chose what appeared to be his room. A Teasmade stood on a bedside locker next to the bed. The wardrobe only contained a few outfits and a shelf of neatly folded vests and jumpers. Two pairs of shoes – shiny brogues and another more casual pair – were arranged on a shoe stand. A black tie hung on the back of the door. The drawers were ordered: socks rolled and arranged according to colour; underwear the same.

A dressing table had been left as an homage to his deceased wife. A porcelain necklace and ring holder supporting a few beaded necklaces and a brush and mirror set had been left in front of the mirror. Natalie caught sight of her haggard face in the glass and turned away quickly.

The second room chilled her. It contained little furniture – only a bed and a wardrobe – but a collection of dolls sat on the bed had been positioned to face the door. They were of various sizes and makes, some chubbier with cheerful smiles, some with long hair and tiny adult faces, and others with serious blank faces. They all had one thing in common: they were all dressed in yellow outfits. Natalie looked away, opened the wardrobe door and remained there for a second trying to comprehend the enormity of what she was seeing. Hanging in front of her, each in polythene protector bags, were two yellow dresses, identical to the ones they'd found.

'Ian! I've found the dresses.'

Ian thundered up the stairs, his footsteps heavy on the thin carpet. 'I might have something else,' he said and lifted the object in his hand. 'There were two dog leads hanging up beside the door. One's thin and looks a little chewed in places where the dog's pulled it, and then there's this one.' The lead he held up was shiny and new and pale yellow.

'Bag it. We've got him. Got to locate him now.'

She raced down the stairs and called Aileen. 'We're sure it's Ned Coleman. There are two dresses hanging in his house and we might have the murder weapon. I'm sending Ian back to the lab with it immediately. Need backup to search the rest of his house.'

'I'll arrange that. Any idea where Ned is?'

'The tech boys are searching for the Yaris. There's a call-out for it too. Ned won't get far. I'm going across to the allotment now.'

She ended the call and gave Ian instructions to wait for the officers then take the dog lead and dresses to the lab. She hurtled towards her car and jumped in. It wasn't far to the allotment. She had to know. There'd been five dresses. Two had been found on the bodies of Audrey Briggs and Rainey Kilburn. One was missing. By now it would surely be on Sage Franks.

Lucy and Murray stood side by side, hands thrust deep in pockets. A chill wind had blown up from nowhere and grey clouds had moved in, providing a suitably sombre atmosphere for the setting. A small team had arrived and were unloading their equipment at the far side of the allotment.

'I don't think I can bear to watch,' said Lucy. 'I just know she's going to be there. I can't imagine how we'll break it to Howard.'

'You'll be okay,' said Murray, who moved closer, the warmth of his body rising towards her.

Their conversation dried. The team were upon them.

'Where do you want us to start?' said a dark-eyed officer.

'That patch,' said Murray. 'The one with the plant marker.'

The men dug with care, lifting the soil spade by spade, beginning at one end of the patch, closest to the stick. The wind blew in gusts that made Lucy sink her hands deeper still into her pockets and hunch her shoulders. Murray remained by her side.

Shovel after shovel of rich brown earth was lifted and placed upon a plastic sheet adjacent to the plot. With each shovel Lucy released a breath, then tensed once more as the spade slapped again into the ground.

Time slowed as she watched the two men work, and then the moment she'd dreaded happened. One of the spades clanged against something. 'Whoa!' she called. 'There's something there.' They stopped digging and knelt to examine the find.

'It's a wooden box,' said the officer with the dark eyes.

Lucy looked at Murray. Neither spoke. The silence was broken by an engine, and a dark-grey Audi ground to a halt near the gates. Natalie emerged and broke into a trot towards the gate.

'Natalie! Here!' Murray's shout filled the air.

They waited until she'd reached them.

'Wooden box,' said Murray.

'Okay. Dig with care,' said Natalie. A sudden pain made her double over. An inner voice whispered *Olivia*. She was terrified of what they might unearth. She couldn't face failing another child.

'You okay?' Lucy rushed to her side.

'Fine. Stitch. Ran too quickly.' Natalie pressed the tender area and, wincing slightly, drew herself upright.

The officers had put down the shovels and were now scraping the dirt away from the box with towels. Little by little a lid became visible. It was a wooden casket.

'Oh God,' muttered Lucy under her breath. She half-turned away.

The officers continued working.

'It's small,' said one.

Natalie pushed the flesh of her stomach hard to halt the throbbing. The wait was unbearable. The officers cleared away the dirt more quickly, scraping with gloved hands, and finally uncovered a wooden casket.

'Looks too small to contain the body of a child,' said Murray.

'Open it,' said Natalie.

The officers worked loose the screws and lifted the top. The inside of the coffin was fitted out with silken material, and lying inside, wearing a yellow dress, white socks and black shoes, with its eyes closed, was a doll with blonde hair.

Natalie's chin jutted forwards and the tension vanished from her shoulders. 'There's nothing else there, is there?' she asked the officers.

'Don't think so.' They scraped away more earth to make sure while Natalie stamped her feet to put some feeling back into them. Murray lifted the doll up. Its eyes opened.

'What the fuck is this all about?' asked Lucy.

'I don't know but I don't like being pissed about,' said Natalie. 'I can't hang about here playing his stupid games. Come on. We're going to find out where he is and where he's taken Sage. Better bring *that* with you,' she added, indicating the doll. 'And the casket.'

She marched away across the allotments, breath coming in sharp bursts. The pain was easing. If she were to be honest, she'd far rather be annoyed at finding a plastic doll than Sage in the coffin. Her only fear was that Sage was hidden elsewhere; a little girl buried in a yellow dress.

CHAPTER THIRTY-NINE

SUNDAY, 30 APRIL – LATE MORNING

Natalie was in a foul mood. She couldn't make up her mind if Ned was deliberately attempting to needle them by burying the doll in a man-made wooden coffin or was genuinely disturbed. Either way, she wanted him found but Ian and the other officers, who'd been drafted in from the technical side to assist, hadn't yet located a dark-blue Yaris on security cameras throughout Uptown.

Using the overhead projector once more, Natalie pulled up the map of Uptown with Ned's house circled.

'We'll have to work it out using old-fashioned logic,' she said, tapping the image with her forefinger. 'We don't know what time he left his house and that's making this all the more difficult. I'm going to base my judgements on the premise Ned is clever and way ahead of us. He's fooled us into believing he's an old man who wouldn't hurt anyone but we've discovered he's devious and able to move about undetected. He is not to be underestimated. So, let's assume he took a route to avoid all cameras. Which direction could he have taken from his house for that to be the case?'

'Left out of his house, past the open-all-hours shop where Audrey was heading and right along that street. That'd take him to the church, and beyond that are lanes leading to two villages, neither of which contain cameras,' said Ian.

'That'd be Kingstone and Honiton,' said Natalie, pointing them out.

'There's a disused quarry at Honiton,' said Ian.

'He might have taken her there. Murray, you head in that direction.'

Lucy spoke up. 'There's not much at Kingstone, only the garden centre just outside it.'

Natalie took a step backwards, a sudden thought taking shape. *Could he?* 'Roselyn told me he purchased plants at Kingstone. I'm going out on a limb here. Lucy, come with me. We'll try the garden centre. Everyone here is to stick to working on the footage in case we're wrong. We'll stay in touch at all times, using the communications units. Anything else comes up here, let me know, Ian.'

Chairs scraped back as one and the room filled with urgent rustling as jackets and communications units were grabbed. They clattered downstairs one after another and peeled off into two cars, Lucy diving into the passenger seat of Natalie's car.

They pulled out of the car park at speed and hurtled towards Uptown, where at a junction they went in different directions. As the car jolted down the potholed lane, Ian's voice crackled through the comms unit.

'Forensics have discovered traces of Rainey's DNA on the dog lead we found at his house.'

Natalie gritted her teeth and drove with even more determination. Hedges flashed past and the first heavy drops of rain tumbled from a leaden sky and bashed against her windscreen. The gnawing in the pit of her belly had returned. *What if we're too late?* Lucy must have been having the same thoughts because she asked, 'What if he killed her yesterday? He might have done a bunk.'

'I don't think he's gone. He probably doesn't even know we're onto him yet. Two of the yellow dresses are still hanging in his wardrobe so he hasn't yet completed his task.'

'He might have already killed her though.'

Natalie shook her head. 'He snatched Sage from where he found her. He hasn't done that before. Also, Sage wasn't at the birthday party in 2015. He's not following the same modus operandi so I'm hoping he hasn't harmed her. I'm clutching at straws here but I have a hunch he's taken Sage to the garden centre. Ava was buried behind a similar centre and I suspect Ned is doing this either because of what happened to Ava or because that's where this all began, and *he* killed Ava.'

There was more crackling and Murray's voice. 'I'm at the quarry. No sign of a Yaris or anyone. I'm going to look about.'

The sign for the garden centre loomed on the right.

'Just arrived at the garden centre,' said Natalie, turning into a gravelled car park. She checked the time on the car display. It was coming up for eleven thirty even though it felt much later. Lucy let out a gasp.

'The car. It's here.'

The Yaris was close to a trolley park to one side of the car park, well away from the entrance. They ran across to it and were met with a sudden yapping. A small, grey-faced black dog raced from one seat to the other, barking furiously.

'Shh!'

Lucy was answered by another volley of barks that got louder and louder.

'Shut up, will you?'

Natalie tried tapping on the car boot lid but couldn't identify any sound from within.

'We'll try inside the centre. Could have taken her there.' As they dashed towards the entrance, she shouted into the comms unit, 'Ned's here. The Yaris is here. I repeat, Ned's here.'

'Where shall we look?' Lucy's head turned left and right. A couple was standing in front of a hanging basket collection. Further ahead, another pair wheeled a large trolley filled with individual plants. Plant displays stood to the left and right of the aisle, which

branched out into an outside area. Overhead signs directed customers to perennials, shrubs, trees and evergreens. The place was
humungous. Natalie had no idea where to head.

'Split up and take the left. I'll go right. Shout if you see him
and be careful not to spook him, especially if he has Sage with him.
Murray, you on your way?' The last remark was into the unit. It
spluttered into life.

'Roger that,' came the reply.

Natalie walked briskly around tables of spring flowers and tubs
and into an open-roofed area. She circumnavigated endless ceramic
pots in violets, creams and pinks stacked under tables of flowers
and plants of similar shades. Then it struck her where he might be.
The tables were colour-coded. She edged away from the table of
pink flowers. Beyond stood another, awash with vibrant reds and
oranges. She skirted around it in search of a table of yellow flowers
and, spotting it three tables ahead, whispered her location to Lucy.
The reply was equally hushed. 'No sign here. I'm near fruit trees.'

'Head this way.'

Walking casually, as if a customer, Natalie continued. It was
surprisingly quiet and she was beginning to lose hope of spotting
anyone at all when she saw another person, dressed in dark clothing,
stooped over and examining the plants by some wooden sheds. She
caught sight of Lucy moving in. Lucy saw her too and signalled
she was moving towards the person. They acted in a pincer movement, each silently and swiftly headed towards their quarry. While
Natalie rounded the table, Lucy advanced from his rear. He stood
up quickly, surprised by the movement around him, then smiled.
'Morning,' he said.

It wasn't Ned. Natalie mumbled a response and they moved away.
'Where now?'

Natalie turned in a steady circle, searching for exits or areas
where Ned might have taken Sage. Her attention was caught by a
flicker of movement. She made out the wheels and wire cage of a

low trolley, out of view behind trellises of climbing clematis not yet in bloom. She hastened towards it, Lucy matching her pace. The owner of the trolley came into view, his back to them.

Natalie sprinted towards him. With each step, she was confident she had found her man. He was the right size and shape. She put a hand on his shoulder and he turned to face her. He cradled the pot containing bare-stemmed roses, his face completely impassive.

'Ned Coleman, I'm arresting you in connection with the murders of Audrey Briggs and Rainey Kilburn and the disappearance of Sage Franks. You do not have to say anything, but it may harm your defence if you do not mention when questioned something which you later rely on in court. Anything you do say may be given in evidence.'

He shook his head. 'You misunderstand. I didn't murder them. They died accidentally.'

Lucy moved towards him. 'Put down the pot, sir.' She withdrew a pair of police-issue handcuffs. He obliged by gently replacing the pot among the others and stretching out his arms.

Natalie stared at the man, who seemed relaxed and unflustered as Lucy cuffed him. His mild manner irritated her further. 'Where's Sage?'

He didn't answer.

'I asked you a question. Where is Sage?'

He blinked several times. 'I was choosing a special rose for her. I decided on this one – Rosa Hakuun. It will look so pretty when it flowers. I wanted to do it properly this time. I didn't want to get it wrong. The other little maids shouldn't have struggled. I was only being friendly.'

'Mr Coleman, I'm going to ask you one last time. Where is she?' Natalie's face was up close to Ned's, dark eyes boring into his, but still he did not flinch. The communications unit burst into life once more. Murray spoke, his voice breathless, his words urgent.

'Outside,' he said. 'I've found her.'

*

There was a commotion in the car park. Ned's dog was still barking furiously, hurling itself against the passenger window, teeth bared. Murray was at the rear of the car, speaking loudly. He caught sight of Natalie and Lucy with Ned Coleman between them.

'There's somebody in the boot. I think I can hear faint knocking when that confounded dog shuts up.'

'Where are the car keys?' Her words were directed at Ned.

'Pocket.' He looked down at his right trouser pocket.

Natalie retrieved them and pressed the release button so all the doors unlocked with a simultaneous click. The dog, spotting his master, wagged his tail and ceased its racket. A tapping replaced the barking. Murray and Natalie dived for the boot and lifted the lid. A slight girl with light-brown hair, wearing a yellow dress, looked up, her eyes huge with fear.

'It's okay, Sage sweetheart, we've got you. We're the police. We're going to take you home to your daddy.' Natalie's voice was thick with emotion.

Murray lifted the girl out. Her hands were tied and a piece of tape had been stuck over her mouth. Lucy marched Ned to Murray's squad car. The sound of sirens approached, their unified wailing increasing as they neared the garden centre. Murray left Natalie with Sage and began ushering the small crowds of people from the car park and out of sight inside the centre. Natalie stood protectively beside the child, released her bounds and stripped away the tape with soothing noises. 'You're safe now, Sage. Your daddy is on his way.'

The little girl began to shake with shock. Natalie knelt and wrapped warm arms around her, allowing her own tears to tumble onto the child's hair. This time she hadn't failed.

CHAPTER FORTY

WEDNESDAY, 26 APRIL – AFTERNOON

AUDREY BRIGGS

'*Mum, there's no cola!*'

Audrey shuts the fridge door, disappointed. Her baby sister, Libby, is wailing, her face purple and tiny fists clenched. Her teeth are coming through and must be hurting her like crazy judging by the racket she's making. Mum's tried teething crystals but Libby screamed all the way home from the dance academy. Audrey tests her front teeth. The top one is beginning to wobble. They're late coming out but she doesn't mind. She hopes the new teeth don't hurt like Libby's do.

'*Can I go to the shop and buy some?*'

'*Can't you have some water or juice instead?*' *asks her mum, lifting Libby. She sniffs the baby and screws up her face. 'I have to change her.*'

'*Mu-um!*' *Audrey urges. 'I'll take my bike. I won't be long.*'

Her mum removes the head from the china frog on the window ledge and tips out the contents – two one-pound coins – onto the table. 'Go on, then.'

Audrey puts the money into her cardigan pocket, races outside, collects her bike and lets herself out of the side gate onto the pathway, where she wheels her bike to the main pavement. It's not yet too busy with traffic. As she climbs onto the bike to pedal off, she hears a shout. She turns around and sees Mr Coleman rushing down the road. He's carrying a plastic bag and holding a yellow dog lead.

'Audrey, can you help me find Rex? He's run off into the park. You've got your bike. You might be able to catch up with him.'

She looks anxious. She's not allowed to cross the road alone but there's no traffic about.

'Quickly, please. I wouldn't want anything to happen to him.'

She thinks about Muffin, her own sweet puppy. He was only eight months old when he ran off and was hit by a car. Before she knows it, she's turned her handlebars and is riding across the road, Mr Coleman by her side.

She rides along the path and at the fork is not sure if she should go right or left. Mr Coleman behind her shouts, 'There, to the right. I see him.'

She pushes down hard on her pedals, head turning looking for the animal, but can't see him. She hears her name again. Mr Coleman is yelling, 'He's in the bushes.'

She comes to a quick halt and leaps from the bike, which falls away into the grass, and darts towards the bushes, shouting the dog's name. There she drops on all fours and hunts for the dog in the undergrowth, but there's no sign of him. She emerges again and almost runs headlong into Mr Coleman. He's looking at her strangely.

'It's okay,' he whispers.

She doesn't know what he means by that. 'Rex isn't here,' she says.

'No, he's run back home.'

He doesn't move and she's suddenly aware they're alone behind the bush. Nobody can see them. He crouches down, his face serious. 'I want you to have this.'

He hands her the plastic bag. She takes it and looks inside. It's a dress; a yellow dress.

'Why?'

'Because you're my friend.' He smiles at her.

She's unsure how to react. She's spoken to him a few times when she's seen him outside, and patted Rex, but she isn't his friend. 'I don't want it,' she says, passing the bag back. It's the wrong thing to say. His face changes and the smile vanishes in a flash.

'Take it. Put it on. Put it on now.'

'I don't want to.'

'Put… it… on.'

She's now scared of him. She surges forwards to run away from him, but in that instant he grabs the top of her arm, and she wonders why he's wearing gloves on a warm day. 'No. Put it on first.'

It won't hurt to do as he says. She'll put it on and then he'll be happy and let her go. She pulls it out. It's a party dress with a large bow at the front. Audrey doesn't like the colour. She'd have preferred pink. She removes her cardigan, drops it on the floor and pulls the dress over her head. It's a bit tight but she tugs it over the leotard and tights until it fits. He seems happier all of a sudden.

'Pretty,' he says.

His face has twisted and the way he's looking at her freaks her out. He's no longer old Mr Coleman, the nice man who lives down the road. He's frightening. He's looking at her like he wants to eat her.

'Turn around. Let me make sure the zip is done up,' he says.

She obliges but before he can reach for her, she bolts. She doesn't get far. Only a few steps and she's lassoed around the neck by the lead he's been carrying, and she's yanked back.

'You mustn't run.'

Audrey splutters, tugging at the lead that tightens around her throat, and lands a light kick on his shin. She can't breathe any more.

'No, Sherry. That's naughty. I only want to be your friend.'

CHAPTER FORTY-ONE

MONDAY, 1 MAY – LATE AFTERNOON

There'd been sufficient evidence to charge Ned. They'd found everything they'd hoped for, including the lipstick he'd used on the girls – it was in the pocket of his trousers, ready to be used on Sage. He'd been compliant and polite but Natalie had been horrified at his confession. Ned had behaved as if it were perfectly normal to steal and kill a child.

Natalie couldn't get over how innocent he appeared as he sat opposite her: a gentle, old man sat next to his lawyer, not at all a vicious killer. She and Murray interviewed him, aware of the rest of the team behind the two-way glass.

'You know why you've been charged. Do you have anything you wish to say?' Natalie asked.

A furrow appeared between Ned's grey eyebrows as if it were all too confusing. 'I didn't ever intend to hurt them. They tried to run away, you see? They shouldn't have done that. I forget how strong I am. I only meant to restrain them.' He shook his head sadly.

'Are you saying you never intended harming the girls? What were your intentions?' Natalie kept a cool gaze on the man, who looked quizzically at her as if she ought to know the answer to the question she was asking.

'To plant them, of course.' He smiled serenely. 'Little maids, all in a row. You must know the rhyme.'

Natalie shook her head. 'I don't know what you mean.'

He ignored the response and continued in a semi-rambling way. 'All in a row, perfect forever, and they wouldn't be alone. I'd made sure of that. They'd have other pretty maids with them.'

'You mean other girls?'

'Yes, little maidens.'

'You were going to bury them in your allotment?'

'Yes.' He gave her another gentle smile. 'Where's Rex? Is he okay?'

'He's fine. He's being looked after. How did you plan on murdering the girls? Or were you going to bury them alive?'

'I was going to send them to sleep. I haven't been able to sleep properly since Lorna died. The doctor gave me a prescription for some medication to assist. I was going to give the sleeping pills to the little girls. There'd be no pain. No suffering. Just sleep. A beautiful, long sleep. They shouldn't have tried to get away from me. They ruined the plan. They should have come away with me. I wanted to go back and fetch them, but it was too risky, and then they were found and it was out of the question to take them to be planted. Such a shame to leave them like that. They ought to have been in the special place I prepared for them.' He rested his large hands in his lap and waited for the next question. His lawyer shifted in his seat but kept his head down.

'The plot at the allotment?'

'Yes. It was all ready for them,' he replied.

'Why did you want to kill them?' Natalie asked.

'Because they're all so pretty and sweet, and I love pretty girls.'

'Do you admit to killing Audrey Briggs and Rainey Kilburn?'

Ned's lawyer gave a cough and spoke quietly to Ned, who shook his head angrily. 'I *want* to explain,' he said firmly, waiting until the lawyer sat back in his seat before continuing. 'It was an accident. I planned it wrong. I had such lovely party dresses for each of them. I carried one in a plastic bag at all times, ready to hand out to a pretty girl. I thought they'd be really happy with the dresses and we'd be friends and then I'd send them to sleep. But you see, they didn't want to be friends with me and tried to run off and… I don't know how it happened, but they broke… like the doll.'

'The doll? Is that the same doll we found in a coffin at your allotment?'

Ned became agitated, his face contorting, and leant closer to Natalie, his hands now flat on the table. 'You dug her up? You dug up Sherry? No. She has to stay there. Put her back.'

His lawyer put a warning hand on his arm.

Natalie wasn't going to stop now. She fired another question. 'Sherry? Why did you call her Sherry?'

Ned sat back, his voice becoming a growl. 'I don't wish to discuss it with you. You must return her to her grave. I have the perfect rose for her. It's going to grow there forever.'

'Ned, did you kill Ava Sawyer?'

Ned let out a splutter and tears began to fall. 'You promise to return Sherry to her resting place and I'll tell you, but only if you promise.'

Ned was slowly unravelling. He was transforming into a muddled old man, pulling first at the sleeve of his shirt and then rubbing at his chin.

'I promise,' Natalie said and waited while he scrutinised her.

'You seem honest enough.'

'Tell me about Ava. What happened?'

'I was waiting for the party to end to collect Freddie. I'd only recently lost Lorna, and Roselyn thought it would be good for me to get out. She asked if I'd collect him, knowing I like garden centres. I still had my own car at the time. I arrived too early and decided to look about. I was looking at some roses and thinking about Lorna, and suddenly Ava ran past me, like a little angel.

She looked so lovely, just like Sherry did all those years ago, in her party dress. I followed her inside a stable. She was hiding under some blankets. I thought she wanted to play a game of hide and seek. I found her. What happened was an accident. She tried to run off and I only put out my hand to restrain her.' He looked far off into the distance. 'I had no idea she'd break so easily. I didn't realise she was dead at first. I spotted a wheelbarrow in the shed and hid her body in it under some polythene and wheeled her to my car. No one noticed me. I went back inside and collected Freddie and took him home, and all the while, Ava was in my car boot. Of course, by then, everyone knew she'd gone missing. I had to hide her. I kept her in my chest freezer at home. I thought I might plant her in my garden, but Rex would have tried to dig her up. Once the hoo-ha regarding her disappearance had waned, I returned her to the craft centre. Obviously, I couldn't put her back where I found her without being spotted, so I went to the rear of the craft centre late one evening, and I buried her among the wild meadow flowers. It seemed the right thing to do.' His hands had returned to his lap and he calmed. 'You must return Sherry now. I've told you about Ava.'

'Can you tell me about the yellow dresses?'

'They're beautiful, aren't they?'

'Why did you only purchase five of them?'

'Ava was five years old. It seemed appropriate to buy five to celebrate her departure from this world. She'll be a pretty girl forever, you know?'

Natalie didn't flinch even though his words chilled her. 'You got them from an Etsy site, using a gift card you bought for your stepdaughter. How did you get hold of the card?'

He shrugged. 'It was meant to be. I bought Grace the card as a present. About three weeks after Christmas, I went to visit her, but she was out and the card was on the ground by the back door. I was miffed. I knew Grace didn't like me much, but to take so little care of something as valuable as that was an insult. I pocketed it. I didn't have any plans for it at the time, but I certainly didn't intend on returning it to her. The idea to go online for the dresses only came to me late last year. I signed up for a course in computer literacy at the local library and used the computer there to find the perfect dresses. Up until then, I'd considered buying them from a shop, but finding the Etsy card had been a sign, and I decided using it to purchase the dresses was a better idea. It would preserve my anonymity.'

Natalie couldn't fault his logic. He'd almost succeeded.

'What happened to you to make you commit these crimes?' Natalie couldn't understand why Ned wasn't displaying any guilt.

Ned looked puzzled. 'Nothing happened to me. I just wanted to keep them pretty forever. And now, I don't want to say anything further. I'd like to go. I want to see Rex.'

'You can't leave, Ned. You've been charged with murder. Your lawyer has explained everything to you. You have to stay here now.'

The lawyer spoke quietly again. Ned studied his flat fingernails and fell silent. The lawyer shook his head. Ned wasn't going to talk any more. Natalie turned towards the glass to signal she had ended the interview.

'I don't get why he did it,' said Ian, sitting on the edge of the desk.

Natalie tried to explain. 'According to the psychiatrist's report, he suffered a trauma in his youth. He was obsessed with a girl in his class called Sherry Hunt. Unfortunately, he was very big for his age, and his advances were clumsy. He scared the girl and as a consequence became ostracised by his fellow classmates. He became a complete loner yet persisted in pursuing the girl. Sherry was tragically killed, along with her family, in a car accident immediately after her birthday. Ned spoke about taking her a present that would have changed everything, and being turned away from the birthday party, but the psychiatrist was unable to extract any further information for the time being. One thing is certain: his actions are linked to those memories. It appears he was deeply affected by Sherry's death. He repeatedly mentioned wanting to be friends with the girl. He admitted he liked young girls and wanted to befriend them. He carried a yellow dress around in a plastic bag with him most of the time, in the hope he'd be able to give it to an unsuspecting girl and then kill her. The victims were all in the wrong place at the wrong time.'

'But why kill them now? Why didn't this happen when he was younger?'

'The psychiatrist thinks the death of his wife was some sort of catalyst. He began to lose his grip on reality after she died in 2015. Ned doesn't believe he's done any wrong. That's what freaks me out the most.'

'At least he can't harm any more children.'

'What about Sage's locket?' Ian asked. 'How did it come to be in the shed?

'It came off when he bundled Sage into the car and he slipped it into his pocket, meaning to dispose of it. After he abducted her, he went to the allotment to ensure everything was ready, took the locket out of his trouser pocket so he wouldn't drop it, intending to place it on her neck at a later stage. He spotted the arrival of some other allotment owners and in his haste to get off, put his gardening gloves down on top of it and gave it no further thought.'

There was a tap on the door. Howard Franks entered. He carried a chocolate collection gift hamper.

'I don't know how to thank you properly but maybe this will go some way towards it. There should be something for everyone. That is, if you like chocolate.'

'You didn't have to do that. It's our job,' Natalie said. 'And, for the record, I love chocolate.'

Ian took the hamper and peered inside. 'Me too. Nice. Thank you.'

Natalie gave Howard a wide smile. 'You want to join us at the pub for a drink? We're almost done here. I'm letting everyone take a couple of days off to recover.'

'Yeah. I'd like that.'

'Good. Okay. Any more questions or shall I call an end to the debrief?' She looked around the room and was met with a collective shaking of heads. 'Then, that only leaves me to say thank you everyone for your tremendous efforts that resulted in a successful operation. I couldn't have asked for more from you. The first round is on me.'

'Now you're talking,' said Ian. 'Mine's a double.' He grinned.

As they picked up jackets and left the office, Murray caught Lucy's eye. 'You still got doubts about being a mum? We can put it off if you do.'

Lucy gave a small smile. 'No. We'll stick to the plan. Seeing the look of joy in Howard's eyes made me realise having a child is a precious gift. There'll be ups and downs but ours will be even more special because it'll be ours – mine and Bethany's. You still happy to take a back seat on this?'

'Yolande and I will have kids when we're ready. I'm cool.'

She thumped him on the arm. 'Yeah, that's why we chose you. You're pretty cool.'

Natalie clambered into her Audi. She'd only had the one drink. It was time to get her life back into some order and be the mother her children needed. Her phone lit up with a message.

If you fancy a celebratory drink and a chat, I'm free.

Mike had been the first to congratulate her and the team on tracking down Ned and rescuing Sage. He'd hugged her fiercely when she'd walked through the lab doors, his eyes shining with pride. No words were spoken. He understood completely what it had meant to her to save the life of a child. She read it again before replying.

Got to take a rain check on that. Best go home.

She paused before sending it. It was tempting to join Mike and talk through what had happened and to share the anxieties and the relief of finding Sage alive. She'd put the demons of the Olivia Chester case to rest for now and nobody understood what that meant to her better than Mike. However, she'd made a promise, more to herself than anyone else. She was lucky to have two healthy children. She wanted to be around them and watch them grow into adults and not rock their boats by causing marital strife that would divide their unit. She needed these moments when she wasn't swamped with work to be with them. She and David would muddle along. They had sufficient history together to work through any grievances. As long as he didn't allow his self-doubt to take over, it would be fine. She fired up the engine and pulled away. It was time to be a mother.

LETTER FROM CAROL

Hello, dear reader,

Firstly, thank you for buying and reading *The Birthday*. I truly hope you enjoyed meeting and spending time with DI Natalie Ward and her team.

I was drawn to the subject of child abduction for this novel, not just because of such dreadful events that occasionally appear in the news but because of an experience I had many years ago, when I lost my three-year-old son in a shop that had both a front and a rear entrance. Those panic-stricken minutes when I couldn't locate him were filled with a myriad of emotions and fears, the memory of which still leaves my skin cold. As luck would have it, he was found in a corner of the store, crouched beside a box of plastic dinosaurs, completely oblivious to my acute anxiety.

If you enjoyed reading *The Birthday*, please would you take a few minutes to write a review, no matter how short it is? I would really be most grateful. Your recommendations are most important.

If you'd like to keep up to date with all my latest releases, just sign up at the following link. Your email address will never be shared and you can unsubscribe at any time.

www.bookouture.com/carol-wyer

I hope you'll join me for the next book in the DI Natalie Ward series, *The Night Out*.

Thank you,
Carol

        📘 AuthorCarolEWyer

        🐦 carolewyer

        🖥️ www.carolwyer.co.uk

ACKNOWLEDGEMENTS

As a writer I am dependent on so many people, and I'm grateful to have such a great team working with me.

It goes without saying that you, my readers, are hugely important, and you keep me motivated and eager to write more.

The Birthday is my eighth book published with Bookouture and I count myself extremely lucky to have their support and guidance. Special thanks must go to my ace editor, Lydia Vassar-Smith, to Leodora Dartington and to DeAndra Lupu, for keeping me on track and for giving me such good feedback. To everyone else from Bookouture who worked on *The Birthday*, a sincere thank you.

I'd like to give special mention to Kim Nash and Noelle Holton, who not only do a phenomenal job organising book tours and handling all media work, but also check up on us all to make sure we're doing okay.

A sincere thank you to the bloggers involved on book tours, who give up their time freely to support us writers.

My hugely grateful thanks to fellow Bookouture authors: a unique bunch of supportive and talented individuals, who kept me sane again!

Once again, a genuine thank you to you, my readers, for reading my books and for staying in touch on social media. You are the reason I love writing so much.